I0536828

HOW BRAVE WE LIVE

By Paul Monash

WILDSIDE PRESS

●

FOR

MY FATHER AND MOTHER

"Man is at best somewhat good, and at worst somewhat bad; there is in him that which is never realized, be it for good or for evil; and it is to those regions within himself where he will not go that I would go, and I will show him what he is but does not dare to be."

. . . *Anaxates*

LARDFORTH: You are, if I may dare speak my mind, much too pessimistic in this account, my lord.

SIR ROGER: I am, you say? How so?

LARDFORTH: Why, sir, you tell the truth.
. . . *William Congreve*

PRINCIPAL CHARACTERS

BREEDON RAWLEY

An unimportant man—until he writes a best-selling novel. His success arouses the enmity of his Greenwich Village friends—and he acquires a mistress.

AARON ROSS

A belligerent artist and a sneak-thief and mugger when he's hard up for food or money to buy paints and brushes.

AMY MACDUFF

Voluptuous blonde giantess who is most always drunk. Breedon worships her even though he knows she's Aaron's ex-mistress.

LOIS WILSON

A singer; passionate, exotic, and one-eighth colored. Goes to live in Haiti where she thinks there's no "color line". Her experiences there make some startling chapters in this book.

OLIVER KITTREDGE

A Park Avenue poet who prefers to live among the low-lifes of Greenwich Village. 'Queer' fellow who has delusions of being a Messiah.

JASON SPIVAK

Sour, mooching writer; envious and jealous of Breedon's success.

PHYLLIS

Oliver's sister; Aaron is her secret lover.

1. Footnote Before Dawn

ONE OF THE MANY novels published toward the end of 1947 was written by a young man named Breedon Rawley and it had to do with several people then living in Greenwich Village, which as you may know is a fairly small community with considerable bohemian pretensions situated about one mile north of the financial core of this planet (and possibly of this universe) and about two miles south of its theatrical axis—admittedly a precarious position for a self-styled center of culture. Breedon Rawley's book was worse than some and better than others, which meant that a number of reviewers hailed it as a striking or promising first effort while certain others dismissed it as unimportant and even trivial. In the natural course of events the book might have been expected to sell a few thousand copies and then expire ingloriously on the remainder counters. But life in these United States often runs so contrary to nature that I contend miracles should be part of our daily expectations; this particular daily miracle consisted of having the editorial board of a famous book club decide to issue Breedon Rawley's novel as the bottom and lesser half of the double selection for the month of December.

I remember running into Breedon Rawley one night as winter was ending, and I remember his telling me that he had finished a novel and given it to an agent. Well, that kind of talk is common in the Village where hope so often substitutes for achievement and people always claim to have some enterprise in hand, so I wasn't very much impressed. Some time later at a bar called the Marino (of which you will hear more shortly) a girl of sorts named Frances Finnerty told me she had read the book and that it was about the Village and really not too bad. Some time

3

later I heard the report that the book had been taken by one of the more aggressive publishers. When advance copies of the book came out we Villagers began to read it to see whether we could identify ourselves with characters in it. (I myself appeared in a disappointingly minor and rather unsympathetic role.) The book wasn't very well received among us. We sided in general with those reviewers who had dismissed it as trivial. Then came the disturbing news that it was going to be distributed to the book club members in their hundreds of thousands. This awesome financial success of someone who until recently had just been a character dropping into the Marino made us all feel measurably poorer and less secure, and many of us busily engaged in pouring the hot oil of our criticism over the book found ourselves scalded by some scattering drops. I remember distinctly how the book began to appear in bookstore windows, ranged in bold red-and-white jackets like British soldiers on dress parade. Those hardy Villagers who ventured beyond the sacred precincts brought back breathless accounts of swarms of office girls carrying cellophane-wrapped rental copies, and by the beginning of January the book was among the favored reading material for trips on the IRT, the BMT and the Independent subways. Breedon Rawley was a success: he autographed copies of his book at Macy's and Brentano's; he stammered through a talk at a book fair, he was given a spread in *Life* (squeezed between photographs of a snake swallowing a frog and an article on How I Would Deal with Russia by an ex-ambassador to that dark land), he had made an ass of himself at some cocktail parties and behaved rather well at others, he had lunched with his publisher at the Algonquin, and four weeks after publication he had received through the publisher's office one hundred and eight letters, of which only fourteen were mash notes, nine from females.

However, that is only a preface of a sort to our real story. We are not so much interested in the meteor course of Breedon Rawley's book as in what happened to some of the people he used as prototypes for characters in a novel being read throughout the country one winter. I am thinking in particular of four of the people I knew fairly well—of Amy Macduff, Aaron Ross, Lois Wilson and Oliver Kittridge. Oh yes, and of Breedon Rawley too. And I'd like to begin

with Breedon Rawley as he was about to enter the Marino
late one night in January. Behind him the cold dark street,
before him the warm crowded bar . . .

•

2. Breedon Rawley Returns in Triumph
Along a Path of Ashes

A BLARE OF BRASS from the five mem-
bers of the editorial board. A deafening huzzah from the
hundreds of thousands of faithful followers. A thick carpet
of reviews rolled out across the threshold. Hail, hail, all hail
Breedon Rawley!

Nothing like that at all.

Breedon Rawley, making his triumphal return to the
Marino after an historic absence of a month and a half,
paused on the street and looked through the fogged windows, trying to distinguish faces through the opaque sheet.
No use. The faces were smudged and smeared, blank pink
combinations. To tell the truth, Breedon Rawley, although
of a courageous enough line, was a little afraid to enter. He
was wondering what they thought of his book in there,
and he was terribly uncertain about how his former (because he had an intuitive feeling they would be former)
friends would treat him.

Even at one in the morning on a Wednesday night the
Marino was tumultuous. It was filled with people and conversation; words seemed to choke the air like great massed
clouds, lightning phrases playing along their edges and
pontifical pronunciamentos rumbling inside them. The
usual gaunt faces leaned toward each other in all the
booths, the jaws all chopping out simultaneous sentences.
Beard almost touched beard in wagged argument. There
was too a restless harried movement, people moving along
the bar and from bar to booth and booth to booth, talking,
talking. These were the young intellectuals of the Village,
drained into the Marino through all the subterranean chan-

nels of American life, now clogging the Marino through a
process of damp yet sympathetic grouping. A couple of
years before, Breedon knew, they had gathered at a place
up the street called the Biretta; in a couple of more years
it would be another bar. There were the young intellectuals,
talking of sex and of drinking, of marihuana and perversion
and poetry, talking about each other and the people they
despised, talking as always with a desperate resolution to
crystallize all the indecencies of their unhappy threatened
young lives into words.

Into this atmosphere, where once he had been a familiar,
came Breedon Rawley the very model of a modern Southern aristocrat, son of Beauregard Rawley, grandson of
Longstreet Rawley, whose own father had seen the incomparable Stonewall Jackson shot in the back during the
gloomy victory of Chancellorsville and had ridden down the
back roads of Maryland with the immortal Jeb Stuart;
Breedon Rawley—portrait by Edgar Allan Poe, deep brown
eyes in a face malarial-thin, the jet hair so common through
genetic mischance and sexual misadventure among the
Anglo-Saxons of the South, the narrow long hands whose
bones moved like visible cables under the smooth thin
skin; Breedon Rawley, suh—the inheritor of a proud name
and a proud tradition, born within fifty miles and three
generations of a white-columned ancestral mansion sur-
rounded by slave shacks; Breedon Rawley—five foot three
and a half inches, exactly.

He stood in the doorway, a little lost, looking for someone
he wanted to see, someone who would give him a sense of
continuing presence here in the Marino. He got a sycophan-
tic toot from a young painter in stained dungarees, and a
girl named Frances Finnerty, a matriculated English war
bride whom Breedon had once given his manuscript to read
in a singularly unsuccessful attempt to make her, saw him
and cried in a surprised fluting voice, hello, well there hello.
Just then Breedon noticed Amy Macduff standing at the
end of the bar and he started to needle his way toward her.
She was standing with one foot on the brass rail, with the
practised stance of a man, the calf of one long powerful leg
slightly bunched, a little drunk as usual. The youth had
flaked off her and her best years were mocked in the
pinched skin around the eyes, but the essential monumental

structure was unchanged, unchangeable. Breedon thought
(approaching her) of how five years before he used to sit at
the window of his mother's apartment in New Orleans and
wait for Amy to come striding up the street, her bright
head bent forward as if with the weight of her massed hair,
taking long quick and yet somehow erratic steps. Later,
when he could make a rough schedule for her, he would
station himself in front of the house so that he could see
for a moment, and remember, the flat planes of her cheeks
where they sloped down from the high bones under her
great blue eyes and her heavy animal lips and then, as she
passed, the piston movement of her full buttocks (so unlike
the flippant signalling of the asses of smaller women). He
had often wanted to stop her there on Rampart Street, but
the speed and power of her walk made him feel, in his own
acutely distressed image, like a small boy trying to flag
down a locomotive. It wasn't until he had watched her for
a couple of months that he had realized that she was almost
always, if not always, drunk as she passed, and that she
walked in a straight line in the same way that most other
people would stagger. Later, when he came to New York
and met her through Oliver Kittridge's abortive theatrical
venture, Breedon told her, after a great deal of hesitation,
about watching her in the Vieux Carre. She had actually
been delighted ("Oh my God, how could you, why should
you? Me!") and after that always treated him with ex-
aggerated affection, making a kind of pet of him. She was
Aaron Ross' girl at the time he first met her, and Breedon
would often torture himself by visualizing their two strong
bodies clashing together, like trains coupling. For Amy's
size had made her Breedon's Everest among women, and as
a virgin twenty-three (except for one desperate unsuccessful attempt with a caved-in New Orleans whore) his reach
could still exceed his grasp.

And now, as Amy stirred at the bar and seemed about
to turn to face him, Breedon felt a kind of fright, and reacting in a common way found it urgent to veer sharply
away and head toward the john.

There, facing the urinal, he faced some more of his past,
because above the stained porcelain was chipped rather
crudely the name of Oliver Kittridge, memorialized until
the remote date when the men's toilet of the Marino would

again be painted. (Possibly never.) Breedon remembered the time when Kittridge, almost a foot taller than he, had furtively peered over the edge of the urinal as Breedon was relieving himself and had seemed about to say something. And how a good deal later than that, their fine avant-garde theatrical venture had come to an abrupt end when Aaron Ross had slugged Kittridge for reasons not unknown.

Then, courage having returned with his relief, Breedon sallied back into the bar.

"Breedie!"

Amy, seeing him as he approached, cried out in her loud rich voice, and in a moment mashed him against her chest. He sank into the smothering softness of her bosom and then recoiled, or rather he was pushed away as Amy held him off to look at him.

"My God, Breedie, in what chi-chi haunts have you been hiding? Why don't we ever feast the eyes on you any-more?"

"I—I've been busy," he said apologetically, knowing he was skittering on the edge of smugness.

"Well, you must have been. You must have been! A drink, n'est-ce pas. We must celebrate the occasion. What will you have?"

"B-bourbon."

"Ah, that ole Souflan', that ole Souselan'!" She called along the bar for a bourbon and another rye. "You don't mind if I join you?" she said, laughing loudly at herself. And without waiting for the inevitable answer: "Tell me about yourself. Tell me what's been happening. My God, I've been excited for you."

There were other people standing around, people Breedon knew in a way, and he felt almost embarrassed by Amy's effusiveness. And pleased.

"N-nothing m-much has been hu-happening," he told Amy (when he actually wanted to carry her off with his success to storm her heights with his triumph). "It—it's bu-been a rat race," he added, effecting a compromise.

"Tell us all about it," said a curly-headed man not much over thirty whose jowls were beginning to slouch. His voice was bitter. "Tell us everything. The whole works."

Amy asked Breedon, "You know Jason Spivak?"

"Of course he knows me," Spivak said emphatically.

"Everyone knows me. What do you say, Breedon, how does it feel to write a bestseller?"

Amy cut in, "Jason is interviewing you. Not now, Jason."

Spivak ignored her. "How does it feel?"

"Well, all right, I ge-guess."

"Come on, Jason," Amy said, "be nice."

"What do you mean, be nice? I'm just curious."

"You're being a bastard."

"Oh for Christ's sake, all I want to find out is how it feels when you turn a load of crap into a mountain of gold. I'm interested in the occult arts."

Breedon felt himself flushing, couldn't say anything. Words were pasted to his dry tongue.

Amy saying, "Cut it out, Jason," and now Breedon ungratefully resented her protective tone. Didn't she think he was man enough . . .

"I'm not doing anything," Spivak said. Then, to Breedon directly, "Am I being offensive?" No answer, so he said, "Well, am I?" Crowing. "You see, he admits I'm only being curious. Real legitimate curiosity. The kind that kills cats. Look, what I want to know is, and this is an important question, why should we knock our heads against a stone wall the way some of us do? Did you ever read my book?" A pause. "No? Well, it was a good book. I put my guts into it for two years and do you know how many copies it sold? And do you know why? Because it was a good book, it was an honest job, a guy had given himself to that goddamned book." Spivak pushed his face closer to Breedon's and his thick breath (beer, tobacco and tooth decay) almost knocked Breedon back. "Tell me something," he said, "just tell me, did you sit down to write a bestseller or was that the best book you could write?"

Breedon tried to rip the words off his tongue.

"Come on," Amy said, draining her drink and grabbing Breedon's sleeve. "Let's get the hell out of here."

"I'd have some respect for you," Spivak was saying, "if you told me that was the best you could do. But if it wasn't, it's people like you, calling themselves writers, who . . ."

His voice trailed off as Amy dragged Breedon away.

Ashes, asses, ashes.

Out in the cold street, Amy said, "I hate these jerks who can't write worth a damn and go around with a chip on the shoulder. No, I don't hate them, I feel a kind of pity for them, even when they're busy being sorry for me. You didn't even have your drink. I apologize, baby."

"Y-you apologize? Wu-what for?"

"For dragging you out of there. Let me make it up to you. Let me take you into the one across the street."

In the bar, after two drinks, Amy said, "Breedie, you mustn't make people try to live up to you. Listen, I'm going to tell you something." Her voice grew thicker with the impending confidence. "I've found out that people love you if they can live down to you. They want to feel superior. Ah yes, but there's the point. They want to look down at you, but not too far down. They want the luxury of disdain without the fear of responsibility. I've lost more friends because they were afraid that some day they might have to be responsible for me." She laughed ironically. "And I'm not even responsible for myself. My God, people stink." She rattled the ice in her glass, the unfailing sign that she wanted another drink. Breedon ordered another rye. "Aren't you going to have something?" Amy asked him.

"I'm not f-finished with this," he said.

"Oh well, haste makes pleasure." She swallowed. "Aaron got that way," she went on. "He became afraid that I'd go down and he'd go down with me. Down with the sinking ship. The merchant marine image."

"You m-mean that Aaron and you . . ."

"Are finito, finished, kaput. I'm a linguist. He's got his own place on Jones Street now." She drank some more. "We were always getting in each other's way and on each other's nerves. I always expected him to get picked up."

"By a g-girl?"

"By the cops. I hate cops."

"Pu-picked up for what?"

"His keen mind, trained by vicissitudes—let no one say I'm drunk when I can pronounce that—has come to a logical conclusion."

"Logical con-conclusion? I—I don't understand."

"Ah, but you're not supposed to understand. Cryptic, I want to be cryptic. Let's forget about Aaron. Come on, Breedie, have something. Don't make me drink alone."

"I—I haven't finished this one," Breedon said, but when she looked at him he had that old terrible feeling of being so much too small and he drank his bourbon quickly, gulped it, trying not to make a face even though he hated the taste all the way down. "There," he said, setting the glass down heavily, making a punctuation mark. Something was going to happen tonight, something good. Aaron was gone (the girl on the rebound) but that wasn't it. It was him, his book, she was impressed by his book, she saw him not as Little Breedie but as Breedon Rawley the Author. Not part a man, but a man of parts.

"That's better," Amy said as he sat his empty glass down. "I mustn't drink alone. That way I might become an alcoholic. Have you ever read the pamphlets? Then you know what they say about people who drink privately. Well," she said defiantly, "I prefer to drink at home. Bars are such gloomy places. They drive you to drink. You enter these surroundings so you can forget them. Look at this place." Ring-stained fake mahogany bar (Breedon looked farther), smeared mirror, rows of bottles, two men and another man alone hunched over the bar, dull grey empty square of the television screen. "Christ!" Amy said in a sudden despairing voice. "Christ! Christ! Christ!" She hit the bar each time with the flat of her hand, the last time pressing it with convulsive force against the wood. Then, "Forgive me," she said, drinking down her rye.

"Is s-s-something wrong?" Was that all the brilliant author could think of to say? Why did his tongue always trip him up?

"Nothin's wrong. Everything's tres gai."

"If I c-can h-help you . . ." (Amy, I mean it.)

"Help me?" She put the shot glass back on the bar, and Breedon saw for perhaps the hundredth time in his life her big rough hands, with the scars of several cuts across the fingers, fingers that made his own look like feeble twigs. "I'm getting out of here," Amy said abruptly. "I've got to get out of this place." She twisted away from the bar, stumbled, straightened immediately, and walked toward the door. Breedon trotted after her, caught up to her on the sidewalk. "I'm going home," Amy said.

"I'll walk you."

"You don't have to."

"I—I'd like to. I haven't seen you . . ."

She dropped her hand on his head, saying, "I like your

hair, did I ever tell you that?" and started up Macdougal Street, with Breedon following as he had in the plaguing days before the publication of his book, taking quick little paces—trot, trot, trot—as he tried to keep up with her. There was always a direct ratio between the amount she had drunk and the speed with which she walked, and now she was going fast, really tearing along. They went past the dark tenements, the stores with the single dim light on all night, a drunk slumped against a stoop, (Amy saying, "Poor bastard, he'll freeze to death, why doesn't someone do something for him?") past the dead cars along the curb, the battered dull garbage cans, the remains of a charred Christmas tree some kids must have burned, past the glamor and glitter of the great gay metropolis. An old man of it might have been forty with a scooped-out face asked Breedon for a quarter, and Amy said give it to him, give him a dollar (give him a million!), and she told the shivering bum to get himself a couple of drinks. Once Amy stooped to pick up a half-grown cat and stroke it several times, whispering to it, and then throw it into the icy gutter, where it landed silently and scampered away. (She would like to kiss and bite the whole world, Breedon thought.) Then she stopped in front of one of the tenements.

"So," Amy said, "we have arrived at my abode. I bid you now a fond goodnight."

"I—I'll come up."

"My God, you can't, the place is dirty, I don't want you to see the place when it's so goddamned filthy. Come and see me tomorrow."

"It—it's too early to go ho-home. I—I . . . (damn it!) . . . it's only one o'clock."

"But God, it's so messy."

"Wu-what do I care?"

She shrugged her shoulders, and he followed her through the narrow mean hall, past the cracked doors and the piles of rubbish, and up two unwashed reeking flights of steps. She seemed to be leading him as she might lead a dog, detached, aware that he was there and that he was going where she was going, and not much more. The third floor hallway was dark, and Amy groped her way forward, saying, "They're hoping I'll break my neck. Ah, but I'm going to fool them. I'll survive every one of those righteous bastards." Breedon heard her key prodding at the lock. Then she opened the door and switched on the light. Entering, he kicked over some rubbish which had been left just outside the door in a paper bag. "You mustn't upset my garbage disposal system," Amy said.

They went into the apartment through the kitchen, a nasty little room with a chipped porcelain sink and a great black stove, a mess of dirty dishes piled in the sink, a few scattered dishes with stale food like droppings still on the deal table, and heaps of yellowed cigarette butts. "Be it ever so humble," Amy said. "The typical American home. One ninety-third of a nation. The man from *Good House-keeping* is due tomorrow to take the pictures." In the tiny studio room there were more heaps of butts, a disorderly studio couch, some chaotic paintings, an empty half-gallon wine bottle on the windowsill. A couple of books had been pulled out from the plank-and-brick bookcase and left on the studio couch. With satisfaction Breedon saw that one of them was his own. He picked it up as he sat down on the couch.

"Why don't you autograph it for me?" Amy asked him. "After all, I stole that copy instead of waiting to borrow one."

"You stole it?" Amy—good old Amy—always full of de-lightful surprises (except whatever she did never really was a surprise). Breedon told himself that he was feeling very relaxed, very companionable, very much the Man of Distinction, holding his own book in his hand. "Why did you steal it?"

"Now you mustn't be angry, Breedie, you mustn't be angry. You get royalties on copies that are stolen, don't you? Besides, it's much more complimentary to steal a book than to buy one. Anyone with money can buy a book; it's a simple business transaction, but only someone who really wants one will steal it. Instead of bestseller lists they ought to have best stolen lists. Why don't you suggest that to someone?"

"I will," Breedon said. He leaned far back. "Sit down, s-sit down here."

But she stayed on her feet, jittering a little as she said: "I must have stolen fifty or a hundred books from the pub-lic library in San Francisco. That was when I lived in the

Monkey Flats. Did I ever tell you about the Monkey Flats?"
Breedon sensed that she was deliberately winding herself
up into a monologue. "Sometimes my conscience used to
trouble me—I have a conscience, damn it, yes I do—and I
used to think I was depriving all the other good citizens
of San Francisco of the books they wanted to read, but all
my friends used to come in and steal the books from me, so
they got circulated anyway, and that took care of my conscience. By the time I left Frisco I felt like a sieve with
books running through me. What do you want to drink?"

"Anything you've got," Breedon told her airily, although
he didn't really want to drink at all. "I'm not fussy." He
waved his hand in what he felt was a broad relaxed gesture.
As she started for the kitchen he stopped her with: "What
do you thi-think of my book?"

She stood in the doorway. "What do you want my opinion
for?"

"Well, I—I value it. Yes, I really do," he added too af-
firmatively.

"I know nothing about literature, nothing about the
higher arts, nothing."

"But what do you think of it?" he persisted.

She sighed. "Ah well, why didn't you write about something you really know?" She went on quickly. "Now don't
be hurt. That wasn't the way I meant it. I meant, well, you
can write, I can see that you can write, but you threw
yourself away. You . . . " She stopped abruptly. "Finish
of the discussion."

"No, no," Breedon said, feeling as if he were asking her
to push him over the edge of a precipice. "T-tell me."

"What's there to tell? You were fascinated by the Village
and you wrote about a lot of characters, me included. So we
made good amusing reading for the people in the sticks, and
there you have it, Breedie, but what the hell, you're young,
and who am I to talk, I can't write anything, not even a
letter."

From the depths Breedon said, "But—but I wasn't writing about y-y-you."

She took a step toward him. "Now come off it, Breedie,
will you? I despise people when they aren't honest. Sit
down," she said sharply as he started to get up. "Honesty,
the lost virtue, the last virtue. Listen to me talk! Why don't

you stop me?" (But how could he?) "I don't give a damn what you write about me just so long as it's not the truth." She laughed and Breedon tried to join in with her, but she wasn't really laughing at all and he was left stranded. "My God, why did you have me committing suicide? You started me thinking about it all over again."

"A-amy . . ."

"Did I ever tell you about the time in New Orleans? I bought a gun once and I was going to shoot myself. I don't remember why it was. Yes I do." Christ, she was talking tonight, she was garrulous, and it was annoying because it interfered. "I thought I'll give myself just one day to clean up all my affairs—ah, not that kind—make my peace with the world, and then that evening I'd end it all. Did you ever want to shoot yourself?" There was so much Breedon could say in answer to that, and he did start to tell her something, but she ran on right through his first tentative sputter. "That was in the morning when I bought the gun. In the morning. I didn't do anything that morning, just sat around and drank a little and looked out the window without any feeling of regret. What the hell, I've always known I'm self-destructive. I felt wonderful, I really felt wonderful. What are most of us living for anyway? We're just hanging on. What's so great about life? I said to myself I'll take care of everything in the afternoon. I believe in procrastination. If I don't do anything I can't do anything foolish. That afternoon I got an idea. There was some bastard I hated and I thought what the hell if I'm going to kill myself I ought at least to kill him first. You might know who I mean. So I went around to his place but he wasn't home. I would have done it too. That gave me an idea and I started to think of some other people I hated—ah, nothing gentle about her—and I made quite a list, I can tell you, because this world is full of bastards, real evil bastards, but most of these weren't in New Orleans and the rest I couldn't manage to locate. They'll never know how close they were, but maybe someday I'll do it again. After a while I began to get tired of the whole idea and I ended up selling the gun in a bar to someone from Alabama or some such place. So ends my story."

Breedon was busily and consciously translating the recital into a story: the girl buys the gun to kill herself, etc.

His agent had been after him for more material: strike
while the iron is hot. It might even make a book. Yes, yes,
suppose she listed all the people she wanted to kill, and
then there would be a chapter for each one, and you
wouldn't know until the last chapter, until the very end,
which of them she was going to kill. A kind of *Bridge of
San Luis Rey* in reverse. What was so bad about that? Idea,
copyright Breedon Rawley.

"What are you thinking about?"

"You gave me an idea. I th-think I can work it into a
b-book," Breedon said impressively. Proudly he added, "it
j-just came to me, just like that."

"A book about what?"

"Ab-about what you told me. About a girl . . ."

"My God, why write about that? Listen, if I had your
talent do you know what I'd write about? Well, look at the
world, Christ, look at the way it's going. Do something,
Christ, write something, make them stop."

"S-stop what?"

"Never mind. Why didn't you remind me," she said, going
into the kitchen, "I offered you a drink." Breedon, listening
to her open the ice box door and start to rummage inside,
felt frustrated. This wasn't what he had wanted at all. He
had envisioned, but vaguely, telling her of his plans, big
things he was going to do, perhaps a trilogy on the intel-
lectual development of a young Southerner, or a long
definitive novel about the Civil War (told from the Southern point of view this once), or his plan to travel and write
a geographical novel about South America, or even (his pet
project) a novel about the Nuremburg Trials. He had never
set down a word about any of these projects, but they were
there, somewhere around the base of his skull. But instead
of talking to Amy about these things and making her see
(if she didn't see already, and she didn't seem to see it)
that he was going to become one of the truly important
writers in America, more, the world, instead of that he was
listening to her grumble in the kitchen, "There isn't a goddamn thing, not a goddamn thing to drink in the house."
She came back into the studio room. "What do you think
of that? Not a thing." Breedon thought there was a trace
of fear in her voice. She walked over to the windowsill,
picked up the empty half gallon bottle, shook it, and set it

down again. He could see even in that dim light that she was biting at her lower lip. Then she came toward him, bore down on him, ducked, and reached under the couch, rising with an almost empty pint of brandy in her hand. She held it toward the light, swished it to see how much residue there was in the bottle. Just a wash of it. "I can't offer you any straight out of the bottle," she said, taking a swallow. "That would be vulgar, tres vulgar, and I must be a good hostess." She finished the bottle and threw it under the couch. "There must be some more. Just let me think." She started to pace the small room, going from wall to wall in four broken steps. "Listen," she said, "don't let anyone ever tell you alcohol destroys ambition. It gives you an incentive. God, what I wouldn't do for a drink right now."

"Honey," Breedon said, luxuriously letting the Southern word slip over his tongue, "s-sit down, take it easy. Here, sit here." He patted the couch at his side.

"I've got to have a drink."

"Take i-it easy."

"My God . . ."

Again patting the couch, "Sit down, honey." But this time he knew the "honey" was wrong.

"I don't want to sit down," she said, and flopped into an armchair at the side of the room. "My nerves are beating me to death." She was sitting with her legs carelessly spread, her skirt tight across her thighs, and Breedon's eyes went to the shadowed white of the insides of her legs, went there and stayed there, while his stomach began a slow whirling with all the tension of fear. "Breedie, baby, get me something to drink."

He stood up, walked toward her on sawdust legs (this is stronger than both of us).

"Go ahead. Get me something."

"A-Amy . . . Amy I—I . . ."

"A good boy. Be good and get me something."

"I just . . ." He was bending over her chair now, running his hands over her shoulders.

"You don't live far. You must have something."

Lord, but her shoulders were broad and how round at the end.

"Christ now, don't be foolish. Just get me something first. Listen, go down to the Marino, tell them . . ." His hand

was following the slope of her breast when she thrust him
away. "Cut that out, damn you!" She was bulking over him,
like a steeple about to topple. "Oh you sonofabitch, here
I'm dying and all you can think about is your lousy hardon.
Get the hell out of here. Find yourself some kid, there are
plenty of cute little kids who'll be impressed by your book.
Get out of here, I said." Breedon started toward the door,
trembling, humiliated, but Amy caught him before he could
open it, wheedled: "Baby, baby now, you mustn't go away
sore. I didn't mean anything. It's just that I feel like I'm
dying. You couldn't know, Christ." She turned him around,
bent down, and laid her thick lips, dry now, inaccurately
on his mouth. "Be a good boy. Go to the Marino. Tell them
it's for me. Tell them I'll pay them tomorrow." She was
starting to shake. "Christ, go ahead." He could see her
stomach pulsing under her blouse. "Go on, baby, go on."
"What should I get?" he asked. "Oh God, anything. Whiskey." She turned him back toward the door. As he opened
it he looked around and saw that she was standing in the
middle of the studio room, unzipping her skirt. Her back
was toward him and he watched her drop the skirt to the
floor, stepping out of it as if it were a puddle of ink (yes,
by God, she wasn't wearing anything underneath), and
then pull her blouse over her head. Naked, a monument
of nakedness, she went through the open door into the next
room and he heard her fall onto the bed. Closing the door
gently, not wanting her to hear the closing of the door
(tiger and prey) he went through the studio room, stepping around her skirt and blouse, and into the box of the
bedroom. She was lying there, her legs loose, one of them
half off the bed like a broken column, her palms cradling
her head, her flesh seeming to glow in the semi-darkness of
the room. He could see that her eyes were open, but she
wasn't looking at him. Her stomach was shaking, the whole
surface bulging and breaking spasmodically. "Lu-let me
help you . . . let me h-help . . ." He sat down on the edge
of the bed and reached out his hand. At his touch she
whipped over on her side. He ran his hand softly along her
back, hoping to soothe her. Suddenly she kicked and kicked
at the wall, grunting savage little cries, and then she began
to moan. Breedon scrambled off the bed. "Amy . . .
Amy . . ." The moans were becoming fragmentary, were

becoming sobs. "Amy . . ." And then Breedon was afraid.
Of what he couldn't say, of some eruption, some insane fury.
He backed to the door, weak, puny, childish, and went out so
blindly that he stumbled with his small feet into the rubbish
pile again and half-skidded into the wall. Her agony was
inside him, but with that defensive alchemy that protects
us from what are called instincts it was being felt as self-
pity. Why, he asked himself, why did that have to happen?
Going down the stairs, holding tight to the bannister, he
thought. Why did she have to let that happen? Yes, why
did she have to get sick just then? Just then . . . He missed
a step and almost fell. Get her a drink? Maybe he ought to.
A drink would settle her and he could . . . At the bottom
of the stairs, anger. What, buy it with a drink! No better
than that whore. What did she care about him, what did
she care what he wrote, what he did, who he was. Out in
the street, self-righteous. What right did she have to drink?
She could have been such a wonderful . . . Who was she
to drink, being big and beautiful? What about him, he
didn't, and God he'd been knocked hard. All his life smaller
than everyone else, his father run away when he was only
a kid, his mother sending him to their kinfolk who treated
him like a backdoor nigger, then with his mother living
in a house where he couldn't sit down because he might soil
the furniture, sick for two years that time in Jacksonville
and lying in bed for one long year while the other boys
were playing and growing, and then when he left the house
and began to walk around (Breedon, you mustn't run, that's
what the doctor said) to find the other kids were giants
now, cruel and frightening. And then the dream beginning,
when he was how old, impossible to say now, but he remembered his mother telling people while they were still
in Jacksonville, Breedon is going to be a writer, I just know
it, I have every confidence in him, his grandfather Jefferson
Rawley wrote the most beautiful letters, I still have them.
The books he'd read, beginning with the year in bed, and
then he found that he was writing more and more, with the
Biloxi paper (when they lived there) publishing his poems.
A whole childhood drenched in misery. He should be drinking, not her. And yet . . . perhaps if he went to the Marino
and got a bottle, not a whole fifth because he didn't want
her to pass out, but say a pint or a half-pint . . . Back to

the Marino? Well, that was the only place he could get a
bottle at this time of night. Or morning. Back to the
Marino? Well, look who's here—Breedon Rawley, the
author of the (epithet) bestseller.

It stabbed him, hilt-deep in all his visions on returning
gloriously, because he knew that he should never have
gone back to the Marino, not before he was ready to treat
the opinions of those lean and hungry and lacerated minds
with indifference. They were now despite himself his ar-
tistic conscience, and his conscience hurt. He wanted people
to tell him his book was good—else why would he have
written it? He wanted to hear people say, and he wanted
to believe, that it was a great book—well no, be reasonable,
that it had the seeds of greatness, those promiscuous seeds.
Go back to the Marino? Not there. He would not get the
assurance he needed there. The contrary. Those gaunt faces
would never approve. However much they might secretly
envy him, they would never grant approval. And when
someone like Jason Spivak asked, "Is that the best book you
can write?" it didn't do much good to ask himself what
Spivak had ever written (one book, and the man was already over thirty) and by what right then, sir, he spoke.
(Since a beggar can cross the path of a king.) He spoke,
and that was enough, because in speaking he brought
Breedon Rawley to the edge of the deep pool of inner fears,
the unreflecting pool into which each writer at times must
sink, some never to be found again, no matter how many
salvoes sound over the surface. In the authorized biography
of Breedon Rawley (four volumes, boxed, illus.) there was
now one verifiable fact: that he was a writer. Agreed.
But what kind of writer? What species—specious? What
genus—genius? What would that name, Rawley, mean in
history? Rawley North Carolina, Sir Walter's head, a brand
of cigarettes (since language becomes more phonetic), name
Breedon perhaps. The adolescent dream of greatness, of
immortality nagged at him. Certainly, go ahead and scoff
at the Great American Novel, think of it as non-existent
as the Continent of Mu or love for your father, but when
he was younger Breedon had known (and he still knew)
that it had not yet been written, it was waiting there still,
and there had been certain times when he had known that
the author of it would be and could be none other than—

hats off!—Breedon Rawley. Yes, he was going to write it
and stand on that foot-thick volume and be taller than other
men. Now—now that he had written a novel and was being
called a success, now with his picture in *Life* (typewriter
in front of him, bookshelves to the rear), now that he had
heard those people cluck-cluck that it was so so *extraordi-*
nary for someone so young to write a novel, now he was
deeply and painfully depressed. The depression gutted him.
He knew that the book was no damned good, and in his
bleaker moments the thought almost killed him. "Was that
the best book you could write?" Yes—he had to admit it—
it was. And thus none of his earnest daydreams realized.
Where was she—the beautiful woman saying: "Breedon,
I've been waiting for you all my life . . ." The reviewers:
"With his very first novel Breedon Rawley, a man to respect, takes a place in the very first rank of American
writers." A letter from George Bernard Shaw: "I wish to
reach across the Atlantic, which so unfortunately divides
us, to take your hand. . . ." Instead: one hundred and eight
letters (to date) of such calibre as: "I was very interested
in your book because I have written one about the same
theme . . ." Or: "Are you the Breedon Rawley I knew
in . . ." And the constant fear that someone would say
to him (did in fact say to him): "Is that the best book
you can write?" He had money, that was true, but his
old fervent dreams had run more to garrets and defiance,
with fame and fortune coming as the result of some struggle. Now he was faced with the obligation of writing another
book sometime, and grinding out short stories for his agent,
and he was already wondering what in the name of God
he was going to write about. He must go forward like a
stoic Roman (quote) where pangs and terrors in his path-
way lay. Perhaps he could take the money he had made
and spend three or four years writing a really great book.
If he could write a great book. If . . . that castrating word.
    Breedon Rawley walked slowly, not so much thinking as
feeling, dredging around inside himself, stirring up those
muddy fears, walked past a few lesbians clustered tough
around the dingy corner of Third Street, the cheap base-
ment taverns for the soldiers and the sailors and the sluts,
along the side of the quiet park (was that Aaron Ross
going away from the Square?), past the apartment house

of Mrs. Franklin Delano Roosevelt (it looked like him),
and the chummy avant-garde bookstore at the end of the
park, up to bright Eighth Street where couples were still
plunging through the cold night from one little joy club to
another. Across the street, directly facing him, was the
Washington Square Bookshop (the probable scene of Amy's
depredation). He crossed the street to it, looked in the
window. Where two short weeks ago there had been a rigid
row of copies of his book, now he could see in the light
that came over his shoulder from a street lamp not a single
copy. Not one. Instead, the showcase was treacherously
filled with a pyramid of bosoms and swords, the garish
covers of the latest contender in the bestseller tournament.
And not a single copy of his book. *Sic transit* . . .

Wait, there was one—there, at the bottom, and off to the
l-left.

"Well, really!"

He spun around, to face Lois Wilson.

"I thought you'd be in Hollywood by now, or Europe, or
anywhere. What are you doing in this lousy town?"

"Y-you make me feel unwelcome."

Her olive face was open with a smile. The light shone on
her oiled hair, drawn back tight and flat from the pale part
that ran like a highroad through it. A small pockmark in
the middle of her forehead had been filled with mascara and
looked like a Hindu caste mark.

"I've hardly seen you since those long-gone days of the
old theatre group. The group that never was," she added.

Breedon remembered again that conglomeration under
the aegis of Oliver Kittridge which had flapped fledgling
wings and never flown.

"I—I guess I've been bu-busy," he said for the second
time that night.

"Well, you're not so busy this moment." She slipped her
hand under his elbow and began to steer him down the
street. "Walk me along and pick me up on what's been
happening to you."

"N-not much," he said, wondering with an attempt at
defiance whether everyone (or anyone) was staring at
them.

"Don't be so modest," Lois said. "I dig that it's been fabulous. Really fabulous." And two fingers coiled into the bend of his arm. Trusting, tenacious fingers.

So Breedon Rawley walked down Eighth Street in the borough of Manhattan of the City of New York in—more to the point—the United States of America with Lois Wilson, stepped behind her as he remembered to take the gentlemanly position on the gutter side, slightly pale and chilled as he fought down those embarrassments acquired through nineteen years of living below the Mason and Dixon Line, walked arm in arm with this girl who would have looked quite natural and still beautiful in Calcutta or Bombay, one-eighth or perhaps one-fourth of whose ancestors might have originated in the old slave shacks on the Rawley Place. Somewhere a shadow fell across a Confederate memorial. And then was gone.

3. Aaron Ross Seizes Upon
A Patron of the Arts

 ̇ THAT WAS BREEDON RAWLEY pattering along the park toward Eighth Street. The shit, Aaron thought, he had a couple of things coming to him for that book of his. Meyer Greenberg—he was supposed to be some character named Meyer Greenberg in that book. A guy who slapped people around just to prove a Jew could be tough. Well, what the hell. He'd never hit a guy without good reason. A Jew who hated the world just because it was a Christian world. Or words to that effect. Holy Jesus! Who gave a damn whether it was a Mohammedan world or a Buddhist world or a what have you world. It was all a sorry mess and it mightn't be a bad idea for the dumb bastards to start pitching atom bombs all over the lot. Get rid of everyone and start out with a clean slate. Start evolution all over again with horses. The Everlasting Neigh. Christ, what a country when a jerk like Breedon Rawley could make fifty thousand bucks or so with a piece of crap. But crap, that's what the country wanted. Screw all that. No time to be a Deep Thinker now. There was work at hand.

The Patron of the Arts was rolling toward Sixth Avenue and if he went along there, what with all the lights and the cars and the people, then he was a lost cause. He'd spotted the Patron earlier on Third Street almost getting hit by a cab, and he'd noticed that the Patron was wearing an expensive overcoat. The Patron was flush, unless he'd pissed it all away drinking. Well, with half a break he'd soon find out whether he was going to be an Associate Patron, a Contributing Patron, or just a plain bust.

Aaron stopped. He was getting too careless, coming up too close to the schnook. Better to trail him by half a block or so and from the other side of the street.

Bad. The Patron was stopping outside a bar, holding onto the building with one hand and trying to look through the window to see what was going on inside. Bad if he went in. Catastrophic. He'd probably stay there until closing. Come on, Jack, keep moving. I need it more than they do. You're not going home with dough on your hip, so spend it for a Worthy Purpose. For Art, Jack. Squeeze tubes of paint out of your wallet. A good Number Five brush. Jack, you'd be astonished if I told you all the things money will buy. Look, Jack, keep walking and I'll acquaint you with the Ross Theory of the Arts. Theory of Life too, because Art is Life, and Life is artful. The artful dodger. Get away from those swinging doors. Art, Jack, requires Time, and Time requires Money, and that's why there are more Business-men than Artists. You can't rush an artist, Jack. He's got to have Time to Develop, only these days a guy gets squeezed drier than his own tubes of paint. People keep asking you, What do you do for a Living? And you tell them you're an Artist. So they look blank and say, Yes, sure, but what do you do for a Living? I know, Jack, because my own father is one of those. My father is an International Banker who as a sideline has a tailor shop in the Bronx and makes a vast fortune sewing buttons on vests. When I came out of the merchant marine he said to me, You've got some money saved, you should open a business with Morris—that's my kid brother, Jack. I said, A tailor shop maybe? And he said, Not a tailor shop, a good business.

I'm not a business man, Pop, I said, I'm going to be an artist. And he said, You're meshugge. That means crazy, Jack. Jack, I can see from the fit of your overcoat that you and my father ought to shake hands. I'll bet you're one of those smug bastards who says, If you're a Real Artist and Have The Stuff you'll work Eight Hours A Day and you'll paint in your Spare Time. Make up your mind, Jack, are you going in there or not? Now dammit, dammit to hell, there was a time when a young guy who wanted to be an artist and had the stuff could go and work with one of the old boys and they'd paint some walls and cast some doors for a few years and then he'd be ready to knock off a few small jobs on his own. No one said, Paint in your spare time. These days, you know what the trouble is, every household from the Bronx to San Diego is filled with reproductions of Van Gogh and Gauguin. The silk screen is replacing the canvas. Culture, Jack, that magic word Culture, comes for twenty bucks framed, so why take a chance on a new guy when you can get a Nineteenth Century French Old Master (and know what you're getting) at the nearest novelty shop. No spare time work, that's not art, you'll pardon me if I say you've got to give your life to it. But a guy needs to eat and he has to buy stuff and maybe he wants a drink now and then, and that's where you fit in, Jack. There has to be Patrons.

"Aaron Ross."

A high-pitched voice, and yet funereal, and if it wasn't Oliver Kittridge. No time for him now.

"I have something to say to you."

Well, look at him. What was he doing—starving himself to death? He had dough. What was this all about?

"I got no time now," Aaron said. Where was the Patron?

"I have something important to say."

"Some other time."

The hell with Kittridge. Getting him and the others together in that theatrical group, telling him he was going to paint the scenery (that would have been a good push), and then that business up in his apartment. He must have known he'd get slugged. Sure he'd known. After Aaron had laid him out, he'd managed to get to his knees, clasping his hands as if he were praying and begging to be hit again and again. So Aaron had obliged him once or twice, with more curiosity than anger, because this was a sick guy and Aaron, being then fairly new to the Village, was interested in sick people's reactions. So he'd knocked him over a couple of times more and then he'd taken twenty dollars out of Kittridge's wallet, mostly to give his act of hitting Kittridge some purpose, and he'd left Kittridge kneeling at the side of the room, beginning to sob. Great stuff. La Vie Boheme. A few weeks later, running into Kittridge on the street, he'd borrowed (really taken) some dough from him, and he'd done that sporadically for a while, until he'd lost sight of the guy. And now here he was again, looking real gone. But he might have some dough.

"Hey," Aaron said, "slip me a twenty, will you."

"I've got something more important than money to give you."

"Just give me twenty. That'll be okay."

"I can give you the Word."

What word? The password for the Kiwanis Inner Circle? The three hundredth word under R in the dictionary? What kind of baloney was this?

And where was the Patron?

Kittridge grabbed at his arm as he started past him.

"Let go," Aaron said, yanking his arm away.

Because there was the Patron going up Cornelia Street, a dead pigeon. Aaron cut after him. Looking back over his shoulder he could see Kittridge watching him turn into the street after the Patron. Hard rocks, Kittridge watching him, but he had to take chances. You never get anywhere unless you do. Wasn't that what they'd taught him?

The Patron was ploughing up Cornelia Street ahead of him. A great street, Cornelia Street, one of the real wop streets, short and concentrated, connecting West Fourth and Bleecker, looking real brutal tonight, the black buildings pressing together, the fire escapes like coarse patches of hair on swarthy skin, the buildings booming toward a grey trapezoid of sky heavy with snow. The Patron was dropping into the street, his dark overcoat merging into the background. He was getting more than anonymous—he was getting obscure. Aaron turned quickly, couldn't see Oliver Kittridge at the mouth of the street. Fighting down his excitement, the kind of excitement that used to catch at him when he'd steal art supplies from the locker at school (until they'd nabbed him red-handed and suspended him for a month), he looked up and down the street carefully. No one coming. Then up at the windows. This cold weather was good; it kept people off the streets and away from the windows. The Patron stopped in the doorway of a store, was hunching forward. Aaron saw a spurt of flame as he tried to light a cigarette. Then he was across the street fast, with a quick glance into a parked car to make sure it was empty, and on the sidewalk right behind the Patron. The Patron didn't even turn around as Aaron raised his arm, clipped him on the neck, right on the first vertebrae, with the side of his hand. It was like using the edge of a board. The Patron gave a little gasp, slumped sideways, going down slowly at first, and then sliding fast along the wall. Out cold. No more work necessary. Aaron looked at the street for a moment, his groin tickling. Coast clear. Get going. He bent down, skillfully unbuttoned the Patron's overcoat, fumbled inside his jacket for the wallet, feeling the broken heave of the man's chest. No wallet. Another quick look at the street. He rolled the Patron over, patted his hips, found the wallet. Without looking at it he slipped it into his own pocket. Then he went through the Patron's side pockets. Couldn't tell about lushes; they sometimes slipped a good deal in there. He found a few bills. And that was all. As he straightened up he saw a car turn into the street. He started to pull back into the doorway, changed his mind. Better to just start walking. The car cruised past as he walked toward Bleecker. He turned around for another look behind him. Was that Oliver Kittridge coming up the street? No, it wasn't. The car, a dark sedan, pulled up to the curb alongside him and he saw the man reach for the woman inside. They didn't care about him, didn't know he was alive. No kicks about that. What they didn't know wouldn't hurt him. He turned left onto Bleecker and walked fast, but not too fast toward Sixth Avenue, Avenue of the Americas. There he stopped under a street lamp, knowing it was foolish, but he had to find out. Sixty bucks in the wallet, three twenties. And seven in loose bills. Par for the course. Enough to make the Patron a Contributing Patron. Dough enough to last a week or two. What he needed was to strike it rich just once. Get some guy who was really loaded. Get enough to take him to

Mexico, let him sit there for a year and paint away, just work at it, get good, get real good. Never make that on seventy bucks at a time.

There was still a crowd at the Marino and he went on in. He wanted to find Amy. Be a good thing if she'd sit for him tomorrow and he could give her a little loot. She could use the dough. He liked to paint her; there was a shaped grace to her that his brush just seemed to follow. He was good when he painted her. But she wasn't at the bar for once. He pushed in a little further and saw Jason Spivak at the same time that Spivak saw him.

"You seen Amy?" he asked Spivak.

Spivak's face was blurred with drinking.

"She was here a little while ago. Went out with your friend Rawley."

"When was that?"

"How do I know? I thought you were through with that bitch."

"Mind your own damn business," Aaron told him, and went out. He'd remembered seeing Rawley going alone toward Eighth Street. Maybe Rawley had taken Amy home. He still had a feeling for her, even though he couldn't live with her. She was on a self-destructive kick, was bent on tearing herself down. In the beginning he'd tried to make her give up drinking; he did everything he could think of, coaxed her, threatened her, knocked her around when she got drunk. She might lay off for a couple of days and then she'd go off again. One time he'd been almost jealous of the liquor; give her a choice between him and a bottle and he'd known which she'd take. He'd gotten so involved with her that he'd begun to take on some of her misery. So he had to let go; it was interfering with his work. Art is Discipline. Besides there hadn't been enough room to paint at her place and he'd found one of his own on Jones Street. Had to give her up. Art is Sacrifice.

He climbed the stairs, taking them two at a time. At twenty-seven his wind was good, he was in shape, he kept himself that way. Just outside her door his foot shot out on something slippery. Some garbage that had been left outside, lying loose. Goddamn—he kicked at the garbage— why did she always have to leave a mess around? He kicked at the garbage again, heard it scatter in the hall. Serve her right if she had to clean it up. Then he knocked on the door, hitting it hard with his knuckles. No answer. He kicked the door a couple of times, just in case she was sleeping There was no bell, only some loose wires like bare fangs. He listened at the door to hear if she were rustling around. Dead. One more kick, a final good-bye kick.

At the head of the stairs he stopped as he heard a door open. Turning around, he saw it was the door next to Amy's. A middle-aged Italian was standing there in woolen under- wear, his fat stomach falling toward his knees.

"Wotcha want?"

"Nothing. It's okay. Go to bed, Pop."

"What for you bang on the door?"

"Go back to bed."

"You—bum!" The door slammed.

Aaron curbed his impulse to give it a couple of kicks, just to show that guy. Aw, what for? He went down the stairs and walked to the Marino, wondering whether Amy was inside her place, passed out. Else where was she? Maybe she had Rawley in there and didn't want to answer. Now what was he getting in an uproar about? He tried to laugh at himself. Only tried. Outside the Marino he shifted the dough to his left pocket, keeping only a dollar in the right. Not smart to flash a wad in there.

Jason Spivak seemed to be waiting for him. "Where've you been?"

"What's the difference?"

"I know where you've been," Spivak said, sounding like a child about to tell a secret.

"Then forget it. Want a drink?"

Spivak eyed him suspiciously. "You're buying?"

"This once," he said. "What do you want?"

Spivak was having rye. Aaron ordered two ryes. He took his straight, looked at his hands. He heard Angelo put the dime change on the bar but ignored it. He had half a hunch that Spivak would snatch it. Well, let him. He was busy thinking of what he wanted to buy. A couple of canvasses and a new stretcher. A Number Five brush. Maybe a sable Zero. Also tubes of crimson lake, viridian and prussian blue. A new sketch pad? He could use one. He had an idea for a painting. City thing. Lots of heavy blocks, real solid feel- ing, you had to feel it. Done in blues and browns, sombre, brooding. The whole thing pulled toward the center, like water dragging a lot of stuff as it went down the drain. Whirlpool. Cesspool. Maybe a bunch of people being sucked under. Arms and legs flying out, fractured, making them look like letters in a crazy alphabet. A little corny. He had to have something, though, to give the feeling that the whole city was being swallowed up, going into the ground. Not a bad idea at that. Just let him get across the river to Hoboken and watch it go down.

He put his empty glass back on the bar.

"Going?" Spivak asked.

"Yeah. Take it easy."

"Okay, Aaron. Thanks." He was at the door when Spivak grabbed his arm. "Where are you going?"

He shook himself loose. "How the hell do I know? Home, where else?"

The sky was heavy. It was bulging in, like a piece of tin with something weighing on it. God leaning his elbows on it. Good explanation. Yeah—great! Up north, over Broadway and so forth, stains of crimson mixed with grey, like a dawn that had gotten smudged. The buildings nearby black and hard, a lot of substance to them, and farther away soft and grey and misty, like mountains in a Chinese painting. It was going to snow and the city would be quiet tomorrow. A good day for work.

4. *Oliver Kittridge Has a Rendezvous With a Very Important Personage*

HURT BY AARON ROSS, but not angry (because he had placed himself beyond anger), Oliver Kittridge, about to turn the corner of Eighth Street, heard the shouting. Then, between the Nedick's and the newsstand, he saw the frail man whose pinched face seemed designed to reflect the pain of his birth. He was holding up his hands and shouting:

"MEN AND WOMEN, NOW YOU LISTEN TO ME. A TIME OF GREAT TROUBLE IS AT HAND. THE ANTI-CHRIST IS HERE. YES, HE IS RIGHT HERE, RIGHT HERE AMONG YOU, AND YOU DO NOT KNOW IT, YOU DO NOT HAVE THE LIGHT." He held his hat in his hand, shaking a few coins in it. "HE IS HERE TWO HUN-DRED MILLION STRONG AND HE IS GROWING STRONGER EVERY MINUTE."

Oliver Kittridge stopped to listen . . .

"THE WORLD HAS ALREADY BEEN VISITED BY FAMINE AND PLAGUE AND PESTILENCE. BUT WORSE, OH I TELL YOU FAR WORSE IS COMING."

. . . and to watch the cynical closed faces of the people passing by . . .

"THE GOSPEL TELLS US, THERE SHALL BE A GREAT TRIBULATION SUCH AS WAS NOT SINCE THE BEGINNING OF THE WORLD. (Matthew twenty-four twenty-one.) I PRAY FOR YOU, MEN AND WOMEN. I AM PRAYING FOR YOU."

. . . and the amused faces of the two young men loung-ing against the plate glass front of the hot dog stand . . .

"I PRAY FOR YOU WHETHER YOU GIVE ME ANY-THING OR NOT TO HELP SPREAD MY MESSAGE."

Oliver saw an elderly woman gingerly yet complacently drop a coin in the stained hat and walk on.

"THE CITIES OF THE GENTILES—(NOW THIS IS WRITTEN IN THE BIBLE)—THE CITIES OF THE GENTILES SHALL BE DESTROYED, EVEN TO THE LAST ONE OF THEM. AN ARMY TWO HUNDRED MILLION STRONG IS COMING, IT IS COMING TO TRY TO CAST THE LORD GOD OFF HIS THRONE."

Why wouldn't she listen? The message meant more than her hasty coin. Because it was true, it was true.

"I SEE A RIVER OF BLOOD TWO HUNDRED MILES LONG FLOWING THROUGH THE LAND." (The frail man had his eyes closed now.) "I SEE A SLAUGHTER SO TERRIBLE IT WILL TAKE SEVEN MONTHS TO BURY THE DEAD." (And he was swaying a little.) "I SEE PILES OF STONE WHERE ONCE THERE WERE CITIES. AND I HEAR THE CRIES OF THE AFFLICTED, I HEAR THE MOTHERS AND THE FATHERS, I HEAR THE ORPHANS . . ." He paused for breath.

Oliver came to his side quickly and said: "That's **right**, you've got to make them listen to you."

The frail man looked up, a little annoyed by the interruption, and said mechanically, while shaking his **hat**: "Thank you, brother, thank you."

"You've got to make them understand," Oliver **said**, glancing at the people walking by.

"That's my mission, brother."

"You've got to prepare them for the Coming."

The frail man took one step away. "That's what I'm doing," he said. "I'm preparing them."

"For the Lord is coming," Oliver said with true affirmation.

"Amen." Another step away.

"He is coming soon."

The frail man was silent.

"Let us pray," Oliver said. "Let us go down on our knees and pray."

"Amen," said the frail man, "let us pray." And he looked apprehensive.

"I have gone through Hell," Oliver said to him, now oblivious to the people going by. "I have sunk myself deep in sin and I was lost but now I have been chosen and I have found the way back."

"Amen."

"And now I am ready, now that I have found the way. Come, let us pray. Together." Oliver grasped the frail man's shoulder and pushed down on it. "Let us go down on our knees right here and sanctify this place and let us speak to the Lord." He sank to his knees on the sidewalk, while the frail man deftly sidestepped to avoid the downward pressure of his hand, saying in a loud and frightened voice: "What's the matter with you? Are you crazy or something?"

But Oliver was already praying. He prayed that this sinful world would be forgiven its awful transgressions, that they would be absorbed in His body and taken up by His spirit and absolved by His sacrifice. He prayed for some time, and when he got off his knees the frail man was gone.

There was a crowd around him, some of them laughing, some of them with twisted half-smiles. He heard someone say, "He's harmless," and then a small young man came toward him, stood before him indecisively, saying,

"O-Oliver, w-w-what's wrong? What's the t-trouble?" He pushed past the small man, barely touching him, and past an olive-skinned girl who reached for his arm, and he walked out of the light and into the darkness. Before him he could see the pale columns of the church, like those pillars by night, and he knew he must go there quickly, because he was sure he would not be disappointed tonight. The spirit was in him strongly. At last he, who had sinned against his father and who had sinned against his sex, stood still on the steps of the church, facing the recessed door, and waited.

He waited a long time for the coming, and as he waited he was pierced again and again by the fear that he had been finally deemed unworthy. He thought of his past sins—of the money he had stolen when he was a child, stolen to buy pleasures, of the times he had wished his father dead, of his pleasure on hearing that his father had died in the airplane accident and that he and Wilbur and Phyllis were to have the money, of the things he had done with the other boys at the academy and his sinful life when he had first come to the village, of the vanity of his writing poetry, of the terrible things he had done. And he waited, but the door stayed shut as it had the past two weeks, ever since he had first stopped there and seen. He prayed for the coming and promised to remove the last impurity from his spirit, but when he looked up he was still alone. Christ was not there. He had not come. Suppose He never came again, despite his promise to let His spirit dissolve into the substance of Oliver's flesh, so that by a renewal of sacrifice the world could again be saved from its folly and greed and wickedness and lechery. Could he, with his own imperfections, have prevented Christ from coming to him? Was the faulty race of men, whom he loved despite all their faults, doomed because he had proven unworthy? Had he failed them all, and himself?

For a long time he waited in the cold on the steps of the church and finally departed, deeply troubled.

Back in his apartment, now stripped bare of worldly decoration, he knelt before the crude black wood crucifix above the fireplace (where once he had hung a gay abstraction) and prayed through the night, only faintly conscious at first of the pain in his knees, and then gratified by it, prayed until he suddenly sank forward, his forehead and his hair in the ashes of a long-dead fire, and he slept like that until late in the morning, when, again conscious of the weakness of his flesh, he pushed himself to his knees once more and prayed.

5. *Lois Wilson Decides That Two Worlds Are Worse Than One*

OPENING HER EYES, Lois Wilson discovered that a square of winter sunlight was plastered on the floor near her bed. It looked cold and pale, like light coming through a glass of beer. She slipped off into sleep again and when she opened her eyes for the second (or third or fourth) .time that late morning, the square of sunlight was gone. Squinting at the small clock on the table across the room, Lois made out that it was just a few minutes before noon. She heard noises coming from the street, mostly the sound of automobiles. A hissing came from the leaky radiator. Twelve o'clock. Noon. Another day, another dollar. Another day, another dolor. What was in the line of duty for the day? She had to see her arranger and try to work out a couple of new numbers. And call a guy who owned a club uptown. And . . . Nothing else. A dull dull day. She closed her eyes again and tried to sleep some more. Sleep, the great escape. Now wasn't that strange, she was talking to Joe Stalin, they had a letter in code but the code was too simple, Stalin was a little angry, now they were walking to a subway station—ah, this was all a dream—and Stalin now had a kinky bullet head and was tall and really built -and he gave a quarter to the man in the change booth and said, Give me two liberty dimes and a nickel. Two liberty dimes and . . .
BRRRRRRNNNNNGGGG
O God!
BRRRRRRNNNNNGGGG

Lois flopped over in bed—damn! her period must be coming, her breasts were hurting—and . . .

BRRRRRNNN . . .

. . . picked up the phone.

Managed to say hello.

"Lois?" The voice was creamy.

"Yes. Who is it?"

"Baby, am I getting you up?"

"No," she lied, shaking herself, "I've been up."

"You sound lousy. You sound hungover."

"No such luck. Who is it?"

"It's me—Tiger."

"Tiger! Where are you?"

"I'm in a phone booth in Whelan's. What's more to the point, where the hell are you? I got your new phone number . . ."

"Oh, I moved."

"Don't be elementary, baby. Let's have some breakfast."

"Well—sure."

"Where do you live? All I got's this phone number."

She gave him the address. It would help, Tiger coming to breakfast, it would help begin the day.

"I'll bring you up something. What do you need?"

She thought for a moment. She needed a lot, but first things first. "I could use some eggs," she said.

"How about coffee?"

"Well . . ."

"I'll use my discretion. Trust that Tiger. Give me that address again."

She repeated the address.

"Okay, baby," he said, "put the fat on the fire." And he hung up.

Lois wrenched herself out of bed, padded across the cold floor to the bathroom, winced as she felt the tiles under her feet. (She suddenly remembered Alonso, an old Cuban boy friend, who used to moan, "Que vida mas cruel!" She brushed her teeth, gargled, doused her face with cold water. Then she stroked her hair a hundred times, counting automatically, until it shone. She hated her hair; it had a way of going stiff and wiry. She parted it carefully, drew it behind and clipped it there, so that it lay tight, almost lacquered. After that she put on lipstick and filled the tiny hole in her forehead with mascara. Looked at her face then, the olive skin, the small nose with nostrils that flared a little too much, the black eyes with invisible pupils, the lying caste mark. Facing two worlds, the white and the black. A face meant to be batted back and forth across the racial net like a tennis ball. Not a nice new tennis ball, all white, a Newport ball, a Forest Hills exclusive special ball, but one, if you please, a little dusty, a little soiled.

The bell. The downstairs bell. She still wasn't used to the difference between them. She pressed the button, heard the buzz downstairs, and then Tiger coming heavily up the stairs.

"Hello there, baby," he said coming through the door, his chest covered with bundles. "Where do I stash these?"

"In the kitchen," she said, and showed him where it was.

After putting the bundles on the table near the kitchen window, Tiger gave the place a once-over. "This ain't bad. Not bad at all. When did you get this pad?"

"Last week."

"What did you do for it, baby, kill someone?"

"Didn't have to," she said. He had just kissed her cheek and she could smell the pomade on his flattened conked hair. "The guy who had it went away."

"Permanently?"

She moved away from him, gently. No stuff. "I don't know," she said. "He went out to Hollywood."

"Well, well, don't that sound groovy. Who was this cat? Did I know him?"

"Name of Breedon Rawley."

Tiger drew the tip of one long black finger along his thick lower lip.

"The name means something," he said. "Why should I know this cat?"

"He's a writer," Lois told him.

The finger pulled away from the lip and shot into the air in recollection.

"Oh yeah, it comes to me now. Someone told me to read his book. Or maybe they told me not to read the book. It don't matter, because I didn't read it anyway. Any good?"

"I suppose," Lois said.

The book was something of a sore spot with her. It wasn't until just before he'd left for the Coast that he'd given her a copy. She had recognized instantly the character which he had based on her, physically at least. But he had missed her, missed her completely. Damnit, he had even maligned her. She was not trying to pass as anything. She had never denied that she was a Negro, even though she had never been convinced of it. There was about seven-eighths of her which was white and in her case nameless and just as well forgotten because the one-eighth of her which had darkened her skin a little came from an African import. The old taint. One drop of that vile Negro blood, ladies and gentlemen, and all that wonderful lily-white liquid which pumps through the arteries and courses through the veins and squirts through the capillaries is rendered impure, is contaminated, is inferiorated. Why, do you know that that little lady, light as she is, can give birth to a baby as black as (searching) as black as the ace of spades. Yes, Mr. Breedon Rawley had missed her, and she hadn't known it until he had left, but that wouldn't have made any difference in her brief relations with him. He had taken her to a couple of clubs where she'd wanted to go and talk to people. And that was good. He was the wonder boy of the moment, so it helped to be seen with him. And he was so little that he wasn't much of an annoyance. But the main thing was the apartment. Her own sublet had been just about up that night she had seen him in front of the bookstore, and she had been looking with increasing desperation for another place. There were always half a dozen leads with nothing at the end but bait and promises. People who only wanted to make out were always coming on with talk of an apartment that was going to be vacant at such and such a time. Nothing to it. And she hated to talk to those real estate agents, lords and masters of the world now, who'd look her over as carefully as if they were thinking of taking out adoption papers, or as if they were art experts trying to determine whether she was School of Giovanni the Florentine or Ambrosio the Flem, with almost all of them scared to death of coming right out with it and asking her the dread question: Just what are you anyway? Obviously they didn't give a damn what she was as long as they knew what her father and mother had been. One of them had made a sneaky approach to it by asking if she were Portuguese. No, she'd told him politely, I am a Negro.

At the word his eyebrows had flown up like flushed ducks and then had settled slowly and cautiously as he'd said. Well, that doesn't matter to me, not at all. I'm not that kind (I'm the *other* kind) but the people who have this apartment, you know how people are . . . Yeah, yah, blather, blather. If she could only have seven-eighths of an apartment and seven-eighths of a bathroom and seven-eighths of this and that to accommodate the part of her that belonged to free America. Well, when Breedon Rawley had told her he was going out to the Coast, she'd taken out insurance of a sort, and now she had his ex-apartment. A girl had to live.

While she was fixing eggs, Tiger called in from the other room: "Say, this Breedon Rawley, what kind of name is that?"

Yes, Lois thought, a little wearily, even we ask that.

"He's from Mississippi," she said.

"Don't tell me." Tiger came into the kitchen. "Mississippi?"

"He was born down there."

"He's white, ain't he?"

Lois nodded, stirring the eggs in the pan.

"Well, sonofabitch," Tiger said, without particular malice. He went and sat at the window.

When she put the eggs on the table, Tiger asked: "What town, do you know?"

"What town?"

"Does he come from?"

"I think Biloxi," Lois said, sitting down. She didn't want to talk about Breedon Rawley and where he came from.

"That's not in Mississippi," Tiger said." That's in Alabama. You know I come from there, Mississippi I mean, that goddamn state, I ain't been there below that Smith and Wesson Line for twenty years say, but I sure remember it. You been there, ain't you?"

"Just once. During the war, with a USO." Lois wanted to get off Mississippi and the South, wanted some chatter with Tiger, some talk about the job he was playing, some news of what was open, what was closed, who was up, who was down—the kind of chatter you'd get if you asked, What's cooking, man?

"This damn country!" Tiger dropped his fork on his plate.

"What's griping you?" Lois asked.

"I'm in one of my fed-up moods. You know how it is. Or maybe you don't."

"What do you mean by that?" Lois asked him, sensing the meaning and resenting it. He was lucky; at least he knew where he stood.

"You know what I'm gonna do. I'm gonna get elected to Congress, just so I can pass one simple law. And do you know what that law's gonna be?" He paused and then went on. "I'm gonna have one day a year, I'll settle for that, just one day a year. I'll call it Turn Black Day, and all them white bastards are gonna turn black and all of us will turn white. Of course there are some technical difficulties."

Lois forced a laugh.

"See, that day we'll lynch a few of them bastards, in a few selected places, and we'll make them come on with that cap'n and boss crap and scratch their heads and do a jig and yak-yak for us and ride over the goddamn wheels in the back of the bus. And use all the stinkingest johns. Just one day. That's all I ask. Turn Black Day."

"What's got you all worked up?" Lois said, a little embarrassed.

"Well, I'll let you know. Just coming here, coming down this street, just today you know, just when I was coming over here, well I hear this voice—Hey boy, get me a nigger wench. I walk a few steps and suddenly it struck me that I really heard it. Well, Christ, I stopped dead and I looked around and there was a drunken old white fool so drunk he could hardly stand, giving me that kind of silly look, you know . . ."

"What did you do?" Lois felt something like the tendril of a cyclone begin to race through her.

"What did I do? What could I do? All right, suppose I jumped him, everyone would see some great big nigger beating up on a little old white man. By the time I got through explaining there'd be the law and everything and next thing you know I'd be standing up in court with that poor little old white man half my size next to me, me looking like a big ape . . ." Tiger shoved his chair back violently. "Oh shit, what am I getting off on this kick for? Stop me, will you, baby."

Lois got up and went to the coffee on the stove. "Do you take it with two lumps?"

"It ain't the lumps in life that counts," Tiger said, grinning, showing his big haphazard yellow teeth.

After that Tiger sat around for an hour or so and talked shop. Things were pretty rough in general. People weren't spending the way they used to, money was getting tight, all the entrepreneurs were bitching plenty. But things might take a turn. His own outfit was making out all right; bop was really catching on and they'd gotten nights when people had listened, really listened. At first bop had gotten them on edge, made them feel insulted by its off beat, but now they were getting educated to it. Tiger said it made him feel good, it knocked him out, playing the stuff. It was the real thing, it was what he'd been waiting for.

At last he stood up and said, "How are you fixed for cash, baby?"

Lois shrugged her shoulders.

"Take a couple of pounds, will you." He slipped a twenty out from under a gold clip, and put it in Lois' hand.

"Gee, really, thanks, Tiger," Lois said. What a good guy he was.

"Forget it."

"I'll pay you back."

"Now Jesus . . ."

With Tiger gone, Lois felt blue. God, how time could drag on the winter days with nothing to do but sit around and mope. If she only had the dough she'd go somewhere in the West Indies, to Cuba maybe, or to Haiti. If she had the dough . . . Things were getting tight. Her father, who sold insurance on the South Side in Chicago had sent her a little on Christmas, and that was the last income she'd had, except for a one-shot at a dance. She'd even tried to hook up as vocalist with some outfit, but no dice. But—courage, chick. It's always darkest before the dawn. That old saw. Like the prosperity around the corner. Well, something might turn up . . . *might* turn up.

At three o'clock she went midtown to see her arranger. In the days when she'd been going great—six months ago, even—she'd always traveled by taxi. That insulated her

from the world, from the two worlds. But now she had to
go by subway, jammed right into humanity. A seedy old
man in an overcoat stained by phlegm sat opposite her all
the way (Lois thought of Tiger's story) and she tried not to
look at him, even though she could feel his eyes going all
over her like wet fingers. When she got out at Fiftieth
Street she saw him get up, after a moment of indecision, and
she braced herself for what she knew was coming.

At the turnstile he came up behind her, not quite touching. "Hey . . ." he said . . . and whispered something she
couldn't quite hear, but she knew what it was. She whirled
around, striking him full in the face with her heavy em-
bossed bag, and he staggered back, gasping. She swung a
second time, knowing she was screaming at him, and missed
by a mile, seeing as she spun around a tall light-skinned
man in a porter's cap come running out of the change booth,
while the old man scuttled down the platform.

"I'll get him," the porter said, starting to duck under the
turnstile.

Lois blocked him. "Leave him alone."

"He can't get out."

"What good would it do?"

"Could call the cops."

She snorted and saw a slow bitter smile come to his face.
"Yeah," he said. He looked around to where three people
were lined up at the booth, staring at them. "I got to get
back to the booth."

Wanting to say something kind, feeling sorry for him,
Lois patted his arm and said, "It's all right. You get used to
it."

"Yeah? Do you?" And he went back into the booth.

The session with her arranger didn't go well. They
worked over a couple of blues, but Lois wasn't in the mood
and the arranger was pretty sour himself. He hadn't made
any money with her for months, and while he knew she was
good and would be hitting soon again, well, his time was
limited, you've only got twenty-four hours a day, etc. They
went through everything in a perfunctory way and presented each other with a little perfunctory optimism and
they were finished in an hour.

That left a lot of time to kill. Lois walked slowly down
Broadway, feeling a little chilly in the raw wind that was

cutting up the street, hoping to run into someone she knew. It would feel good even to say, Hi, man. But she didn't see anyone she knew. She went into the lobby of the Paramount Building and debated whether she should drop in on a middle-aged man named Steinert who distributed foreign pictures, and decided that was from hunger. Standing in the lobby, holding firm against the sudden discharges from the elevators, she looked through her black appointment book. Not a thing. Not a thing for that evening, and she began to feel sorry for herself, and a little puzzled. By God, could she be through? What, when she was twenty-four, when she was good, when she had the stuff? No, this was only one of the black periods, she told herself, and almost believed it. She thought about going to a movie, but she didn't like to see a show alone. She couldn't sit through one that way, no matter how good it was. She remembered the hundred and more times when she'd been out with some character and wished she were home, alone, the radio on, unbothered, reading a book, washing her hair, taking it easy. But tonight she knew she didn't want to be alone—not when things were breaking this way.

She took the subway at Times Square, sitting stiff on the dirty straw seat, her legs pulled back, half-expecting to see the old man again. But across the aisle was a wall of afternoon newspapers, a horizontal listing of the latest catastrophes which are called the news.

At Penn Station a tall black man about thirty with a knobby face got on. He started talking to himself, in a loud voice, every now and then slapping his hand against the front of his Eisenhower jacket. Lois saw the white people in the train look disgusted or smile covert smiles, thinking he was drunk (there's a real drunk nigger), but even though she couldn't hear what he was saying she could see he wasn't drunk, he was goofing off. A white girl in a stupid green hat and a cheap fur coat moved away from him quickly. Lois felt her stomach crawl and crawl, against her will, felt it crawl with apprehension while she said to herself, The hell with them, the hell with them. A well-dressed Negro sitting opposite her was looking with intense anger at the man in the Eisenhower jacket. Lois knew how he felt, and he must know how she felt. At Fourteenth Street Lois felt her stomach settle a little, and she hated herself for it, when the man in the Eisenhower jacket went out of the train, pushing aside the people who were trying to enter. She felt that everyone was looking at her, to see her reaction, but she knew her face was composed, if pale. When she got up at Sheridan Square the well-dressed man across the aisle didn't even glance at her. He was busy forgetting.

Coming out of the station she almost collided with Aaron Ross, and she finally had someone she could say hi to.

"How are you, kid?" he asked.

"Fine. Aren't you cold?" He was only wearing dungarees and a paint-stained sweatshirt.

"I'm okay. Just going home."

"Come into the Rikers with me. Have a coffee." She wanted a little company before she went home.

"Okay," he said and walked across Christopher Street with her.

In the Rikers she asked him about Amy.

"She's in bad shape," Aaron said. "We don't live together now."

"Cause and effect?"

He looked sideways at her. "No. Why should it be?"

"You'd know better than me," Lois said. "Where do you stay now?"

"I got a goddamn cell on Jones Street."

Drinking her coffee, Lois watched him obliquely. She hadn't seen him since the end of summer, and she remembered how he had looked that time, sitting in the circle in the park, wearing dungarees and a T-shirt, showing his large body held tight by muscle. His arms were a little too thick and hairy, but there was an exciting play along his forearms whenever he moved his fingers. What she really liked was his skin; it was dark, and she hated the blotchy pinkish-grey bark that was generally called a white skin.

"How's the painting going?"

"Don't ask."

"Why?"

"I haven't found myself yet. I'm years away."

"Don't get discouraged."

He looked directly at her for a long time. "If I were discouraged," he said, "I'd quit right now. I'll get there, you'll see, but right now I think I stink. What's in me and what I'm putting on the canvas haven't gotten together yet. You know what I mean? Sometimes I lie in bed and I can think up really terrific paintings. I see them complete, color, texture, everything. I've got something really good. And then when I try to get it down, it isn't there anymore. A kind of a gap, I've got to close it. When I've done that, then I'll be a painter. You understand?"

"Of course I do," Lois said.

Aaron said slowly, "I think you do." He went on, "I don't want to be a pretentious jerk about it but I've got myself committed. I'm going to be a painter and that's all that matters. Maybe in a few years from now I'll wake up one day and find I don't have the stuff. I have nightmares about it. Maybe I'll never close the gap."

Thinking of all the people she knew who thought they'd already arrived, when they hadn't, Lois felt a certainty, founded on nothing more than an instinct and a memory of a tight-muscled body, that Aaron would make the grade.

"What will you do if you don't?" she asked.

"If I don't close the gap? Then . . . I don't know. It won't be too pleasant." He finished his coffee. "Christ," he said, "I'm hungry. I must have a hole in my gut. Haven't chowed all day."

"Why not?"

"No dough."

"Aren't you on the fifty-two-twenty?"

"Me? No. I was a slacker in the last war. In the merchant marine. I thought you knew that."

She remembered. "Oh yeah, I forgot."

"No benefits, no nothing. Boy, that was a mistake. If I'd only gone into the army or the goddamn navy I could go to school under the G.I. bill and so forth. But we guys in the merchant marine . . . Oh well, what the hell. I'll tell you what. I can promote some loot somewhere. What do you say we chow together?"

"I have an idea," Lois said. "I have some stuff up at my place." She thought of Tiger coming through the door with a chest covered with bundles, and she suppressed a smile. "Just some eggs and stuff."

Aaron shook his head negatively. "Look, kid, I'm really hungry. I can promote . . ."

Still thinking of Tiger, not feeling in the least that it was a betrayal, Lois said, "I've got some money."

"Okay, let's get a little hamburger for bulk. What do you say?"

They went across the street again, this time to the A & P, and then walked to Charles Street. When Lois guided him into her house, Aaron said, "I didn't know you lived here."

"I just moved in," she told him.

"That guy Rawley lives here, doesn't he?"

"Not any more," Lois said, and she felt almost triumphant (over what?) as she said it. "I've taken over his place."

"Well, what do you know," Aaron said.

After dinner he borrowed five dollars from her and went down to buy a bottle. They killed it by nine o'clock, and then they lay on the couch, the fire going and the radio soft. And it was pretty terrific. "How come we didn't ever get together before?" she heard Aaron ask, just before she began to doze.

Lois awakened to find Aaron getting dressed. The fire was out and it was a little cold in the room.

"Where are you going?" she asked sleepily.

"I've got to get some dough," Aaron said. "Where's the key?" He saw it on the mantel and put it in his pocket. "I'll be back in a while," he said, going toward the door.

"Where are you going to get it?" Lois asked, not really caring. Oh God, she was knocked out.

"It's around," Aaron said. "I'll find it. I got patrons."

Then he went out, and she heard him go down the stairs. Lois shivered with cold, pulled her legs up under her, and hoped that he'd come back soon, even if only to turn on the radiator.

6. Breedon Through the Looking-Glass (or, What Alice Was Spared)

"MISTER FIELDING WILL SEE you now," said the secretary, rising and opening a paneled door for Breedon Rawley.

At last, on the thirteenth day of his employment with

Superior Films, Inc., Max Fielding, the man who was going
to do his book, had decided to see him. For two five-day
weeks and Monday, Tuesday and Wednesday of another,
Breedon had done nothing but conscientiously read old
shooting scripts and bother Fielding's secretary. The nights
had been terrible. The first couple of nights, carried by the
momentum of his expectations, he had eaten in Dave
Chasen's and Romanoff's, but sitting there in the midst of
all that studied gaiety and careful camaraderie he had felt
more than ever alone, in a half-world somewhere between
the diners and the waiters. Some evenings he had walked
along the streets, but all the attractive girls pained him by
their apparent unavailability. He found it impossible to
stay at home and read, mainly because he had no home.
He was living in a characterless modern cabin situated
behind an imposing low hotel. The cabin's furniture and its
appointments were so sterile, despite the bright colors and
polished light woods, that he could never feel he belonged
there and he came back to it only to sleep. A phrase started
to play over and over again in his mind that first week—the
world's a sad and lonely place—the world's a sad and lonely
place, an none I think do there embrace. Several times he
stifled his impulse to call Lois long-distance, and say—say
what? His secretary, contrary to all his hopes and wishes,
was a parched blonde named Elizabeth Tanner, whom he
addressed as Miss Tanner, please, and who called him Mister Rawley, even though all the other writers and secre-
taries, from what he could gather, called each other by their
first and sometimes Christian names. But once they had set
their own particular precedent, Breedon had been too shy
to break it and (he suspected) Miss Tanner too uninter-
ested. During the second week he had hired a convertible
and, feeling free and powerful behind the wheel, had driven
out to Santa Monica and out to Venice and through the
Mexican and Negro sections. One night, in downtown Los
Angeles, he had discovered a dance hall patronized almost
exclusively by Filipinos and featuring for their enjoyment
large peroxided partners. He had danced excitedly for ten
dollars worth of tickets with a fleshy Venus, who seemed all
ageing meat and perspiration strained through layers of
cheap powder, and had made a date to drive her home at
three in the morning. And he had waited for her too,

squirming in the front seat of the convertible, until he had
seen her come out with a Flip (as he had already learned
to call them) hanging on either arm, and that was the end
of that adventure in sex. His attempts at friendship with
the other writers had been impeached by his diffidence and
his damned stuttering and by a certain resistance on their
part whose cause he couldn't ascertain. One or two had
said, "Read your book," in a very off-hand way, but no one
had added any comment, and Breedon was beginning to
feel as if his having written that book was a sign of his
shame and that his photograph on the back cover was in the
same class as a postoffice photo, front and profile. Breedon
Rawley, Wanted for Writing. Always in the background of
his life in Hollywood was the figure of Max Fielding, the
producer, whom Breedon already knew was about two thousand dollars higher in the scale than he. During his thirteen
days of waiting, Breedon felt that Fielding was assuming
legendary proportions. Whenever he called in an attempt
to arrange to see him, he was told that Mister Fielding was
inspecting a location, was on the lot, was seeing rushes, was
checking costs with the accountants, and so forth, and so
forth. Breedon began to believe that there were three or
four Max Fieldings, and that each of them was continually
busy.

But now he was being shown into the office of Mister
Fielding, or one of them.

It was, as he had expected, a large office, with afternoon
sunlight brought in through the venetian blinds, books solid
on one wall (did he actually read them?), a long leather
couch which made Breedon think of a psychoanalyst's office,
a lawn of green broadloom, and near the window an im-
mense carved desk that might have been looted from the
Palazzo Venezia. Behind the imposing desk sat a small
plump man with a tanned bald head and tremendous shell-
rimmed glasses that seemed to cut into the lofty bridge of
his nose. As Breedon crossed the room, shuffling through
the broadloom, the small plump man stood up (and proved
to be about two inches taller than Breedon) and reached
across the desk to take Breedon's hand. Their short arms
barely bridged the gap.

"I'd been hoping to meet you sooner, Mr. Rawley. I hope
you'll excuse any inconvenience I may have caused you."

Breedon was unaccountably surprised that he did not speak with a foreign inflection. "I've been very busy these last few weeks."

"Y-yes, your s-secretary told me."

Breedon saw him whisk away a look of surprise at the stuttering.

"How long have you been here now?"

"Over two weeks."

"Well, I hope you've been putting your time to good use."

"I've bu-been reading some s-scripts . . ."

"Have you gone over the lot?"

"Y-yes."

"Well, you're getting into the water slowly and that's a good thing. I'm not one of the school that says, Throw him into the water and let him sink or swim. I remember when I was a boy we threw another boy into the East River because he was afraid of the water. He drowned. Do you know, my analyst discovered that I had a guilt complex because of it. You're not being analyzed, are you?"

"No," Breedon said, and added for some reason or other, "N-not at the mo-moment."

"It would be good for your stuttering. You'll pardon my being blunt but I've seen wonders worked. We had an actor under contract . . ." A buzzer interrupted and Fielding flipped a tiny lever. Breedon heard a tin voice say, "Mister Carney is here." "Well, send him in," Fielding said, flipping back the lever. "I'm going to have George Carney work with you," Fielding said to Breedon. "He's a good man and knows the ropes." The door opened and Breedon turned around to see Fielding's secretary, who was as full of juice as his own was parched, ushering in a tall thin man who impressed Breedon immediately as having the furtive face of a safecracker. Fielding came around the desk to greet Carney democratically. "How are you, George," he said, shaking hands vigorously. "George, this is Breedon Rawley. I've been telling him about you and I suppose you've read his book. Pretty young, isn't he?" Carney's hand was bony. And cold. "Sit down, sit down, boys," Fielding said, going around his desk. Carney took a plywood chair, Breedon dragged up another. "Now," said Fielding, letting himself down in his own upholstered chair, "lct's get down to business." He glanced at his watch. "I've just bought a story L want you boys to work on." Breedon reflected that this was a strange way to refer to his book in front of him. "I think it's something with a lot of guts to it, or it will be by the time you're finished with it. Huh?" Carney nodded, and Breedon edged forward on his chair.

"What kind of picture is it going to be?" Carney asked.

Breedon started to tell him about his book, but Fielding was already speaking: "It's a Western . . ."

Breedon heard himself say, "A Western!"

The eyeglasses swiveled toward him like a hostile battery.

"B-but I thaw-thought . . ." Breedon couldn't go any further.

"Oh, I meant to tell you, we can't do your book just now. We're having some difficulties with the Johnston Office . . ."

"B-but . . ."

A sympathetic look penetrated the twin sheets of glass.

"I know how disappointed you must feel, but you can rest assured that I'm going to do your book, just as soon as I can. I don't buy properties to let them gather dust on the shelf, do I, George?"

"Not that I know of."

Fielding leaned forward across·the desk. "When I say I want you to write a Western that doesn't mean I want you to throw off some formula job. I want you to bring your fresh talent, your proven talent, to bear on an honest story about real people, people who happened to live in our West. I'm not interested in turning out a formula job. I expect you to give me a story about cowboys, yes, but real cowboys, doing a job, facing danger, unafraid, you know, men with grit and courage and guts . . ."

"The real American qualities," Carney said solemnly. Breedon looked at him to see if he were joking, but he looked serious, dedicated.

"Yes, the real American qualities," Fielding said. "The qualities that have made us the greatest country in the world."

Breedon half-expected a fife-and-drum corps to come marching through the door.

Fielding opened a desk drawer and put a copy of the *Saturday Evening Post* in front of them. Carney pushed forward. "This is the story I want you to use," Fielding said, flipping the pages. "I'll tell you about it and we can kick it around . . ." He looked again at his watch, ". . . for a while."

Fielding and Carney did all the talking, with Breedon barely following the thread of the discussion. He couldn't make out whether he was relieved or angry that they weren't going to screen his book, at least not for the present. It made no difference financially, and he was now past the point where he could securely regard the book as an accomplishment. So he listened, not listening, to the discussion about the two main players in the script he was supposed to work on, their capabilities, their limitations, about the budget of the picture, watched Fielding get up once and prance around while he illustrated a scene, saw Carney do the same thing in detailing another scene a minute later. From time to time he heard himself shouting, "I quit, I quit," but he knew he was sitting silent and a little stunned and perhaps nodding in approval (oh no!) when Fielding made a point. Then Fielding looked at his watch again, pressed a buzzer on his desk, pushed the copy of the *Saturday Evening Post* into Breedon's hands, and started him toward the door. Breedon walked across the green broadloom, which seemed longer now, following Carney. At the door he stepped aside to let a thin ageing blonde come into the room, and as he went out he could hear Fielding's voice say in a greeting as warm and transparent as weak tea, "Hello, darling, it's been ages." And the blonde starting to shrill something . . .

They went to Carney's office, which was somewhat more plush than his own, and dismissed Carney's secretary, who seemed far better irrigated than Miss Tanner. They sat at Carney's desk and Carney took out a bottle of scotch and two dixie cups.

"So now you know the worst," Carney said, trying to make his furtive face look friendly.

"Yes."

"A Western. It could be worse."

"N-not much," Breedon said. He took a swallow of whiskey and gulped. Carney flipped his down deftly.

"A Western isn't so bad," Carney said, pouring himself another drink. "Want one? They never lose money and if you keep writing pictures that make money you hold your job. It's like the old saying, You never go broke taking a profit."

"B-but I wanted to w-work on my book. I thought . . ."

"I came here ten years ago to adapt a novel about a newspaper editor. It was a good book, not quite a bestseller, but I think it doesn't date. Read it? *Deadline Deferred.*" Breedon had never heard of it, but he nodded diagonally, noncommittally. "It was the third book I'd written. I was married at the time and I used to work for a couple of hours every day before I went to sleep. I was full of all kinds of ambition then. When I went to college I used to write poetry and I used to think of myself as Shelley first, and then Byron. But no money in poetry, so I went to work for the Chicago *Tribune*, which makes a lot of people in the Screenwriters Guild still suspicious of me. I was convinced when I wrote my books that I was satisfying my creative impulses, but I know now that all I wanted was to better myself. In other words, to make dough."

"B-but if you want to be a s-sincere writer . . ."

"Sincere writer!" Carney let a laugh trickle from his tight mouth. "What's a sincere writer? Anyone who writes one of those intense incompetent things that sells a thousand copies calls himself a sincere writer. Anyone, and I mean anyone, who has a manuscript rejected by a dozen publishers immediately becomes convinced he's a sincere writer. Listen, kid," Carney said, laying a paternal hand on Breedon's knee for just a second, "a book is something in which a writer gets together with a lot of people. The more people who read his book, the more money he makes. I don't go for this stuff of people saying they don't write with an audience in mind. They ought to."

"Yes but . . . the qua-quality of the aw-audience . . ."

"Who determines that? Some half-assed intellectuals with baked-out brains? A few precious smarty-pants who always pretend to be better than you are? I'd rather write something that Joe Blow, the average guy, enjoys than turn out one of those things that's going to get all the horn-rimmed lads waving their scarves. Forget them. They don't count, they're not worthwhile. Don't let them scare you. I'll bet some of them got you down about your book. Didn't they?"

"Well . . ." Breedon liked what he was hearing, and he was trying hard, hard as he could, to accept it.

"I read your book and it's a good job. I can see why the club took it. You've got a good plot mind and you can make the grade out here. Make money. Put money in thy purse. This is the place to do it. A lot of people, those scarf characters, will tell you Hollywood is fraud, fake, phoney. Well, it's not. It's real. It's materialistic and it admits it. No pretensions about it. Everything here is based on money. There's a kind of social ranking here. Everyone above a thousand a week belongs to an aristocracy. At a thousand you're a count or a marquis, then you become an earl at fifteen hundred, at two thousand you're a duke, at twenty-five hundred you're a prince, and above that you're God." Carney poured more whiskey into Breedon's dixie cup. "And for Christ sake," he went on, "stop worrying about your sacred mission as a writer. We're writers out here. Don't let anyone kid you that you're not. A studio's paying us, not a publisher. This picture we write will be seen by about a hundred million people throughout the world. Talk of translations, they'll dub it into Spanish and French, they'll give it Italian and Chinese sub-titles."

"B-but . . ."

"Wait a second now. Just listen to me." Carney crumpled his dixie cup and Breedon saw some drops of whiskey roll onto the desk. "Let's stop thinking in terms of books. They're finished. Soon people won't be reading them anymore. I know what I'm talking about. The human mind is a lazy mechanism. Why should it bother translating words into images when it's got outfits like Superior Pictures doing an expert job for it and giving it a neat package, all ready for use? You want to become immortal? A second Shakespeare, another Tolstoy? We've missed the boat on that. Even if we have the stuff, we've come too late. To become immortal you've got to have a posterity, and we don't have any. Even if the human race does survive, and I have my doubts, it won't be able to read in a hundred years. It won't have to. What do you think kids read now? Well, you ought to know. Comic books. And television, who reads when there's a television set in the house? The human race is progressing from a race of morons to a race of cretins."

"I-I'm not so pess-pessimistic," was all Breedon could say.

"Well, you're young yet. But the hell with all this. I get that crap off my chest every now and then so I can justify my being here. Listen, I . . ." Carney stopped abruptly. "The hell with it."

"W-what were you going to s-say?"

"Nothing. Let's get to work." He picked up a sharpened pencil and put a pad of yellow paper on the center of his desk. "What do you know about the West?"

"J-just about nothing."

"That doesn't matter. Pick up a few pulp magazines and read them."

"Pu-ulp magazines?"

"Where do you think people get their ideas? Well, let's see. Fielding wants an opus, a job with real guts to it." The pencil started moving over the pad. "Now here's an idea Metro used about five years ago, but they didn't develop it right. Now what they did . . ."

7. Mathematics:
Ross' Quest Plus Kittridge's Mission Equals Xes

IT HADN'T BEEN A good winter. It hadn't been a good winter at all. Aaron Ross, sitting on a bench in Washington Square Park, his head drawn in protectively, his hands dug into the pockets of his pea jacket, felt the gloom of winter still inside him. He was hardly touched by the promising breeze that pushed up fitfully from the south. He hardly noticed the faint green film on the tops of the trees or the patches of fresh green in the muddied sere turf. On the benches opposite him the first checker players of the new spring were gathered around two boards, while a little distance away a line of old Italians in black overcoats and black felt hats lifted their faces to the sun. People were walking through the park briskly, with that first freedom of spring, the release from their pinching apartments.

But things were going badly. Lois had long spells of being morose, generally about the color question (as it affected her), sometimes about her inability to get work. They had gotten on each other's nerves a good deal—a lot of squabbles, a lot of making up, no calm at all. His work hadn't gone well that winter. He hadn't known just what he wanted to do. He needed to study with someone, but he didn't have the dough. The Patrons had suddenly become uncooperative; the last one had had two dollars and change and the one before had begun to scream bloody murder (the guy had been turning when he'd hit him and he'd only managed to catch him on the side of the neck). He was depressed about Amy too. The last time he'd seen her she'd looked like hell, like she'd been going through hell, and she had hardly been able to stand on her feet. Every time he saw some drunken old biddy lapping it up at a bar he thought of Amy, Amy in ten years. If she lasted that long. The last time he'd gone up to her place to see her she'd started crying. "I'm going to be dead soon, I'm going to die soon, it doesn't matter, I've been dead for thirty years." That's what she'd said, and even though he'd known it was just maudlin bilge it had cut into him, cut into him deep enough to make him think, Go ahead and die, it's the best thing for you.

This was something new, this feeling of depression, this feeling that someone had twisted fingers in his guts. He'd never had it until now. Generally as long as he'd kept active, kept doing something, usually something physical, he'd felt good, felt able to do whatever he'd wanted. And he hadn't begun to lose faith in himself until this winter. When he'd first started to draw he'd said to himself, I've got something. During the war when he used to spend his spare time on shipboard sketching he knew he'd had it, that it was good. And when he'd first come to the Village and when he'd been living with Amy it was there, the knowledge that he was a good artist. But somehow this long cold winter, between the bickering with Lois and the enforced physical inactivity, when he'd sometimes hit the walls of his place with his fist, and his feeling of guilt over Amy, the feeling that he should have done something for her that he could

not. somehow the idea that he was a good artist and that
he was destined to make his mark had gone, had gone
down the drainpipe, had been flushed down the toilet, had
crept out one of the ratholes.

He knew what it was. He was getting old. Twenty-seven,
the Age of Discretion. The Summing-Up. The Where-Do-
We-Go-From-Here? Worse—Do-We-Go-From-Here? In
the life of every Artist (the lecturer who looks like God
says) there must come a Time of Doubt, which is the Fire
that tempers the Steel . . .

The sun was blocked off. Jason Spivak was standing in
front of him.

"Well, everyone's crawling out of their dens," Spivak
said and sat down next to him. "I hate spring," he went on,
making himself comfortable by slumping until he was sitting on the base of his spine. "April is the cruelest month,
breeding lilacs out of the dead land."

"It's still March," Aaron reminded him.

"It's almost April, and I can exercise poetic license, even
if it is T. S. Eliot's license. You know what I think about
Spring?"

"You told me. You hate it." Aaron didn't want to be
bothered; there was too much to think about to listen to
Spivak's chatter.

But Spivak was sailing on. "Spring is a coward. It won't
come in all at once. It's too coy for that. I hate coy things.
It knocks at your door and then when you open the door it
runs away. It breathes on you and then it's gone like a
ghost. I hate it."

"It seems to me," Aaron said without feeling any interest,
"that you hate a lot of things."

"And so do you," Spivak said aggressively. "We all do.
It's the curse of the century. We've learned that we actually
hate all those things we used to think we loved. Our poor
parents, to think we ever let them believe we loved them,
when actually all we felt about them could be summed up
in one complex or another."

"What brought this on?" Aaron asked.

"I've been thinking all winter long. Didn't have much
else to do. This is just one of the things I've been thinking
about. Buy me a beer."

"Where am I supposed to get the money?"

"All right. But I tell you this . . ."

"For free?"

"Don't kid. I'm serious. I'm telling you that this whole generation of writers and artists, and I include you among us, is sick, and that's precisely why we're artists. We're the advance agents of the future of man. We post the billboards. Our sickness is just a sample of the mass sickness that's to come. You know what this date is? You think it's 1948 A.D.? Maybe that's right, but there's another date, a date that means more. About 4 or 5 B.F. B.F., Before the Finish."

"Spivak, why do you keep on living?"

"I don't know. Maybe curiosity. Why do you?"

"Because I'm not so sure of things as you are."

"That's because you haven't thought enough."

"Maybe."

"Of course it is. Let's go to Hoboken."

"What for? To escape the holocaust?"

"No, Jesus, I want to go to Hoboken to get some steamed clams. I know a joint there where you can get a couple of dozen steamed clams for a dime." Spivak stood up to reinforce his suggestion. "Come on, we can take the ferry over."

Aaron didn't move. "I don't want to go. I've got to do some work today."

"It will keep."

"So will the clams."

Spivak sat down with a great show of reluctance. "Where's it going to get you?" he asked.

"Where's what going to get me?"

"Working hard. Breaking your ass. Suppose you're good, what difference does it make? You've got to bootlick the galleries, you've got to bootlick the critics, and then you've got to do the same damned thing with the jerks who buy paintings to stick up on their walls."

"Now hold on. There've been plenty of artists who haven't gone down on their knees . . ."

"I'm not talking of the past," Spivak said angrily. "I'm talking of now. Look at me. I won't compromise. That's why I can't get my new book published. It's gone to eighteen publishers, it's with some jerky house now, and every goddamned one of them wanted me to tone it down. I could have had it published long ago, if I wanted to give in. But I

won't do it. The hell with them. Either the book gets published the way I wrote it, or not at all. Okay, so it will be
not at all. That's what you were going to say, wasn't it?"

"I wasn't going to say anything," Aaron told him. He
was feeling tired and irritable, and Spivak did nothing for
his spirits. Near the play area he could see some kids
throwing a ball around. Maybe he ought to toss it around
with them, get some exercise. That was what he needed,
some exercise; he was getting sluggish, getting some fat
on his gut.

"What's eating you today?" Spivak asked querulously.

"Nothing's eating me."

"You can tell me."

"I said nothing's eating me." Aaron managed to keep his
tone mild . . .

"Get it off your chest."

. . . but Spivak was going to get clipped . . .

"What's wrong, trouble with Lois?"

. . . if he didn't let up.

"Is that it?"

"No."

"You're still with her, aren't you?"

"More or less."

"Is she working?"

"Not much."

And he wasn't letting up.

"That's the good thing about us," Spivak began. "I mean
people like you and me and most of the people we know.
We're always in training for the depression. I laugh when
I read in the papers that a depression is coming. When it
comes we'll be all set for it. We're used to doing without
money. It's the goddamned middle-class people who'll be
jumping out of windows. Only there won't be a depression.
Do you want to know why?"

"No," Aaron said wearily.

"Because there'll be a war first."

Here was old familiar ground.

"The people who run this country are humanitarians,"
Spivak said in a loud voice, looking around to see if anyone
was listening. No one seemed to be, but he continued: "No
one realizes it but they really are. They don't want to see
the Thirties all over again. People thrown out on the street,

Bonus Armies, guys going through garbage cans for something to eat, Hoovervilles. They've got the right idea: the only justifiable cause for war is acute unemployment. Know something?"

Aaron kept quiet. He'd stopped listening, stopped reacting.

"They've got a device in the Pentagon, a kind of thermometer that registers the number of unemployed in the country. When the thermometer reaches a certain level, called in Brass Hat parlance the Level of Fever, a bell will go off, electronic what-nots will start automatically to press buttons, and the air will be crowded with rockets and atom bombs. That will be the war. Russia has the same thing, only it measures the number of anti-communists."

"You've been thinking about that all winter?" said Aaron, getting to his feet.

Spivak got up also. "Where are you going?"

"I've just thought of where I can borrow some dough," Aaron told him.

"Borrow dough!" Eagerly. "Where?"

"A guy named Kittridge."

"Who? Oliver Kittridge?"

"Yeah."

"That nut?"

"He's got dough," Aaron said. "He inherited a bundle. I got some out of him when he was starting that great drama group."

"Yeah, but he's a nut. He's off on some religious kick now."

"Since when?"

"I don't know since when. But this guy's going through a typical fairy metamorphosis. He thinks he's Jesus Christ, or something. You know how they go. You ought to see him."

"I ran into him the other night, maybe two months ago."

"I saw him about that time. Haven't seen him since. His teeth were practically showing through his cheeks. And with a beard. No kidding, the guy looked like one of those cheap engraved Jesuses. I had a good look at him late one night standing in front of that Catholic church on Sixth Avenue."

"What was he doing?"

"He was talking to himself."

"Could you pick up on what he was saying?"

"No. He was kind of mumbling. I'm not kidding you, Aaron. This guy has really blown his top."

Aaron started walking.

"You're wasting your time," Spivak called after him.

Maybe. He'd see.

He heard Spivak saying, his voice fading, "I'll bet you don't get any dough out of him."

He might be right, but still it was worth the chance. And he wanted to get a look at this Jesus Christ character. Funny about those queers—when they went off the deep end they always tried to be something impossibly good. Still and all, what had this to do with the prime object of promoting some of the wherewithal? There wasn't a single law of the land which said you couldn't borrow money from a nut. And even if there were . . . Maybe, since the guy had blown his top, he ought to raise the ante. Maybe the guy had all his dough hidden under a mattress now or under the rug. Maybe . . . Maybe this and maybe that. Out of the realm of speculation now (because there was Kittridge's place) and into the realm of reality.

Aaron went up the stairs to Kittridge's apartment and knocked on the door. There wasn't any answer, but when he knocked harder the door shook as if it weren't locked and . . . what do you know . . . it wasn't locked. Aaron opened the door, a little stealthily, because it had struck him that if Kittridge weren't home and he had a little time he might have a windfall. Too bad he had told Spivak he was going there. Although that didn't matter. Spivak wouldn't talk, especially if he threw a scare into him.

But—cancel out everything—Kittridge was home. Aaron saw him sitting on a straightbacked chair in a dark corner of the livingroom, his whole body conforming exactly to the rigid lines of the chair. As he walked toward him slowly, Aaron noticed that Kittridge didn't look toward him, and as he came closer he could see that Kittridge's eyes weren't following his movements. He tested him, going first to one side and then to the other, but Kittridge's eyes were as fixed as the hunks of glass taxidermists jam into the eye sockets of dead animals. Maybe the guy was dead. But no— going right up to him, Aaron could see an almost covert rise and fall of his chest under the rough brown bathrobe.

"Kittridge."
No movement.
"Kittridge."
Still.
"Hey, what's the matter with you?"
The left arm twitched and then froze again.
"Are you okay?"
What a dumb question.
"Hey." He caught Kittridge's chin in his right hand and
began to shake his head from side to side. There was no
resistance; the head followed his hand as if it were a free
ball, but the second that Aaron took his hand away the head
snapped back into its fixed position and stayed there. This
was a hot one. The guy was nuts. Catatonic, they called it.
I'm an analyst yet. How did the guy live? When did he eat?
Christ, did he even go to the toilet? Come to think of it the
apartment stunk, like there was a cat in heat around.
    "Kittridge, hey, snap out of it." He began to work Kitt-
ridge's head back and forth vigorously. "Come on, come on,
kid, snap out of this." He remembered once when they
were going through an attack by a U-boat—he was on a
tanker that time—one of the kids had sat down on a hatch
and begun to cry, and he'd slapped him a few times to
bring him around, only it didn't work. "Come on, Kittridge,
you're going to be okay, come on, kid, it's me, Aaron Ross,
your old pal, come on, relax, relax, will you?" He tried to
loosen one of the arms, but the fingers seemed to be glued
to the right knee. Jesus Christ, what was he supposed to
do now?
    The phone started ringing. It sounded loud as the clanging
of a fire bell.
    "Your phone's ringing," Aaron said, and wanted to laugh
at himself. What a stupid remark. He left Kittridge and
picked up the phone.
    "Hello, Oliver?" came a woman's anxious voice.
    Aaron thought a moment before replying. "Who's this?"
    "Is Oliver there?"
    "Sort of."
    "What do you mean—sort of?"
    "It's hard to explain. Who is this?"
    "I'm Oliver's sister. I've been phoning and phoning for

days and I haven't gotten any answer. Is there anything wrong?"

"Where are you now?" Aaron asked her.

"What's wrong?" There was fright in her voice now.

"I can't tell you. Where are you?"

"I'm at home."

"Yes, but where?"

"On Sixty-fourth Street."

"Well, you'd better hop a cab and get down here right away."

"Can't you tell me what's wrong? Is Oliver in trouble? Who are you?" Irritation was mixing with the fright.

"I'm a friend of your brother's. I just came over here to visit him and I found him sick."

"Sick?"

"Not that way. He's just sitting here, you understand, without moving, won't say anything, just sitting here. Now stop asking questions and get down here. And fast."

"Oh my God," he heard her say. Then he hung up.

There wasn't anything to do while he waited for her. What a mess. He tried talking to Kittridge again, and he wondered whether Kittridge would move if he put a lighted match to his hand, say. He lit a cigarette and blew smoke at Kittridge's face, curious, scientific. Kittridge blinked, but that was all. He snapped on a couple of lamps. Kittridge's pale face shone like wax in the lamplight and his beard was the same faded brown as the rough bathrobe. Aaron saw a couple of paintings leaning, face in, against a far wall. He turned them around. They were scrawls of color, bad, very bad, as if someone had deadened every color by mixing it with black and then had begun to whirl them over the canvas, like a frenzied ice-skater. It was like photographs of star clusters, splash and point and slash. What a waste of paint, what a waste of canvas. You didn't have to be a Great Brain to see that the guy who'd done those was off his trolley. He looked for Kittridge's name on the paintings, but they were unsigned. Well, that showed some discrimination. It might not be a bad idea to take the canvases. He could paint over them, or use the backs.

The door of the apartment was thrown open suddenly and a tall woman in a long mink coat, Aaron guessed it was, rushed in. She took a second to get her bearings, and then ran across the room to Kittridge, saying in a low and frightened voice, "Oliver, Oliver." She pulled his head against her stomach, calling his name again, and then abruptly pulled her arms away and stepped back. "Oliver, it's Phyllis. Oliver, look at me." Aaron heard her suck in her breath each time she had spoken her brother's name. He felt a kind of anger begin to go through him as Kittridge sat there immobile. What was wrong with the guy? He must hear her. Why didn't he come loose, even for a minute? Now she was saying in a shrill voice, "Oliver, stop it, do you hear, don't sit there like that. Oliver." She got down on her knees in front of him, the mink coat spreading warm brown on either side of her. "Look at me, please, please, it's Phyllis, it's Phyllis." She began to repeat her own name over and over, as if it were a charm. Finally Aaron came behind her and said, "I don't think that's going to do much good." She stood up, aiding herself by pushing on her brother's set knees, recoiling when she realized that she had touched him.

"What's wrong with him?" she asked, her voice close to breaking.

"I don't know," Aaron said. "I came and found him like this."

"How long has he been like this?"

"I don't know."

"Are you a friend of his?"

"Sort of. I know him from when he started that theatrical group."

"Oh, yes, I heard about that," she said, recollecting. Then, "What can we do? What can we do?"

She was a little over thirty. Aaron saw, with a face that had been scraped and chiseled into fine unmoving lines, even in emotion a composed face, with eyes that were a little dull and thoughtless, skin that had doubtless been patted and creamed and powdered into constant smoothness, and hair styled and set and brushed and brushed—the face, Aaron told himself, of a rich woman.

"What can we do?"

Better leave me out of this.

"Should we get a doctor?"

That was her problem. He had enough of his own without getting involved in this.

"Please, please help me."

Reluctantly Aaron found himself saying, "I'll do what I can." But what?

"I don't suppose he'll do any harm to himself," she said, her voice questioning.

"Not without moving," Aaron said. "And he don't seem to want to move."

"Can he hear us?" she asked.

"I guess so," Aaron said, and regretted it, because she immediately and inelegantly flopped to her knees in front of her brother again and began to plead with him. Finally and somewhat urgently Aaron helped her to her feet, his fingers buried deep in the rich fur of her coat. She started to cry, and he turned her toward him and held her head forward against his shoulder, while the fingers of his left hand ran softly and appreciatively over the fur. Something about it excited him; that fur, that mink, was the symbol of the world of opulence, the world of big cars and sleek women and plush warm apartments, the world which he sometimes thought he hated and the world which he often knew he wanted. There came to his mind a scene from a movie, *Scarface*, a sign flashing on and off at the end of the picture, as he remembered it, a sign saying: THE WORLD IS YOURS.

The World Is Yours. What world? What would he have to give up to enter that other world, the world of good things to eat and good things to wear and women in gowns instead of dungarees? Because you always gave up something to gain something, that he knew.

She was out of his arms now, recovering, dabbing at her eyes. Christ, women were almost as shallow as men. She took a deep breath (he could see her breasts become prominent) and when she spoke her voice was steady.

"I think I'd better call my doctor," she said.

"That might be the best thing," Aaron agreed.

She went to the phone, looking at Oliver only once, and started to dial a number, missed, and had to start all over again.

"Want me to dial it for you?" Aaron asked.

"No," she said. "I can do it. Thank you."

This time she made it, asked for a doctor by name, and

told him in a quick and urgent voice about Kittridge. She told the doctor to come right down, gave him the address, and hung up. Then she went over to her brother again, stood before him undecided, and after a few moments turned away. She fumbled in her purse, brought out a gold cigarette case, and took out a cigarette. "I'm sorry," she said, "I forgot. Do you want one?" "Thanks," Aaron said, and took a cigarette. "It's Turkish," she said. He took the lighter from her (it was gold and heavy) and lit her cigarette, then his.

"Better sit down," Aaron said.

She sat on one end of the couch. He sat on the other. From a distance of five feet he looked at her, frankly, with objective eyes. She had good lines, a tight stomach, thighs with some bulge to them, long legs with subtly swollen calves. She puffed on her cigarette several times, ground it out, forced herself into an easy position on the couch. Then she looked at him, and he watched her eyes follow the curve of his body.

"I want to thank you," she said.

"What for?"

"For being so patient."

"It's nothing," he said. Should he reach out and pat her hand reassuringly? No, what for?

"What's your name?" she asked.

"Ross. Aaron Ross."

"You said you were a friend of Oliver's?"

"Not exactly. We know each other, just kind of."

"What do you do?"

"I'm a painter."

"You look young," she said.

"Maybe I am."

Out of the corner of his eye he could see Kittridge's frozen figure, as impersonal as the chair on which he was fixed. Did he hear all this? Did he care? What was he thinking? Was he thinking, if he was listening to the two of them, sitting there in his presence, or what might be loosely thought of as his presence, going through the age-old preliminaries, familiar to both of them through so much usage, was he thinking: What kind of people are they?

Well, Aaron asked himself, looking at her, looking inward at himself for a moment of feared introspection, what
kind of people are we anyway?

8. The World of Amy Macduff, A World of Fear and Trembling

IT HAPPENED TO HER as she was coming
out of the state unemployment office at Forty-third Street
and Eighth Avenue. Maybe it had been the standing on line
with all those shabby beaten people. Maybe the brusque
superior attitude of the woman behind the counter had
brought it on. ("Why haven't you found a job? Have you
been looking for employment? Have you been offered employment?") Or perhaps it was going down those narrow
spit-covered and butt-covered stairs out into the spring
sunlight that fell with wasted grace onto the grey and
dirty street. At any rate, now she was going into one of her
white faints. It seemed that the world was a photographic
print taken from a badly overexposed negative. Everything
was bleached and faded. No clarity or distinction to any
of the lines she saw, so that everything appeared to be far
off, and growing more distant. And now the shakes began.
Amy could feel the earth starting to pitch under her feet,
erratically, as if she were trying to remain standing in a
rowboat caught in a cross-current. She leaned against the
building; her weight seemed to press it backwards, to make
it slide away, as if after all it had been nothing more than
a large cardboard carton. She felt the perspiration break
out on her hands and on her feet. People walked by, not
looking at her; there was no way she could reach them,
there was nothing she could tell them. They were in some
remote safe and sound world. Now she couldn't breathe.
Something had tightened around her chest, and she couldn't
breathe. This time I'm going to die, she thought, knowing
that she'd said that to herself each time this had happened.

But this time, this time it would happen. The appalling picture of herself lying neglected on the sidewalk broke into her mind. Yes, yes, they always said you could die in New York, you could die on the street and no one would take any notice. Her heart was pounding against the wall of her chest; it seemed to be trying to break through with its hammer strokes. Spasms began to run through her, starting around the diaphragm, which contracted and went loose with irregular but terrifying violence. Down the street she could see the sign of a bar. Automatically she began to move toward it, afraid with each step that she would fall flat on her face. If she could make it to the bar, she knew, she would be all right. A couple of drinks, and then it would be all right. Someone darted in front of her, almost knocking her over, but she managed to keep upright, maintaining a precarious balance, until she reached the bar. Her hands almost slipped from the polished wood but she hung on desperately. The bartender came toward her from some dimness and stood before her, looking in his white apron and white shirt like a hospital attendant. Amy dug in the pocket of her trench coat for her money, feeling her fingers tear at her thigh. A couple of coins stuck to her wet palm, a quarter and a dime. She fumbled in her pocket again, couldn't find anything more. Thirty-five cents—my God, was that all? Why hadn't she cashed her check? Oh Christ, why did this thing have to happen to her? She dropped the money on the counter; the quarter started to roll away but the bartender knocked it flat with his hand. He said something to her—she thought he was asking what she wanted —but she couldn't talk. The words were big dry blobs that couldn't work up through her throat. They had jammed together there, so she couldn't breathe. She watched mutely while the bartender filled a shot glass and pushed it in front of her. She felt some of the whiskey spill over the back of her hand as she carried it to her mouth. It went down hot and raw, wonderful for a moment, as it hit her stomach, and then it began to roll around and around there, like a ball of ice. And the shakes began again. She felt her chest bang into the wood of the bar, bang and bang again, while she tried to suck air into her lungs, and she could hear the dry gasping from her own throat while she looked at the bartender, the hospital attendant, trying to tell him somehow that she had to have another, just one more and then she could make it, she wouldn't bother him anymore. But he was already moving away. God, how could he do it? Couldn't he see . . . couldn't he see . . . I'm going to lie down on the floor and die, she thought. Then they'll all know, then they'll all know. There was a man standing next to her—where had he come from—a short man with a fat dark middle-aged face layered with grease, as if it had been cooked for just a little while. She felt his fingers on her arm and she could sense that they were sweaty even as they pushed through the gabardine of her trench coat. "What's the matter, lady?" he was saying to her. "You sick?" She jerked her head up and down several times, and then she couldn't stop the jerking. "Hey," she heard him shout, "hey, give this lady something. Can't you see the lady's sick?" The bartender's hand was there in front of her, the long needle nozzle of the plastic fixture at the top of the bottle tilting forward as the level of the whiskey rose slowly in the shot glass—he was trying to torture her—and then she had snatched the glass and poured the whiskey down her throat. It seemed to dissolve the blockage there. She could breathe now. She took a deep breath, throwing her head back, drawing in the air through her open mouth. "You want another?" the fat dark man was asking her. She shook her head yes, abjectly, feeling now that she was released from her terror a sense of acute shame. This time she tried to drink more slowly, with a little more dignity, as befitted a woman, as befitted her, trying to show that she was now in control of what had been only temporarily a bad thing, but she had emptied the glass before she was aware of it. Still, as she put the empty glass back on the bar, she felt better. One more and she'd be completely all right, completely all right, able to get home.

The fat dark man had a hairy face. He was looking at her with his small eyes, made small by the surrounding creased butter of his flesh, and his eyes were watching her without sympathy. No, they were too calculating for that. And she knew what he was calculating.

"How's it now?" he asked—and she could feel the pudgy hand, the hand of a man who worked in the kitchen of a cheap restaurant, a hand that went a hundred times a day into soup and gravy, press her forearm, the thumb pinching a little flesh against the side of the forefinger. "You okay now?"

"Yes, I'm all right now," she said, hearing her voice take on the trace of British accent that came from God knows where at times like these.

"I know just how you feel."

The hell he did.

He said, "I've had plenty of rough nights in my time, plenty of rough mornings."

She had to thank him. After all—okay, we'll forget his motives—he had helped her out.

"Yes," Amy agreed, "you must have been around."

Well, that was nice and ambiguous.

"Damn right I've been around," he said, swelling a little, showing some of his bright plumage. Oh, these little bastards. "I've had plenty of good times, you know what I mean." And he actually winked. "And I ain't through yet. I'm a guy likes a good time. What the hell, what are we here on earth for, to have a little fun. Huh?"

"That's right. That's a good philosophy." Now where did that word come from? Plato to Spinoza to Bergson to have a little fun. His hand was going, finger over finger, like a mountain climber edging up a steep rock face, to her arm, and now his thumb was subtly, with the infinite subtlety of a slap on the behind, nudging the side of her breast. His eyes were sharp and excited, seemingly attempting to escape from the soft dough that held them. This was the moment of decision. This was the time for action.

"Do you have a dime?" she asked him.

The thumb recoiled.

"A dime? What for?" He seemed as surprised as if she had asked him whether he had the Taj Mahal in his pocket.

"I need a dime."

The long black hairs that dangled from his nostrils quivered a little. "Well sure," he said, "here, take a buck."

"No, I only need a dime."

"It's okay. Take the buck."

Well all right, if he insisted. She slipped the dollar into her pocket. It would be insurance, just in case she got one of her attacks again before she could cash her check.

"You want another?" he asked.

It wouldn't be fair, she thought, but then his urgent

thumb decided her. It was all an investment for the dirty
little bastard, and his thumb was paying the first (and only)
dividend. All investments don't pay off.

"Thanks," Amy said. "I'd like one."

This time she drank slowly, patiently, the tension gone,
the fear of dying gone, and in place of that fear a small
and ridiculous annoyance at the hand on her arm. The fright
replaced by the trite. Yes, everything was going to be all
right now. Storms in the morning, clearing at noon, a few
scattered clouds toward evening. Barometer rising. Thumb
rising. Yes, when she got home she'd cash her check and
buy a bottle, not a fifth, mind you, but just a pint, only
enough to settle her and nothing more, because she had
to start tapering off. In a sudden swell of optimism a host of
plans dangled before her. She would get herself a job, buy
some new clothes, fix up her place, start keeping regular
hours, go to the Clay Club some evenings and do a little
sculpting, go to the neighborhood swimming pool, keep
busy, keep active, keep well.

Now she could look around the bar. God, it was a gloomy
run-down awful place. Most bars were. She sometimes
wondered how she could ever have spent so much time in
them. Time plus money and you have your life. There were
the red-lettered signs pasted to the mirror behind the bar.
BAR WHISKEY—25. SEAGRAM'S—35. FOUR ROSES—
35. A little farther along: OLD-FASHIONED—40. A reasonable pub, a good cheap bar this, the kind of place
needed in the Village. The booths at the side were empty,
the tables absolutely bare. The floor had been swept so
clean that all the trampled-in dirt showed clearly. In the
rear a couple of stark fluorescent lights were on. That reminded her of an idea she had for a make-up light for
women—a two bulb affair for bathrooms, say, with one
bulb simulating daylight for daytime make-up and the
other less glaring for night or evening make-up. There was
money in the idea; she'd have to think of someone who
could help her develop and market it. Yes, there was money
to be made in this world, and she could make it.

Or could she?

She put the empty glass back on the bar—had it been the
fourth or fifth?—and slightly and not offensively moved
away from the fat dark man. "I want to thank you," she

told him. "I appreciate what you've done very much. I just don't happen to have any money with me . . ."

"Well, that's okay," he said quickly.

"If I ever see you again," she said, "I'll pay you back."

"You're not going now?"

"I'm afraid I have to." She tried to sound pleasant, to give him the impression that forces stronger than herself were taking her from his side. Inflexible powerful forces like a previous engagement.

"Have another drink," he said, shrewdly calculating that with one or two more she wouldn't be able to stop. Ah, but that was where he was wrong, because she could always stop. "Come on, have another." He started to call to the bartender, who was at the far end of the bar talking to two men in the uniforms of a delivery service. "No, I'm sorry, I can't," she said, smiling, firm.

"Why not?"

"I've got to go somewhere."

"Where?"

"I've got to go home."

"You live around here?"

"No, no," she said, "I live in Brooklyn."

"What part of Brooklyn?"

He was closing in.

"Just in Brooklyn. Across the bridge."

"What do you have to go home for?"

"Well . . . my husband's expecting me."

He was looking at her hands.

"You ain't got no husband," he said, his lips pulling back so that the jagged blackened edges of his teeth showed. "What are you giving me that for?"

She laughed to show that she wasn't embarrassed. "I never wear a ring," she told him. "I don't believe in it. Don't you think it's a barbarous custom? It goes back to primitive times and we're much too advanced now. Besides," she added, "I pawned it last week."

"Listen," he said, "you don't have to go to Brooklyn now and you know it. If you got a husband he works, don't he? He ain't home now, so you don't have to go home."

"He's on the night shift."

"He's on the night shift? Where?"

"Look," she said, lighting a cigarette—a lit cigarette always came in handy at such a time. "I've told you that I appreciate what you did for me and if I could repay you I would . . ."

"Who's saying anything about paying me?"

"Well, what do you want?"

The blunt question made him think for a moment.

"I want some company a little while. I tell you what, I got some stuff up my place, it ain't far from here, we can take a taxi. I got some good stuff, not like this crap you get in bars. You come with me, it's safe, I ain't going to try nothing. I just want some company, that's all. I just want to talk to you."

Of course, of course, so pure in heart.

"I am sorry," Amy said, speaking slowly, precisely, not trying to force warmth into her voice now, "but I really have to go home and I do have a husband and I haven't been lying to you. If you want to come home with me and meet my husband, well, that's up to you."

"You kidding?" he asked suspiciously.

"No, I'm not kidding."

He didn't know what to make of it.

"Okay," he said finally, "I'll come along."

"It's out in Brooklyn," she told him.

"I know. That's okay."

"I don't think you'd better come," she said, and began to walk toward the door.

She heard him say behind her, "Goddamn whore," and then she went out through the door. She heard the words once more, trapped and squealing in her mind, and she tried to laugh them off. But when she couldn't do that, when the words stuck there in her mind as if cement had hardened around them, she tried to bury them in a wave of anger. Oh that dirty little bastard, oh that greasy sonofabitch, why hadn't she taken her cigarette and burned it into his eye, why hadn't she kicked him in the balls, oh that crummy little louse, let his guts rot out, let him only get sick some time the way she'd been sick and let someone spit in his face, the bastard. The hell with it, she couldn't be bothered with a petty thing like that. But damnit to hell, why did men have to have their minds centered between their legs. Oh well, he was just an ignorant sonofabitch. Out of sight, out of mind. Dead, gone, finished, forgotten.

But if she ever saw that little bastard again . . . It must be good to be a man, to be able to take someone and smash his face in, to just let him have it, to work all the evil out of your system with a few blows. Just work it out. Modern psychiatry, sanity through judo.

On the subway platform, waiting for the train, she began to feel good again. The weakness was completely gone from her legs. Her breathing was free and easy. She held out her hand; it was steady. But dirty, she'd have to wash it. And get those nicotine stains off. God, she'd been letting herself go to hell throughout the winter. Well, now it was spring, birth of the year, rebirth of her. No time like the spring for a new regime.

Sitting in the train she decided she would write a letter to her mother in California, telling her that she was all—was well. She hadn't seen her mother for almost five years now, not since that disastrous time when, feeling depressed and emotionally isolated in New York, she had gone back to her family in California (two sisters, a brother, and her mother, her father having died when she was fourteen) in the hope that she would feel some tie, some bond, some sense of love being given and being received. Instead, when she had felt nothing on seeing all those old remembered and yet unfamiliar faces and listened to all those old remembered and still doltish opinions, she had gone into a complete tailspin. Her mother had told her, "You need a rest, dear, and we're going to send you to a quiet place where you'll feel better," and the next thing she knew she was in a state hospital with a lot of people who were, obviously, nuts. She had succeeded in getting out a couple of months later, after the usual warm tubs and restraining sheets, with a burning hatred of her mother, which had flickered out in the next couple of years. As a matter of fact, not long after V-E Day, she had decided to go back to California again, just to prove to herself that she would be all right. Unfortunately, she had had a good deal to drink to brace herself for the train trip, and when she had insisted violently on her right to sleep in the aisle of the pullman instead of in the constricting confines of her berth, and when her insistence progressed to beating the conductor with her broad leather belt, they had thrown her off the train in Philadelphia and clapped her into jail. (She had had to pay a fine, but on the other hand had received a rebate on her ticket from the Pennsylvania Railroad.) So when she wrote to her mother to tell her all was well, it was a way of proving to herself that all was actually well, because any contact with her mother seemed to mean automatic disaster, and if she felt strong enough and willing enough to write, why then it was apparent that she was all right. Q.E.D.

Ah, but she had led a strange and complicated and devious and stupid life. There was something inside her, she was convinced, that made her want not to be happy. Every time she had been on the verge of getting the things which in the ordinary course of events (whatever "ordinary" might be expected to mean) might make her happy she had managed without apparent effort to foul things up. Of course, consciously she wanted to be happy, but subconsciously . . . and there we slide into all that Freudian bull. Every now and then (which was pretty often) someone would suggest politely that she go to an analyst. Or, as Aaron had put it: "You ought to have your head examined." Well, she had gone to see a couple of them, but found that she couldn't talk to them: she knew immediately that she could never tell them what was going on inside of her. She had known one psychiatrist well two years before; he had been her age (thirty at that time), he had been a worried lousy lover, he had been by way of being a bit of a jerk.

There was too much to tell, too much of a wall between her and what people thought of her. When they told her she was big and beautiful (men did, and she knew they were sincere) she could listen to them and try to believe them, knowing all the time that she was overgrown (not merely big) and grotesque. Women, especially those with some latent lesbianism, admired her, grew very fond of her, which meant nothing. She should have been a man. She should have been a football player, a boxer, a stevedore. Or, being a woman, she should have been made in the image of those pretty little women who fitted into size ten and twelve dresses and could easily become a drop in the puddle of a group. The other day a guy had come up from

New Orleans and stopped in on her. Thank God it was so dark in her apartment, so he couldn't see the claw marks of the past winter on her, so he could say, "Down there they still talk about you and everyone says you'll be coming back someday." She was a kind of female Paul Bunyan, a Blue Ox. The Times, Trials and Tribulations of Paula Bunyan. In this anonymous society there must be a pleasure in being anonymous, to become part of the whole as completely as the cream in homogenized milk. Ah. well, ah well . . .

Coming out into the sunshine (and now the sunshine felt warm and real and appropriate) at the Washington Square stop she decided she would pay a little visit to Aaron, just to let him see her in a cheerful mood. During the winter they had run into each other a couple of times. He had been with a dark·and beautiful what-not, a singer named Lois Wilson whom she had met somewhere or other, at some party perhaps, a girl whom she had envied immediately for her exotic beauty and her reasonable proportions. They had exchanged elaborately unembarrassed salutations and small talk, ·although she had felt bad, bad as hell, knowing that she was still drawn to Aaron. Well, now she'd just drop in on him with a couple of bottles of beer, and a darling how are you and tell me what's been going on. That was all. Keep it casual, keep it remote. A look at his new painting—Christ, he'd be painting her now; what did that matter? Finish the beer, and then goodbye, Aaron, come around · sometime. In answer to previous questions:· I'm going to get a job, I'm going to stop drinking, I've decided to take your advice and start doing some work in clay. Yes, she wasn't going to have him going around feeling sorry for · her.

She bought two bottles of beer—the money having been thoughtfully provided by the gentleman with the sweaty hands—and walked to Jones Street, feeling as brisk and gay as the new season demanded. The bottles clinked gently against each other inside her sheath of brown paper; it was a pleasant sound. She walked on the sunny side of the street, not minding that the sunlight was striking her full in the face, and turned at a right angle to cross the street and go up to Aaron's place. Entering the narrow vestibule, she saw a woman in a mink coat with elaborately done hair, trying to make out the scrawled and scratched names in the battered rectangles under the bells. The woman looked around as Amy came into the vestibule. The two of them filled the cramped space. Amy saw a cool, or cold, symmetrical face, the face of a well-bred in-bred person, the kind of face that you knew instinctively chewing gum could never enter. Amy disliked that face; its perfection of detail made the broad lines of her own appear even coarser, grosser.

"I'm sorry," the woman said, straightening up, "I can't seem to decipher these names."

"They're not put there to be deciphered," Amy said. "They're meant to deceive and frustrate. We keep in step with the modern world down here." Certainly the mink coat did not belong to the Village.

"What a curious thing to say."

"No, it isn't," Amy said, pushing open the inner door. "Not when you think it over." She started to go in.

"Oh, excuse me," the woman in the mink coat said, stopping her, "could you tell me which bell belongs to Aaron Ross?"

Amy pushed aside the temptation to say she didn't know. She'd never been like that, a common bitch, and she wasn't going to start now. If the mink coat wanted to find Aaron, so much the better for Aaron. Someday she might tell him of her unselfish and almost incomparable behavior. And then again she might not. She showed the mink coat the bell and watched the long slim finger press it. A few seconds later—while Amy remained in the doorway—came the sound of the buzzer. Amy held open the door as the woman in the mink coat—Aaron's guest—went in.

"Thank you." Then, as Amy turned to leave, she said, "Weren't you going in?"

"I changed my mind," Amy said.

The woman hesitated for just a second. "You weren't going up to see Mister Ross?"

"What a curious thing to say." And Amy went out into the street.

She was halfway down the block when it started to come on. She started to walk quickly, telling herself that she would make it, clutching tight the bottles of beer, hoping that her momentum would carry her home before the shakes really began in earnest.

9. Aaron Ross Prepares to Enter One of the Upper Classes

WELL, THIS WAS A surprise. An unexpected surprise? Not exactly an unexpected surprise.

Aaron said, "Sit down," and watched as Phyllis née Kittridge made a difficult choice among a stool, a wicker chair with a torn seat, and the cot; she took the chair. "What do you say I make you some coffee?"

"Don't bother," she said. "I can't stay long."

The lines of the classic gambit. Aaron offers coffee. Phyllis declines. Takes king's chair. Aaron to kitchen to make coffee anyhow. Phyllis to feet to look at paintings. Aaron to check and mate in five moves.

Yes, there she went. In the kitchen, putting up the water to boil, Aaron heard her get up from the chair and begin to move around. The once-over. Has he talent? Hasn't he talent? Coming back, he found her standing in front of his easel.

"That's quite good," she said, adopting the tone of a person who may not have expected much.

"It's not finished," Aaron said, moving to her side.

"But I like it."

"That's too bad."

"Too bad?" Should she be offended?

"Yeah. Because if you like it now you won't when it's finished. How can you judge something that the painter's still working on?"

"I didn't know it wasn't finished," she said, and added quickly, with a smile of false apology, "I know very little about art." She had a high bosom, Aaron noted, probably due to an expensive brassiere, and what in hell was that perfume? "I know everyone must ask you questions like this"—a slight pause—"but just what does that represent?"

"Nothing."

"Nothing?"

Not bad hips and a good gentle curve to her behind.

"That's right," Aaron said—he'd almost said, You heard me. "It's what's generally called an abstraction."

"Oh." Teach me, Daddy.

"It's just the way I feel while I'm painting the thing. I put down the colors to reflect my mood. I'm painting from emotion." What kind of baloney is this? "That's the big advantage of modern art," Aaron went on, hoping to take the curse of pompousness off himself. "You can paint nothing and get away with it."

She laughed.

Okay, laugh.

"But I do like it," she said.

"That don't change it any. It's no good. As a matter of fact, it stinks. I got to finish with the coffee." He went back into the kitchen. Next thing she'd be telling him she liked the composition or the use of space, going off into one of those routines used by people who liked to pretend they got a real kick out of art. The kind you heard at museums or exhibitions—Oh, Charles, look at the color in the Matisse; Anita, don't you *feel* that red?—brightly putting into words the things you shouldn't even try to put into words. Phonies. A year before they'd been laughing and saying, A six year old child could have done this, but then they'd discovered that wasn't nice, and moreover it was unfashionable in a world where you were supposed to admire simplification and Grandma Moses sat on the left hand of God, who if you looked real close you could see was none other than Pablo P. Picasso. He threw some coffee into the boiling water—rude methods are best—and listened to her stirring in the next room. Beneath that Paris original dress, beneath that scented and oiled skin would soon flow Coffee à la Ross, grounds and all. He watched the brown mess erupt in the boiling water and then turned off the gas and let it settle. There was a good smell in the room; it took the odor of the heavy perfume—Chanel Number 3.7—away.

Bringing the cups of coffee in, he asked her, "Do you like yours black?"

"Do you have cream?" She had been doing a little brows-ing among a stack of paintings against the wall.

"Cream? No. I don't even have milk. I can go down and get you some," he said hypocritically.

"Don't bother," she said for the second time.

Sitting on the couch, he drank some of the black coffee, conscious that it was not festive champagne. She sat rather stiffly in the chair, holding her cup and saucer in the approved manner.

"Tell me about your brother," Aaron said.

"He's much better now," she told him.

"What was wrong with him?"

"It was a nervous breakdown." It was always a nervous breakdown. In the old days they used to come out with it and say someone was nuts; now it was only a breakdown. "We've put him in a rest home temporarily."

"How long is temporarily?"

"Well, that depends. But my elder brother is going to Europe soon—Oliver's youngest and I'm next—and he's thinking of taking Oliver with him."

"Will that be any good for him?"

"Oh yes, I think so. Oliver has always liked Europe. I think it's been this environment down here. He's very sensitive, you know, and a little different."

"Different from what?"

"Well, you know, from most people. He was always very sensitive."

"What makes you think most people aren't sensitive?"

"I don't . . . Do you think they are?"

"I think they are. Or at least they're getting that way. Maybe you'd call it being touchy, jumpy, except for people who can express themselves. Then it's sensitive. It comes to the same thing for me. People are always getting rubbed on these days, and that makes them sensitive. Ever notice how many people walk around talking to themselves? Or how many people are drinking themselves to death?"

"What about you?"

"Me?"

"You're very unhappy, aren't you?"

"Christ no."

"You talk as though you are."

"Why should I be unhappy? Listen, I won't be unhappy

until I know I'm a failure, and I don't know that yet. Where there's life there's hope." There's hoax.

She was nodding her head. Then, "Where do you come from, Aaron?" There was an intimacy in this first use of his name.

"I come from the Bronx."

"What did you do before you became a painter?"

"I sold bathing suits door to door."

"Please."

"Okay, I went to school."

"School? Where?"

"In the Bronx. High school. I went to De Witt Clinton. That's an exclusive preparatory school on Mosholu Parkway. Anyone can get in."

"What did you do after that?"

"When I got out? I worked as a sailor."

"Were you in the army during the war?"

"That's when I worked as a sailor."

"Not in the navy?"

"That's not working as a sailor, that's being a sailor. I was in the merchant marine." He'd just as leave skip this.

"Why did you do that instead of joining up?"

What was he supposed to tell her? How he and Marty Greenwald had talked it over—this was when oil from the sunken tankers was washing in on the beaches of New Jersey and you could sometimes see them burning from the shore. How he'd felt screw the army and the chicken shit routine, might as well go where he could still be an individual even though he was in the fight? How he had made up his mind then and there that he wanted to be ineligible for the G.I. Bill? (Bitter laugh.) Well, Marty was ineligible anyway, because he was mixed up with some mud and debris at the bottom of the North Atlantic. This damned why-weren't-you-in-the-army business. They'd gotten enough of that during the war, hitting the beach in civvies and people looking at them in that way.

"I'll tell you about it sometime," Aaron said at last.

She sipped her coffee delicately—that lousy brew—and then said, "I make you feel uncomfortable, don't I?"

"Why should you?"

"Because you think I've got a lot of money."

So she wasn't rich after all. In a good story he'd now

leap to his feet, or at her feet, and say, I'm so happy, your money was all that stood in our way. My God!

"Well, don't you?"

"I suppose I do." Well, good for her. "Yes, I am what you'd call rich. Are you one of those people who hates the rich?"

"Sure."

"I don't think you are. I think you'd like to have a lot of money. I think you'd like to surround yourself with fine things, things you'd like to see and touch. You people have that feeling, you want to own good things, and that's one of the things I like about you." She stopped and seemed to look at him a little more closely. "You are Jewish, aren't you?"

"Yeah," Aaron said, "I'm a Jew." He never said, I'm Jewish. Always, I'm a Jew. It was a kind of point, hard to explain.

"I thought you were. Your name."

"You couldn't make a mistake, lady," he said, trying to put down the rise of anger. What was the use?

"I couldn't tell looking at you," she said. "You don't look Jewish."

Bless you, madam, bless you for saying that—you bitch. The Great Compliment. You don't look Jewish, boy, laddie my boy, old son, you look like you might even be—now hold your breath—you might even be One Of Us.

"Thanks," Aaron said.

She got up, put her coffee on the low scarred and stained table in front of the cot. "Show me some more of your work."

"Why?" he asked, putting his own coffee down. "Do you want to buy some?"

She patted him on the arm as he stood up. "I might," she said. "Do you know, you're a very strange young man. I don't know why I'm saying this to you, but I think you're a good deal sweeter than you pretend."

"I'm not pretending anything."

"I think you're afraid people will think you're a nice guy. Do you ever laugh?"

"When there's something to laugh at."

"I'd like to see you when you laugh. I know that girl." She was moving away from him, toward a head of Amy that he had stacked in a corner. "She was downstairs when I came up. I asked her if she were coming to see you . . ."

"How come you asked her that?"

"Intuition, I suppose. I felt that she was coming to see you. Now don't ask me how. She's a strange-looking girl. I think she'd been drinking."

"Who, Amy? She never touches it."

"I thought . . . Do you know her well?"

"Sort of. We used to live together."

"Oh. Oh, I see. What happened?"

"Nothing."

"You don't still live with her?" And he could see that she was really concerned. Oh, this was too easy. And the rewards? A new Patron of the Arts? No rolling Patrons in doorways or on dark streets, never no more. Just roll me over, roll me over, and do it again. Less risk, less self-respect. But the voice of the Professor: You are doing nothing shameful if you use your talents well.

Her eyes had flicked toward a study of Lois. "Who is that?"

"Some girl."

"I can see that. What is she—Javanese?"

"No. She's a Negro."

"Really? That's odd."

"Why?"

"She doesn't look like a Negro."

"No one looks like what they're supposed to be. I don't look like a Jew and she don't look like a Negro. We do that to confuse people."

"Aaron, don't try to be unpleasant."

"I'm not trying."

"Well then, don't be." She approached the study; it was a charcoal drawing, a preliminary sketch. "She's very beautiful."

"Yeah."

"Is she a model?"

"No. Just a friend of mine."

"Do you have many friends? Women, I mean."

He shrugged. The modest masculine answer. I'm the boy, but I can't admit it. Crap.

"It's economic necessity," he said. "I can't afford a model, so I paint people I know. That's all there is to it."

She turned around and faced him full. "Do you know something," she said, "I think I'd like to have you paint me."

"You mean a portrait?"

"Something like that. I'd like to have a painting like that. Of myself." She indicated the study of Lois; it showed Lois nude to the waist, some drapery over her upper thigh— Aaron wasn't pleased with the arrangement—stretching her arms behind her neck, so that her rather long flat breasts were drawn high. "Would you like me to pose for you?"

Aaron thought for a few seconds. "Okay," he said then, "Strip."

"What?" Astonished.

"I said strip."

"You mean . . ."

"I mean take your clothes off. We might as well start right now."

10. In Which Oliver Kittridge Reveals
That He Knows What He's Doing

OLIVER SAT WITH HIS brother Wilbur on a bench under the heavy branches of an oak, and from where they sat he could see in the distance, seemingly shadowed, the long smooth backs of the Berkshire Hills. The sunlight came in fragments through the branches and the now-opening leaves, so that at times his brother's face was in sun and at times in shadow as he moved his head, speaking.

"It's good to see you feeling so much better."

This was the country of his boyhood summers, of their boyhood summers, spent in the big grey house of Aunt Martha near Pittsfield.

Wilbur: "I've just had a talk with Doctor Heller." (Wilbur could not know how significant that name was.) "He says you can leave whenever you want. What would you like? Would you like to stay here and rest a while longer?"

"I might as well leave," Oliver said, indifferently. And it didn't really matter.

"You'll have to take things easy for a while." Wilbur's brotherly love was obviously struggling with a good old New England aversion to mental illness, at least to that kind of mental illness which overstepped the bounds of decency delimited under the name of .eccentricity. "Of course Doctor Heller doesn't recommend that you live in New York again. At least not for some time. But I suppose he's spoken to you about that."

"Yes, he has."

Mr. Kikaus or Glaucose or Raucous was standing in front of his white cottage, a companion cottage to all those little white cubes spotted around the grounds, cutting viciously at the air with a stick. He was duelling again.

"Oliver, you understand that Doctor Heller has discussed everything with me." And so the word *everything* at last became a euphemism. "I don't want you to think that I condemn you or anything like that. After all, well, to speak frankly, well, at school . . ." The frank speech faltered, died. "I'd like to help you overcome that . . . that tendency. Believe me, I understand it. I . . ."

"We don't have to talk about it now," Oliver said gently.

"But we will. I want you to talk about it, or anything else. You know, being ten years older than you . . ." Wilbur found it difficult to finish a sentence containing a complex thought.

"You have more experience," Oliver said for him.

"Yes. We'll be open with each other, won't we?"

"Of course."

"That makes me feel better. Doctor Heller told me that you . . ." An effort. "That you've been holding yourself in too much."

Yes, and Doctor Heller, who was a Viennese and therefore an ex-pupil of Freud, had explained the conflict between his deviation—as he called it—and his morality and its consequent resolution into what he termed a religious hallucination. And naturally, of course in the course of nature, it was all a hallucination. Quite clearly so.

Wilbur saying: "I've had a letter from Phyllis."

"So have I."

"She says her husband is remarrying."

"Yes, I know."

"But that won't affect her. He still has to provide for her."

"That's fine."

Cloud-dappled-dappled skies above.

"She tells me that she's met a friend of yours."

"Yes, I know. She wrote."

Glory be to God for dappled things.

"Who is he, this Aaron Ross?"

"I don't know."

"What?"

For skies as couple-colored as a brindled cow.

"Oh. He's a painter."

"She said so. What does that mean?"

"He paints. Paints."

Fresh-firecoal chestnut-falls; finches' wings.

"Oliver."

Yes, the world had taken on meaning for him that dark winter when he had first read Hopkins.

"Oliver."

"I'm sorry. I was only thinking about something."

"You suddenly went blank."

"Oh, no, I wasn't blank at all."

"I was talking about this Aaron Ross."

"Yes, I know him."

"Do you think he's after Phyllis' money?"

"I couldn't say."

"I don't like his name. Aaron Ross. I get a picture of one of those . . ."

He fathers-forth whose beauty is past change.

"All right," Wilbur said, with elaborate consideration. "We won't talk about it." •

A wrench back to the trivial. Wilbur and Phyllis and the question of Aaron Ross. But he was already too late. The question of Aaron Ross vis-a-vis and tete-a-tete with their sister was laid aside, tabled by a motion. Down there, on the flat lawn near the main house, Mr. French was playing croquet with Mr. Harmon. It was Mr. French who had managed to leave twice, while he had been there, each time being picked up, or rescued, in the nearby town, drunk, besotted. Mr. Harmon was a tortured soul; he was given to crying for no perceptible reason, his sensibilities being very well hidden. And yet, and above all, it was people like them whom he had to . . .

"Oliver, how would you like to go to Europe?"

"Well, I : . . . I think so."

"Remember ten years ago, just before the war. You were only a kid then, but I was twenty-three, and I've always wanted to go back. Without Father. I don't suppose I should have said that. Doctor Heller says . . ."

"Where would we go?"

"Well, I have some business to attend to, some orders for the mill, and I have to go to France and Italy. And while I'm taking care of the business, why, you can do what you like, visit museums and galleries and . . . churches. What do you think?"

"It sounds exciting," Oliver said, hoping that he was putting some emotion in his voice.

"Great. I'll make all the arrangements."

"All right."

"You might as well stay here, as long as you like it, I mean, unless you'd rather stay with me in Fall River until we go."

"No, I'll come to Fall River a couple of days before sailing."

"That's fine. I'll have someone come here for you."

"Thanks, Wilbur."

For such, but not of such, is the Kingdom of Heaven.

"So then . . ." Wilbur was standing, his hand stretched out to take his in a vigorous assertion of masculinity. Shake. Of whose masculinity? And why had Wilbur never married? Why—the actual why—had he broken his engagement to Miss Pamela Sawyer? Or . . .

A few more words before Wilbur went down the hill toward the main house, probably to make a dutiful and fruitful report to Doctor Heller. Oliver watched his brother's back diminishing, saw him pass the croquet players who looked up for an uncurious moment, and then go into the main house, the home, the nest, the den of Doctor Moritz Heller. Oliver leaned back against the oak, pressed his ear against the thick rough warm bark of the tree, and heard the sap flowing upward through the core of the tree. It was a loud rushing sound, like the sound of the rapids in a stream. A heart-gushing-rushing sound, a May sound, the life pushing through the cylinder of the trunk to explode in the green leaves of all the fingered branches. God in the sound, everywhere. The earth suddenly darkened. A cloud had passed before the sun. A cloud no larger than a hand. The hand of God? Looking up through the branches at the cloud, Oliver saw it take the shape he had known it would, and then, closing his eyes, he heard.

Yes, yes, everything was going to be all right. Yes, he would have to be discreet—odious as it was to truckle and deceive, to play for the time the Peter and not the Paul—until that moment came which was already ordained, and would come, that moment when he would be called upon. If only that moment would come soon. But no, no, he mustn't, mustn't become impatient.

Would the human weaknesses in him dissolve in that moment when the holy ghost entered in? Or would . . .

A sudden sharp sound. Death, destruction, cataclysm? Opening his eyes, Oliver saw Mr. Harmon sitting on the grass while Mr. French seemed to be gesturing at him with the croquet mallet. The door of the house shot open and Doctor Heller bounded down the steps. Wilbur was in the doorway, first looking at Doctor Heller, who was now separating the players, and now up the hill at him. Oliver turned away, closing his eyes again, and conscious that he was merging for the time with all the earth and all the universe, leaned against the tree, and through the rings of three hundred years and through the bark and along the passages of his ear there came to him again the sound of life flowing upwards, and nearer.

11. Lois Wilson Views with Alarm, But Fails to Sound the Tocsin

Lois: "Why lie about it?"
Aaron: "I'm not lying."
"You are."
"Oh Jesus."

Some chow mein fell back on his plate.

"I told you," Aaron said, jamming his fork into a heap of greasy chow mein, "she's posing for me. Now will you let me alone?"

"No."

"What the hell's wrong with you?"

"I don't like this lying routine."

"Okay, what do you want me to say? Want me to say that I'm laying her?"

"I'd rather you did."

"Why?" An affected injured tone.

"Because it's true."

"Okay, you want me to say it, I'll say it. Now can we eat?" His mouth closed with finality over a forkful of pseudo-Chinese food. His jaws worked over the soft mess, chewing it with unnecessary vigor. Then he looked up. "Aren't you eating?"

"No." The muscles of her throat tightened, fighting down by some strange linkage the spurt of tears. She mustn't cry.

"Baby." He reached across the table with his free hand, the other still engaged by the fork.

"You're a louse," she said.

"Thanks."

"You'd lay anything, wouldn't you?"

"Sure, anything. Now listen . . ."

"To what?"

"You wanted me to say I was making Kittridge, so I said I was. All she's doing is posing for me, and she's going to buy the damned thing when it's finished. What do you think we're eating on tonight?"

"You didn't have to say that."

"What's the matter with saying that?"

"Nothing."

"Okay, now let's stop hashing over that thing. If you want me to stop painting her I will." A moment. "Well, what do you say?"

"I'm sorry," she said at last.

His hand patted hers. "Now stop bothering yourself about it, baby."

Subject discussed, examined, exhausted.

What every woman knows: that you must believe some things which you cannot believe, that you must accept some things which you cannot accept. A blues tune, lyrics being: A woman's a weak thing, a mild and a meek thing, an end of the week thing, a dee dee dee, a da da da da, wah, wah, wah. Or, syncopated: I'm slowing down, honey, so why don't I come to a stop?

Lois sensed that an almost inexplicable process of humiliation was rounding to its close. This had been the winter of her discontent, the winter of her sorrow. From riding high, she had taken a great fall. A few months, a year before, she had been going up up up in that sixty lives a minute elevator, zoom and bang toward the top, that is and to wit, into the patented land of champagne parties, clothes from the best shops, gifts of 18-carat gold plated with platinum, trayfuls of trifles and truffles. Spell it in a word, Number 17 Across, SUCCESS. You could define it also in agents' fees, in men crawling after you, in the sleek feeling when you woke up in the morning to conquer an- other day. A pole vault across the color line, across all lines and barriers, through the wall of sound. And then— hey, what's this?—all gone. Where to? How come? A job canceled, get another, don't get another. Two weeks on the sidelines, agent has a long face. Things have tightened up, honey. A fight with a guy and he doesn't call up the next day. Why? Getting old? No, not that. Law of averages, it has to happen someday. But not all at once. Where the hell is Number 17 Across? A real frightening winter, where you begin to feel that maybe you aren't you and never have been you, and to come out of that into a spring where you find yourself pitched with a guy who isn't straight as a die. A guy she had once thought, mostly from looking at him, was a sturdy character, but whom she could now see was on the run, like everyone else, and shooting backwards from the hip. On the run, like everyone else, and like everyone else bringing pain, bringing hurt. And a guy who didn't know it yet, who didn't realize where he stood, or where he was falling. Brought down, chopped at the knees, ripped and torn and all but slain by the thing which goes under the name of the Twentieth Century, the Century of Progress, the Century of the Common Uncommon Man. Laugh. A yak, a guffaw, a boffo, and a minute of silence one day a year.

"What's the matter?" Aaron asked her.

From the distance, from the blue. "Nothing."

"Baby . . ."

No, cut that, none of those hand-pats, none of this two-for-a-quarter easy-to-pour never-go-dry syrup. None of those babies and honeys and darlings, nor even the sweets and the you lovely bitch.

And there was the hand-pat. Tap, tap, tap, Morse Code, everything's okay between us, pat, pat, pat. SOS. SOB.

Not that she hated him, but with this business of that other woman, who had nothing really but a white skin, a mink coat, and seven bank accounts and nickels and dimes, with that business he had become the sign and symbol of her decline, and so to hell with him. This night, right here in this phoney Chinese restaurant, amid the chop suey and the egg foo yung, this was the end. There were other men, men with money, men with cars, men with cigars and hands, men whom she could like, or if not like tolerate. Once it was known that she was back in circulation, the word spreading from mouth to mouth with the speed of a brush fire on a soggy night, there wouldn't be many lonely nights. Only boring nights. And she could take it all casually, as she used to, not really caring a damn for anyone or about anyone, until came the turn of the luck and she zoomed up to Number 17 Across.

"You finished?" Aaron said.

Finished with what? With thinking? Not what he meant. With eating.

"Yes."

He got up first, helped her on with her coat with a suspiciously thoughtful gesture, his hand smoothing her shoulders. Lover Boy. She waited outside on Fourth Street while he paid the check. Two college kids trudging off to night school gave her the eye. Goodbye, friends. A tall guy in a dramatic trench coat belted tight stopped for a moment, looked at her, wondering about his approach. But then there was Aaron coming to her on the sidewalk, taking her arm, and the trench coat cat shuffled off.

"What do you want to do?" Aaron asked.

"I don't much care," Lois said, seeing the trench coat cat look back. "I might as well go home."

"It's early."

"I'm tired."

"Well, let's get a little air first. It's a great night. What do you say we walk down to the Marino?"

Time enough later to tell him no more crossing the threshold. No more bouncing the springs.

He held her arm as they turned in at Macdougal Street, starting toward the Marino, and he was still holding her arm, with a kind of tenderness (she admitted), when they passed the stoop. There were two men on the stoop, one of them sitting on the second step, the other lounging against the rail. Two other men were sitting on the fender of a new car parked at the curb. They were in a sort of uniform—sharp tough suits with enormously padded shoulders, sport shirts and no ties, nice shiny pointed shoes. Looking at them, Lois felt a sudden and instinctive dread, because of the way they were dressed and because of the way they were staring at her. She hesitated a moment, but Aaron's forward progress dragged her along. And then one of the men moved forward from the fender of the car and bumped into her, thrusting her against Aaron.

"What's the matter, you want the whole sidewalk?" the man said. His lean sallow face pulled to one side when he talked.

Aaron stopped. "What's eating you?"

The man who had been sitting on the stoop was standing now.

Lois saw Aaron look around quickly.

"What are you trying to pull?" he said.

"I ain't talking to you," the man with the sallow face said.

The second man came off the fender, smiling.

Aaron pulled her arm. "Come on, baby."

She was cemented to the sidewalk.

"Come on."

"I'm talking to your nigger bitch."

Aaron pushed her. "Get going, baby."

She felt something dab against her face, like a wad of moist cotton, and then she realized someone had spit in her face. But now she was a few feet up the street, turned around from the impact of the push.

She heard someone say, "Want to make something out of it, you mockey bastard?"

The words didn't fall into place right away; she wondered why one of those characters would say "motley bastard." Black and white?

Mockey bastard. Oh.

She wanted to scream.

Couldn't scream. \

She saw Aaron swing at the man who had first spoken to them, saw the sallow bastard fall back against the car. She saw Aaron jump forward to take another swing at him. Look out. One of the men from the stoop kicked him from behind. Aaron crashed into the fender, caught one of the men—which one?—and smashed his head against the door of the car. She was screaming. No, she wasn't, it was the man, it was a hoarse dirty scream. The man went down and Aaron kicked at him. Why didn't one of them hit him back? (Where had that come from? Whose side are you on?) Someone leaped on Aaron's back, starting to drag him down. Another guy hit him in the face a couple of times. Aaron was shouting something. She heard someone behind her say, Get a cop, and a woman saying, Terrible, terrible, with a kind of sadistic relish. That was Jason Spivak over there, watching. Why couldn't she scream? One scream and it would all be over. Aaron was down, lying flat on the sidewalk, and one of the men was kicking him in the head. Stomping him. Spivak disappeared. A woman was screaming, but muted, as if she were holding a handkerchief in front of her mouth. Me, Lois thought, but knew it wasn't her. Aaron was on hands and knees. A kick caught him in the stomach and he went down again, rolling over and over. He stopped, lying on his back, his hands pressed to his stomach, lower—caught him down there, ah—and one of the men ground his heel in his face. Aaron's legs jacked up. Lois was trying to say something to the man next to her, but she couldn't hear herself talking and she didn't know what she was trying to say. Scream, damn you, scream. Aaron was on his hands and knees again, crawling toward the railing. One of the men was trying to pull him down, but he was managing to get to his feet. There was a movement beyond Jason Spivak, who had reappeared. Someone was coming through. Lois heard the word, Cops. The men stopped, warned, turned, began to come toward her. A face near hers, and wet. She swashed at the saliva with her hand, smearing it over her face, and . . . ughh . . .

Lying in a spinning turntable in the dark, lots of static, round and round and round we go, and up it comes, up, up, the turntable rocking, something hard against the back, the sidewalk, yes, the sidewalk, the wall of a building at a crazy angle, growing straight up out of her head, faces like pink squashes over her, like outsized Japanese lanterns taking shape, separate, one, two, three, four, are you all right? turntable slowing down, down and up and steady as she goes, you okay, miss? face with a visor, cop, I'm all right, I'm all right.

She was standing now, one of the cops holding her, in a hole in the crowd, and there was Aaron, sitting on the stoop, his head down between his hands, his back shaking.

"What happened?"

A ferret face of some snivelling guy alive with the expectation of great events.

She was sitting on the step next to Aaron now, asking him if he was hurt, but he kept his head down, his back shaking, and by God, he was crying. There was a tear of blood on his temple. Are you hurt, she asked him again.

"Leave me alone."

She heard someone say they were sending for an ambulance.

Ah, look at those faces, greedy for excitement, grubbing for it.

Aaron stood up.

She heard one of the cops say, "Better sit down, bud."

"I"m going home."

The cop took his arm. "Take it easy now."

"Let go of me," Aaron yanked his arm away.

She came up to him. "Better wait here," she said. "You're hurt."

"Not hurt." There was blood all over his face. "I'm going home." His face was contorted, as if someone were grabbing it and pulling it tight from inside. "Going home." He pushed her away. "Leave me alone." He was heading into the crowd. "Get out of my way. Get out of my way." The crowd closed behind him.

One of the cops asked her, "What's his name?"

"I don't know," Lois said.

"Where does he live?"

"I don't know."

The cop seemed undecided. He had a black leather note-book, a small one in his hand. Now he flipped it closed. "Okay," he said, "that's your lookout."

She wanted to follow Aaron, but turned back before she touched the inner edge of the crowd. She went in the op-posite direction, not looking to see if anyone were coming after her. But a man was there.

"Can I help you?" he said politely.

"No."

"I saw . . ."

But she didn't listen.

She got home, took two sleeping pills, threw off her clothes, and crept into bed. She remembered she hadn't washed her face, and she went to the bathroom, and once there scrubbed and scrubbed her cheek, and then threw up. She took another sleeping pill—there were only two more left, running out—and got back into bed, and about three interminable hours later, her legs feeling numb and a pain in her chest, she fell asleep.

12. Aaron Ross Comes Back with Murderous Intent Through the Same Door Where In He Went

THIS THING BROUGHT BACK memories, a lot of memories. The thing in his hand itself brought back sitting in a waterfront bar in Genoa and the ex-partisan named Dante Something giving it to him and saying, I take it from a S S. And not wanting more than a handshake and a drink of friendship for it. And getting only that and a pack of American cigarettes, worth their weight then in women and gold. The thing being a shaped weight of blackened steel, grooved for the fingers. Snap of the wrist and twelve inches of heavy steel spring shoot out, hardly quivering. This thing could kill, had probably killed, might kill again. Aaron swished it through the air, satisfied by its heft, then pushed the spring back and went into the kitchen, where

he looked again at his face in the small grimy mirror over
the yellowing sink, making a catalogue of visible damage.
His right eye was discolored and beginning to puff up badly, and the skin of his cheek was scraped and raw. Otherwise not much, visible. His ribs pained him a little when he
breathed and every now and then he got a twinge in the
back. He'd had it worse before, especially the time he and
Earl Johnson had gotten their lumps in a fight with a bunch
of sailors from another Liberty ship, in Liverpool. Yeah,
but this time there was a difference. This time he had to get
those goons. Had to.

That was the downstairs bell ringing. Who could it be?
Lois? The cops? Didn't matter. He didn't want to see anyone. The bell again. Hell with it.

Aaron put on his jacket and slipped the blackjack into
the side pocket. He kept his hand wrapped around it. A fine
weight, an outspoken weight.

He knew why he had to do this, and it wasn't the kind of
thing he could talk about to anyone he could think of at
the moment. Maybe his brother, and if Marty Greenwald
were still alive, then with Marty. They would know what
that word mockey meant to him. Funny thing, in a way
that creep Breedon Rawley had been right in his book with
that business about hating the world because it was a
Christian world. That didn't hit it on the head, but it was
close. A proposition in logic: the world is a screwed-up
mess, the world is owned and run by the Christians in it—
okay, so-called Christians—therefore the world is a
screwed-up mess because the Christians are running and
owning it. And the worst thing to be in a Christian world
is a Jew. Change that—make it white Christian world.

Aaron opened the door, listened for anyone coming up
the stairs to his place. No one.

Go back to when he was a kid, living in an Irish neighborhood. The other kids calling him Christkiller and
sheeney and so forth. He had been a fat kid, bulky and awkward, and he had been stubborn, and about once a week he
got the shit knocked out of him. But he knew that he had
never cried and he had never backed down, and sometimes
now he wondered what there had been in him that prevented him from giving in. Until he was about thirteen,
when he had begun to grow and harden, he had had to catch

it from those other kids. He would go to bed at night dream-
ing of beating up on the other kids. And then, when he got
his growth suddenly, the situation had begun to change.
That time he had beaten up Ray Morley, who was supposed
to be the toughest kid around, ending up getting him in a
stranglehold and damn near killing him. They'd begun to
leave him alone after that, but by that time he was getting
independent of the neighborhood, since he was going to high
school and had friends there. It was in high school that he
had met Marty Greenwald. Then his father had sold his
shop and gotten another in a Jewish neighborhood, the one
Marty lived in, a piss-poor run-down neighborhood in the
South Bronx, where Porto Ricans were first beginning to
move in. Once or twice he had gone up to the old neighborhood, but it had all seemed changed now, and insignificant.
But not forgotten. The times he and Marty Greenwald and
a couple of other kids from their neighborhood had taken
the bus up to Fordham Road, where Irish kids like Ray
Morley were selling Father Coughlin's sheet, watching
those guys spiel about Asiatics and Chosen People and International Criminals—never calling a Jew a Jew—watching them insult old men and women, watching the amused
and conspiratorial smiles on the faces of the goyim, seeing
them buy a Social Justice with the air of making a chal-
lenge. And he and Marty and the other kids had jumped
the Social Justice boys and taken their stuff and knocked
them down and stomped them right there on Fordham
Road, one of the busiest streets in the Bronx and broken
through the hostile hordes of goyim and gotten home. Did
that twice, but the third time they'd gotten theirs from a
bunch of guys who'd been hiding, waiting for them, in doorways and parked cars. Still it had been worth it, because
they had made their point. That point being that for them
at least the whole business of Jews getting slapped and
saying thank you was over.

And this was part of it tonight. This was all the same
thing. No one was ever going to call him a mockey or a kike
or a sheeney or a Jew bastard. No one, nowhere, at no time.

Aaron started down the stairs.

All right, his father would say, Don't you know there are
a hundred Christians to every Jew? How can you fight
them?

Dialogue: Okay, Pop, so what are you going to do?
What have we been doing for two thousand years?
Where has it gotten us?
We're still here, aren't we?
What for?
What for? What for, you ask.

That's right, what for, why live, why crawl around, why
give the others the satisfaction of having something they
could kick? Make them afraid. He'd never been able to put
it in words, at least not when he was a kid, but he had
sensed that the antis felt protected. They were, he knew
now, within the law and within the tradition and they could
go out and commit mental murder every time they saw a
Jew. When a guy said mockey or sheeney or kike, Aaron
told himself, There's a bastard who'd like to kill me, if he
had the guts. And in terms of boyhood and in terms of what
had happened in Europe to six million Jews, it was true.

Like the time he was riding in a subway train—this was
just before the war—and some drunk had come in and
started to holler, Goddamn kikes, hate the goddamn kikes.
Had gone through the train, in fact, hollering, Goddamn
kikes. This was at the time when Aaron had first begun to
notice the black crayon scrawls in the subway stations:
Kill the Kikes. Or on the advertisement for a Jewish ceme-
tery: Good Kikes. He had watched and waited as the drunk
came toward him. There were other Jews in the train, but
they froze up, holding themselves in, disciplined by their
two thousand years of exile. When they got home they'd
shake and tremble, but now they were sitting in fortresses
of pretended indifference. And up the train came the drunk.
And no one, Jew or Christian, said anything to him. Then
Aaron had stood up and holding the back of the drunk's
head with one hand had smashed him in the face with the
other a few times, feeling the cartilage give under his hand,
and only then had let him drop. One of the women in the
train had screamed at him in a Jewish accent and had bent
down to help the drunk. Well, that business about turn the
other cheek, who had started it anyway? Aaron had walked
down the aisle of the train, consciously going back over the
same steps the drunk had taken, and gotten off at the next
station, just in case there was trouble.

As a matter of fact, until he had gone into the merchant

marine he had never known a Christian whom he didn't regard as a potential enemy. And for reasons given. But on the ships he had discovered there were good Joes, guys who would stand up for him and whom he could stand up for, and that had made the world a little bigger. And here in the Village, among themselves, meaning the artists and the writers and the other intellectuals of one persuasion or another, among them there wasn't prejudice, just back-biting.

Yeah, but when you came right down to it—Aaron going out the front door—you stand alone. You live alone and you fight alone. And every man is an Ilande unto Himself and around that Ilande is a lot of prejudice and hate and other nonsense.

And there was Jason Spivak. Now where in hell had he come from?

"I was ringing your bell," Spivak told him.

"I heard it."

"How are you feeling?"

"Okay."

"I saw them do that job on you."

"Yeah."

They started down the street.

"Where are you going?"

"Nowhere."

Because every man is an Ilande unto Himself.

"What do you want?" Aaron asked Spivak.

"Just wanted to see how you are."

"Why?"

"Well, to see if I could be of any help."

Aaron stopped. "Didn't you just tell me you saw them give me my lumps?"

"I know what you're going to say."

"Okay, so why bother coming around now."

"Now wait a second," Spivak said, pulling at his arm and trying to make him stop. Failing, he kept on walking, and talking. "I'm no hero. I wasn't going to jump in there and get myself beat up. What good would it have done? Would it have made you feel any better?"

"No."

"Well, you see." Point proved.

"I don't see anything," Aaron said. "I can think of guys

that might have jumped in to help me, not that I can't fight my own battles. Trouble is, those guys aren't around anymore. All that's left in this stinking world are guys like you. Now scram, will you. I want to be alone."

"You'll always be alone," Spivak said angrily.

"That's right," Aaron said. "I'll always be alone."

And so what? And so nothing. Get to the point finally where things don't touch you anymore, and you live for your work. Yeah, but then suppose you begin to wonder: Who am I working for? Why am I doing this? Why go through hell to put a lot of paint on canvas for a bunch of jerks to see? Because you have to, because it's in you and it's got to come out. Crap. Reason being because you want other people to see what you can do, see the things you can do that they can't do. And if you don't care about them, those other people, why bother? Reason rejected. Back to the original premise, that you do it for yourself, that you do it because it's in you and it's got to come out. Got to come to some kind of thinking like that, otherwise why cruise around looking for those goons.

There were lights all along Fourth Street, lights and colors, with a lot of people milling about, couples stopping to look in the modernistic jewelry store windows, browsing in front of the bookstores, just walking around. A good spring night. He had tried to catch this in something he had worked on the last week—blobs of raw color without connection against a background of thick purple night. It hadn't come off; the thing had been too chaotic. It had been pretty bad.

"Hey, Aaron, what happened to you?"

He kept on walking, not even looking to see who had called to him.

Now he felt his fingers tightening on the grip of the blackjack, now that he was passing the restaurant where he and Lois had eaten an hour before. Turning the corner into Macdougal Street he felt as though his fingers would press through the steel handle as though it were putty. There was the stoop and there was a car, but was it the same car? No one on the stoop, no one leaning against the car. Situation changed. He had a savage desire to punch the car as he went by, but he kept his hand in the pocket of his jacket. A couple of the local Italian boys were on the corner of Macdougal and Third, and he looked at them closely, but they weren't the ones. They'd be around though, somewhere. And he'd find them.

On a hunch he went along Third to Sullivan and then turned down the dark street. This was Enemy Territory. Those goons came from somewhere around here, from these black tenements. He looked into a cafe expresso joint; just some old men playing cards. Nothing doing in a pizzeria. At the corner of Sullivan and Bleecker there was a gang, but this was a different bunch of boys. Bleecker was full of bums from the Mills Hotel. He crossed it, going deep into the Enemy Territory, right into the heart of it, Man Alone. The Quest for Revenge. One Against Them All. In the dark he took the blackjack out of his pocket, snapped out the spring, and slugged the air with it a couple of times. This could even be corny, but it had to be done. Houston Street was full of crosstown traffic, but no one standing around. He walked over to Thompson. It was Sullivan in reverse, going up this dark street the way he had gone down the other. The process repeated. And all in vain, for nothing, for Hecuba. He kicked over a garbage can as he crossed Bleecker, just because he felt like it. Aaron Ross passed here. Pissed here? Why not? He had to take one, so he let go against a wall. The Mark of Zorro. Coming back to Third Street, passing the honky-tonk clubs with their scabby pictures of glamorous babes pasted up outside, he felt disappointed, almost depressed. The thing was still hanging over him; it had to be done. But where were those bastards? The thing had to be done tonight; tomorrow the steam might be out of him. And then he knew what would happen: he'd pick a fight with some innocent character and take it out on him and afterwards feel lousy, a crummy on-the-beach feeling, the kind you could get from some broad . . .

Hey, hold up.

Those the guys? Them?

Damn right they were.

They were coming out of one of the cellar taverns on Macdougal, one of the raided premises where the minor league hoods and the cropped lesbians banded together in a strange and Christ-knows-why incorporation. Those were the guys. This the time and this the hour. He counted them.

One, two, and so on to five. The guy in the grey topcoat was new. His tough luck. Chaplain stuff.

They were coming toward him, so quick, into a doorway. They were laughing about something. Better yet. And here they were, two in front, three behind, a sawed-off triangle of them.

Snap. The coil spring was out and he was right in the middle of them, laying about him with his jawbone of an ass. Down went the Philistines, one, two, three. One of the guys had a knife. Aaron cracked him on the arm with the blackjack; the guy yelped and dropped the knife and Aaron backhanded him across the face with the jack. He dropped. Someone had him from behind, around the neck. He came down hard on the guy's instep, broke away, and came around with the blackjack, missing as the guy ducked. The guy lunged to tackle him, but Aaron stepped back and clipped him on the head. His lunge carried him to the sidewalk and he lay there, still. One of the guys was standing up, groggy. Aaron let him have it in the stomach and he folded in and went down. He could only see three of the guys now, one of them doubled over on the sidewalk, the other, the guy who had tried to tackle him, sprawled out on his face. The third guy was trying to hoist himself up. Then he saw a cop with his bill out, running toward him. No use getting in a tussle with a cop. He began to run, looked around, saw the cop racing after him. And the cop was hitching up his tunic, reaching for his gun. A long street ahead of him, no place to duck into. He heard a shot and stopped cold, almost waiting for an impact. The cop was almost on top of him now, so Aaron dropped the blackjack. Peaceful gesture. There was a splash of red, followed by a wave of grey, and as he began to fall he realized the cop had swiped him with the billy. The sonofabitch. What for? He groped on the sidewalk for the blackjack, and while groping, passed out.

Coming to, he found a couple of cops wrestling him into a squad car. They got him in the middle, sitting on either side of him as rigid as two rocks. He kept shaking his head and breathing in through his teeth. As they drove along he could see a third cop hanging onto the side of the car. Christ, you'd think he was a criminal. He felt nauseous. They had to let him out of the car for a minute.

"Hey," he said, "stop, will you."

They slid around a corner.

"Stop it, will you, just for a second."

The car went on.

Okay, they wouldn't stop, he'd throw up on them.

He heard air break up through his throat, but nothing solid came.

Now they were stopping, it was about time, but what were they doing? They were hauling him out of the car, roughing him up, and then pushing him up the steps between the green lights prisoned in their old-fashioned standards. What was the idea of all the shoving? They had him standing in front of the high desk and a beefy cop was looking down at him, like a fat God from heaven. Things were coming to him in a disjointed way; they didn't link up. Now he heard one of the cops saying something about felonious assault and the Sullivan Act.

"What for? What for?" he asked them, but they were already pushing him up the stairs. They pushed him into a cell, and when he heard the door locked behind him, he began to shout at them. Grabbing the door of the cell he started to shake it, feeling at the same time a curious sensation of playing a part in a gangster movie, until one of the cops chopped at him with his night stick.

The dirty bastards.

13. Footnote at Meridian

SHORTLY AFTER THE ARREST of Aaron Ross I was brought for a while into closer contact with the events of this book by the establishment of the Defense Fund. Frances Finnerty, who took some money from me to help pay for Aaron's lawyer, gave me her version of the whole story, while Amy Macduff, with whom I had several drinks at the Marino one soggy night, furnished me with certain details, some of them at variance with the Finnerty story. But no great matter. The Defense Fund became a manifestation of the solidarity of the embattled intellectuals —if you will excuse my calling them that—of the Village, and almost all the money was collected at their captial, the Marino, with one notable exception. (Of that later.) I'd like to make it clear that personal feelings toward Aaron Ross had nothing to do with these contributions. A clan was sticking together.

About Greenwich Village. The mere fact that a district has a name does not mean that it has a single character. We are accustomed to thinking of places as homogeneous entities: Pittsburgh is a smoky city, Africa is a dark continent, Italy is sunny. But in the Village there are several distinct levels, and while they come together through the decision of geography they do not mix and mesh. And between two of these levels there is a basic conflict.

Fundamentally the Village is a slum, the blocks of tenements being broken only here and there by scatterings of the kind of houses known as quaint, i.e., houses which date back about a hundred years. The Village slum, or the slum that is the Village, is as vicious as slums by their very nature (did I write *nature?*) must be. It is ugly, it is sullen, it is explosive.

Italians, casuals, and intellectuals—those are the three main groups of people living in the Village. The Italians live in the tenements. The casuals live where they can. The intellectuals have the quaint houses, and some others. By casuals, incidentally, I mean the people who live in the Village for the simple and understandable reason that they couldn't find apartments anywhere else, but their yearnings are toward Sutton Place and towards Westchester and Long Island.

Every night, and especially Saturday nights, come the pleasure-seekers and the thrill-seekers, crowding into the cheap garish night clubs or coming to the bars to gawk at the characters. They are less than casual, they are transient.

The older Italians are settled. They have worked hard in this country, and while they have received perhaps less than they may have expected at one time and perhaps less than they may have deserved, they are reconciled. In the good weather they sit in the park and talk and play checkers;

in the bad weather they go to the little cafe expresso places
and play cards and dominoes. Before the war they used to
dream of going back to the old country, but as everyone
knows the old country is in bad shape now. Their sons and
their grandsons, the young hard boys who move like schools
of restless sharks through the neighborhood, they are not
reconciled. They have a code, a code of violence. Their
heroes are gangsters and pugs. Bookies are princes among
them. They are physical. They admire the body, the male
body, muscle, and they want action. They walk slowly and
deliberately, masters of their sidewalks, their feet coming
down hard, their shoulders accenting every step. And yet
they are savage without being robust. When they talk, in
that flat clipped way of theirs, they score their hatreds with
their curse words. They have no use at all for women other
than their mothers, their sisters and the girls they are going
to marry. If one of them finds a girl he can lay he passes
her on to his pals. In the classic sense they are not intro-
verts, not at all, but they live in tight introverted circles.
Beyond the circle of their pals, the guys they have known
for years, there exists for them a dark world of suspicions,
and when they cannot resolve their suspicions they lash out.
They are generally in gangs, not because they are cowards
as some people say, but because in their small knit groups
they find a sense of belonging that is denied to them by
society entire. And yet there is directed against them no
prejudice comparable to that directed against Negroes or
Jews or Chinese or Mexicans. They are victims of a subtle
feeling that is never put into words.

I have often tried to see the Village through their eyes—
to see the fairies and the lesbians as they must see them, to
see with them the fantastic shapes in the windows of the
bright handicrafts and jewelry stores, to see the men in
berets and the girls in dungarees, the bookstores with
esoteric titles of books they will never read. I have seen
enough to understand some of their hate for the intellectuals.

I can tell you something, not everything, about them too.
They are a sad, confused and declining group, these intellectuals, and I often get a sense of the end of our civilization
not so much through what I read in the newspapers, bad
as that is, as through what is happening to people I know

well. I may be wrong, but I do not think these people have
ever been so lost and so hurt as they are in our time. The
sense of hope was blown up by the atomic bomb; it disappeared in the fumes of the debates of the United Nations,
Strictly Ltd. They are the younger generation of creative
people, and they are sick, much much sicker than most of
the young men and women who went to the Continent after
the first World War. They have cut loose from the professed
principles of a society which doesn't bother to live up to its
principles, but they have been able to formulate no positive
standards of their own. They are almost afraid to be happy,
because they can understand better why they should be unhappy. For them at this time there is no quietness, no peace,
no certainty. Recently I came across a quotation used by
Herman Melville in his story, The Encantadas. It is: "How
brave now we live, how jocund, how near the first inheritance, without fear, how free from little troubles." That was
true of one time, some time. Now it only underlines the
insecurity of my friends. And the frightening thing, the
really frightening aspect of all this, is that they may be
seeing the future clearly in all its hopelessness; they may be
right. So they sit night after night in places like the Marino,
and they talk, and they drink, and they find a girl, or they
don't find a girl. Their friendships are tenuous; their love
affairs have only the most temporary substance. One or two
of them will go on to become representatives of our culture,
as Breedon Rawley has started to do—that is, they will
become famous—but for most of them the rest of their
lives will be desert.

Between them and the young Italians there is a state of
undeclared war, the aggressive actions always coming from
the young tough boys. Quite a few have been beaten up in
isolated actions, and usually for no apparent reason. Some
have been mugged and robbed of what little money they
might have had on them, but most have been simply beaten
up. And not much they could do about it. So when Aaron
Ross struck back, he was striking for them too, and when
he was arrested it was felt that he should not be let down.
That is why the Defense Fund was set up spontaneously and
in due course raised, to a limited extent, the money being
given to Lois Wilson, who for reasons about which you
know was judged qualified to act as treasurer. The quarters

and the dollars mounted up, but not far enough, until help came from a generally unexpected and unadmired but not unenvied source—Breedon Rawley in Hollywood.

And here is how that happened to come about:

14. Breedon Rawley Enlists (others) In a Good Cause

BREEDON RAWLEY WAS PAINFULLY writing a poker episode for WHERE THE BUFFALO ROAMED (working title) when Miss Tanner brought in the letter. At that moment (CU OF DEALER LOOKING DIRECTLY AT BLACKIE) he would have been glad to receive any kind of communication which would interrupt him and give him some release from the intricacies of poker (which Carney had explained and demonstrated to him, winning a fair sum) and the stupidities of the script. When he saw that it was a letter from Lois his heart gave a little skip and a bound and he stuck himself in his left index finger when he awkwardly stabbed at it with his letter opener.

The contents were not too pleasing. The letter skittered from the very personal to the fairly aloof, and mainly it dealt with the tribulation and the forthcoming trial of Aaron Ross, who came through the narrative as a defender of the underdog and American womanhood (though Negro). Included in the letter was a frank appeal for support of Aaron's effort to win his freedom, with the touching phrase: "Of all the people I know you are most able to help." Warmed by the remembrance of pleasant dalliance with Lois, contrasted with the involuntary abstinence of his stay in the cinema capital, Breedon bravely determined to do what he could.

But here he was torn between his limitations and his pride. He wanted to make a grand gesture, something that would be incorporated into the financial folklore of the

Village, a magnificent ducal dispensation of perhaps a thousand dollars, flung casually across the continent in an airmail envelope. Impossible, unfortunately. He had discovered that his weekly check, although for a sum which had once seemed so staggering, was being drained into a hundred and one unavoidable channels, and that what remained to him was an almost accidental trickle. The government of the United States effectively diverted a major portion of his wages, while his agent received a steady flow. The convertible, first hired as a temporary expedient to relieve his sense of loneliness, was now a prime necessity. His occasional dates didn't amount to much except in terms of outlay. The little gambling games at the studio commissary cost him dear. His vision of living parsimoniously in Hollywood during the period of his contract and saving enough to write and write and write was only that—a vision. As Carney said to him, "You're not getting rich, but you're living well." Yet he wasn't happy. He felt more insecure than at any previous time of his life; he had so much to lose. There had been a time when he could have lived for half a year on a thousand dollars; now it would last him three weeks. And since he had always looked at money, in part, as being a commodity with which he could buy time and space to work in, he was suffering an increasing poverty as he grew richer.

So Lois' demand presented him with a dilemma. Could he neglect the demand altogether? Well, that would mean cutting himself off from his friends forever, because he would have been wanting when they wanted most. Could he send twenty-five or fifty dollars? Not very well from this legendary place where the dollar sign usually preceded a string of four or five digits, not without being held up as an example of a cheap forgetful heel. Then the only thing left for him to do was to dispatch the magnificent sum, which was manifestly impossible.

In times of need Breedon had grown accustomed to relying on the thin reed of Carney, whom he could at times magnify into a pillar of strength. Therefore, leaving the dealer still in a closeup with his eyes fixed on Blackie (who was shortly going to fall victim to the dealer's deadly derringer) Breedon went into Carney's office, forgetting to

knock, and catching Carney playing an advanced game of
footsie with his well-watered secretary. He began to back
out of the door in profound confusion, but Carney stopped
him and dismissed the secretary with an air of business-
before-pleasure and no show of resentment at all. Instead
he went through his customary motion of offering Breedon
a drink and gulping down one himself, and then settling
comfortably in a swivel chair behind his desk, all ready
to tackle the problem at hand. He was, as a great favor to
Breedon who obviously needed the seasoning, permitting
Breedon to write the major part of the script, of course
following his suggestions, and he would courageously take
the script into the office of Max Fielding at appointed inter-
vals and go to bat for it. This was an eminently satisfactory
arrangement for Breedon, who dreaded repetitions of his
first couple of stammering interviews with the great man.

Now, after listening to Breedon recite his plight, Carney
came up with a helpful suggestion.

"All you have to do," he said confidently, "is to go
around the studio collecting money."

"Bu-ut what will I s-say it's for?"

"Well, what does it say in the letter?"

"It s-says that it—it's for a de-defense fund for Aaron
Ross."

"Okay, there you have it." And Carney showed his palms,
like a magician who has just finished a trick.

But not so fast. "Yes, b-but no one knows Aaron Ross."

"Then don't tell them it's for this Ross guy."

"B-but . . ."

"It's the cause that counts in these things, not the man.
The principle, not the individual. Right?"

"Yes."

"Agreed? Then I'll show you how we can go about this."
He started to write on a piece of foolscap, then changed his
mind and pressed his buzzer. His secretary wedged her bust
through a partly-opened door. "Honey, get me a piece of
good bond paper, the best."

"Just one, Mr. Carney?"

"Just one, honey."

She came into the office a few moments later with a
single piece of stiff rag paper.

"Thanks, honey."

"You're welcome, Mr. Carney," she said, and listening to her well-trained polite reserve Breedon began to think that he had imagined the by-play which he had so foully interrupted.

"Now," said Carney, putting the paper on the desk in front of him. "This is what we'll do." With infinite care he printed the words DEFENSE FUND at the top of the sheet, blocking in the letters so that they appeared very substantial. In smaller letters, directly under DEFENSE FUND he wrote *contributions,* underlining the word. Then, shoving the sheet over to Breedon, he said, "Write Anonymous, Fifty Dollars."

Breedon wrote obediently, finishing before he asked, "W-who's going to pay the fif-fifty dollars?"

"I am," Carney said.

Breedon was overwhelmed.

"I don't want anybody to know I contributed. This is a good cause, but I don't want to get on any sucker lists. Whenever I make a contribution to something I do it anonymously. Besides, it's more impressive that way." He took two twenties and a ten out of his wallet, looked closely into his wallet, thought a moment, and said, holding back a twenty and the ten, "I'll have to owe you thirty. I'm a little short right now and I've got to go somewhere tonight."

"That's all right," Breedon said, taking the twenty.

"But leave me down for fifty."

"Oh, ah—of course.

"Now, how are you doing on that poker sequence?"

Breedon explained certain difficulties owing to his lack of familiarity with the game, so Carney took a deck of cards (which they had used before) from his top desk drawer and proceeded to give him another demonstration, during the course of which he regained the twenty dollars he had contributed toward the fund and won about seven dollars besides.

"Remember," he said as Breedon left, "a flush beats a straight and a full house beats them both," and Breedon, turning, could see his secretary sliding back into Carney's office.

But he had, actually, nothing to complain about. Carney's

idea proved a good one. Wherever he went he gathered sums of money, even from the parched Miss Tanner, his own secretary. As a matter of fact, curiously enough, many of those who contributed treated him with a certain amount of respect and fellowship after they had finished shelling out their money, even though almost invariably they followed Carney's lead and made their donations anonymously. In three days, by dint of plodding around the offices and skipping from table to table in the commissary, feeling a waxing enthusiasm for his own efforts, Breedon achieved the sum of one thousand two hundred and thirty-five dollars, including his own contribution of twenty-five dollars. He was about to write out a check and send it to Lois, accompanied by a warm letter (which would not, however, detail his means of achieving the sum or account for its odd figure) when, after a perfunctory knock, Melvin Blaker came into his office. Blaker was a top writer, still young and sturdily tanned, who once upon a time had written a couple of plays which had been performed successfully on Broadway, quite an achievement considering that the plays were still presented occasionally by what remained of the left-wing theatre groups.

Breedon stood up, respectfully, and Blaker wrung his hand in an enthusiastic handshake.

"Can't stay long," he said. "I'm busy." He made a quick patrol of the office. "This isn't bad. You should have seen the hole they threw me into when I first came here. Ah, but stick around, hang on a little, and you get more cubic feet. How do you stand on The Ten?"

Breedon wasn't sure that he had heard the question correctly. "The T-ten?"

"The Ten," Blaker said, a little impatiently. "You're with us in this, aren't you?"

"W-well, ye-es."

"Good. I thought you'd be. We've got to stand together, all of us. This thing threatens not only our own position as writers, it threatens the civil liberties of the entire country. We happen to be at the center of the storm, and in a way that's a privilege. How much should I put you down for?" He produced a sheet of white rag paper, labeled HOLLY-

WOOD DEFENSE FUND, underneath the words being *contributions*, underlined. There was a long list of contributions, headed by Melvin Blaker, in a bold scrawl, after which came, One Thousand Dollars. Occasionally the following list of anonymous contributions was courageously salted with a name. On first glance Breedon couldn't see a donation of less than a hundred dollars, but then, searching desperately, he found one, anonymous of course, of fifty dollars.

"We're all in this," Blaker said, with pride. "I was surprised, I'll admit, at how people kicked in. Some whom I never expected to. This is a basic issue and we've all got to go down the line on it. It's not only what's happening to The Ten, it's what can happen to any one of us, it's what can happen to anyone in the country, if we don't stand together and beat this thing before it really grows. Yes," he said, leaning forward with a warrior light in his eyes, "we grow soft between fights and sometimes we think we've lost our guts, but then when something like this comes along . . . How much should I put you down for?"

"A-a hundred," Breedon said, regretting every cent. What in the devil's name was The Ten?

"Do you want this to be anonymous, or do you want to show where you stand?" Blaker said challengingly.

"I—I don't care."

"Okay," Blaker said, writing, "Breedon Rawley, One Hundred." Then he wrung Breedon's hand again.

"I—I'll have to wr-write out a check."

"That's okay. Send it to my office." He was at the door, hand on the knob. "Oh, and listen, Rawley, I'm having some people out to my place tomorrow night. Some good people. I want you to come out. Can you make it?"

"Yes, sure, s-sure."

"Great. I'll look for you then." And he was gone.

Breedon sat down, a little weakened by the suddenness of the attack on his purse. He thought carefully, wondering who or what was The Ten, considering the inroads made on his finances for a cause that was his own, assuredly, but unknown. Finally he saw a way to make up his personal deficit. He slowly wrote out a check to Lois Wilson for one thousand one hundred and thirty-five dollars, having by a simple feat of bookkeeping transferred an entry for one hundred dollars from one good cause to another.

But what was this about The Ten?

.

15. Aaron Ross Discovers That Sometimes Jail Is Better Than Bail

JACK THE RIPPER STOOD facing the wall while a cop frisked him with hard and practised hands. Jesse James signed the release slip and was given the manila envelope containing his wallet and his wristwatch. Killer Aaron Ross, the Villain of the Village, went through the wire mesh door to where Phyllis née Kittridge was waiting for him, very superior to this sordid jail vestibule in her Hattie Carnegie original suit. She took both his hands in an affected way and smiled up at him, saying, "Aaron, my jailbird."

Jail and farewell.

"Was it bad?" she asked, her face assuming a serious expression.

"No. A week's never bad, no matter where you are."

"Yes, but you didn't know it would be only a week."

"That's just it."

A bad week? No, a pretty good week actually. He had made a couple of sketches and then one of the guards, prodded by a promise of a portrait drawing of himself, had gotten him some decent drawing paper and a couple of charcoal pencils. Now he had a bundle of good sketches, stuff he could compare to the sketches he had made on shipboard to see just what, if any, progress he'd been making. And a lot of new pals, unwilling candidates for everything from thirty days to life, the very Salt of the Earth. And just as on shipboard they'd fallen all over him to get themselves drawn, Man being the animal that he is, and they'd come through with the usual but heart-felt and heart-warming criticism of, Hey this is pretty good.

They were outside now and Aaron took a last look at the
pile of rough grey rock that had been his hotel. It was a
squat powerful structure, the kind of building that ought
to have cannons nuzzling through the windows. He thought
he saw someone at one of the windows wave at him, and
he waved back. His checking out might be only temporary;
he wasn't out of the woods yet. His trial came up in Special
Sessions in a couple of months and it might be hard rocks
for him. Still, what could he get? A year? At the most.

"I'm sorry I couldn't bail you out sooner," Phyllis told
him.

"That's okay. I didn't expect it."

A year? What was he getting so casual about? That was
a long time.

"I came around to see you a couple of times and you
weren't home."

"No, I was here."

"Then I ran into a friend of yours and she told me you'd
been arrested."

"Who was that?"

"The woman I'd met at your place."

"Woman? At my place?"

"The one I told you about, the one who'd been downstairs,
the strange-looking woman . . ."

"Amy?"

"Was that her name?"

"How was she?"

"She was drunk." Reproachfully, "I thought you told me
she didn't drink?"

"I said that?"

"That's what you told me."

"Oh well, a white lie. You got to protect a girl's reputation. Besides, what's the difference? It's her business how
she kills herself."

"You say callous things."

"Yeah," Aaron said. "Yeah, I do."

Goddamn, what was he supposed to say about Amy? He'd
been in love with her—wasn't that enough? He still had a
yen for her, right through and beyond the others, Lois and
this babe. But she wanted to stay on the skids and there
wasn't anything anyone could do about it, except duck.

They got into a taxi. Sitting in the cab, Aaron looked at

his broken brown shoes next to her crisp alligators, at his loose black socks next to her tight sheer nylons. Rags and Riches. The Pauper and the Princess.

"Do you need money?" he heard her ask.

By God, this was intuitive.

"I can use some."

"Suppose I let you have a hundred."

"That's a lot of cash."

She was dipping into her bag.

"Is this what it is when you're being kept?" Aaron asked her.

She laughed at him and slipped a couple of bills into his hand. They were fifties. As he put them into the pocket of his old trousers, he had a feeling that they must be uncomfortable there.

"You must think I'm something like a lousy whore," Aaron said, "and maybe you're right, but I can tell you something. I'd do anything to be able to keep on painting. I'd steal the dough . . ." He stopped and laughed to himself.

"What are you laughing at?"

"Nothing."

"It must be something."

"Hell, didn't you ever laugh at nothing?"

"Yes," she said. Then, "You like me, Aaron, don't you?" In her voice was the uncertainty of her years over thirty.

"Sure I do," he said.

"Why?"

"Why?" Oh no, he wasn't going to be trapped into that. He took her hand in dumb answer, and she squeezed it and rolled her thigh against his. Oh Daddy, Daddy. The Age of Jazz. He firmed his thigh, giving her something solid to roll against, and then pressed back, thinking he was being politic, but he was surprised to feel an instinctive and ready response down there. It was really the first time, here in this taxi toward the end of the afternoon, that he had ever gotten that with her so readily. A week in jail did things. And legs in nylons. The Age for Jazz. He slipped his arm around her and pulled her close, throwing his mouth against hers and feeling her tongue play like a wet little lizard.

"Cut it out," he whispered, but into her ear, so that she shivered and began to murmur.

He pulled back from her, but she was after him, **playing** with his hair, and then she ran her hand down his **body**, smiling with success as she let it fall slowly from his stomach to his thigh.

"This is very vulgar," she said.

"Well then wait."

She leaned over and started to kiss him again.

But after they had been at his place a couple of hours, lying on the narrow cot, he began to grow impatient. He wanted her to go home, to leave him alone. The light was going out of the sky. He wanted time to himself, and then he wanted to go down and walk around a little and maybe drop into the Marino. At least he didn't want to be with her anymore.

"Baby," he said, "you'd better go."

"Let's have dinner. I'll go out and get something. You might not know it but I can cook."

"Good for you, but let's skip it tonight. I just want to be alone. I've got things I want to think about."

"I haven't seen you for two weeks."

"I know but, Christ, you know I'm a funny guy. The way I feel now I've got to be alone."

"How do you feel?"

"I told you, I want to think."

She was slow in getting dressed and he had to kiss her again and again before he finally managed to ease her through the door. When she was gone he had a sense that his place was populated again, by himself and the things he had done, the things that counted.

He looked at his paintings for a long time, leaning them against the wall and standing back to get perspective. On them. On himself. He didn't know now, he didn't know whether he liked their harshness. The paintings were getting to be too much like himself, and what was he getting to be? Where had the others been at twenty-seven? Picasso, Matisse, Bonnard. They'd been academicians mostly, working with soft lines and easy colors before they broke out into reality. But he'd started where they were leaving off, or maybe at a point a little beyond that. Damn it, he might have been trying too hard, maybe he had to go back to fundamentals. He began to think of a few paintings based on his prison sketches, playing off the postures, flexible, against the rigid bars and straight lines of the walls. A courtyard scene, men in a pacing circle in a frame of walls. Maybe some naturalistic work, basic, maybe broadened close to caricature, working carefully on the detail of faces, hands. Yeah, yeah, he'd started to get too abstract, he'd been taking off. Back to earth. Descent from the Stratosphere. Fall of the V-2. Back to Rembrandt and Hogarth. And a portrait in the manner of John Singer Sargent. How far could you go with this? What was that Strauss waltz? An Artist's Life. Hah.

And again the question: Why go on with it? He'd thought about that in jail, and now he knew. He knew that whatever else he might do, whatever ease he might find, his hand would inevitably go to the brush and the brush would go to canvas, because without that he was nothing. Yes, the answer: It is in me. But why that was, how it had ever come about in the beginning, what there was in his genes or in his childhood to make it so, that he did not know, this dark process of selection.

He stacked the paintings together again, feeling dissatisfied but not unhappy, not unhopeful. The battle was joined. Forward the Light Brigade.

He went down and walked in the warm evening, feeling in a good and generous mood. It was like a shadow of ripe age, this easeful feeling with himself. He looked for nobody and he avoided nobody. Suddenly he realized that he felt free and, by God, he was free. Free—with a year in jail hanging over him. A Sword of Damocles. Well, the thread wasn't cut yet. Bridges should be crossed when . . . He stopped for a couple of minutes, explaining to a guy named Castro and a girl named Doris (he'd have to go see Lois) that he was out on bail, and he heard for the first time about the Defense Fund. A feeling of gratitude actually swelled inside him. They were/standing up for him. What did you know. He made off toward the Marino, home of good fellows, stalwart companions, comrades. All pals together, birds of a feather. Going down Macdougal he felt a stab as he passed the spot where he had been beaten up, but he could look diagonally down the street and see where he had gotten his revenge. Good. These two places would always mean something to him. He'd never be able to pass them without thinking about . . .

On the corner they were standing. No, not the same guys, but guys wearing the same uniform, the draped jackets, the slightly pegged pants, the hats pinched at top and worn brim up on the backs of their heads, and no ties. Not the same guys; their brothers. They didn't seem to look at him as he walked past, but some of the expansive mood had been stolen away.

He went into the Marino through the restaurant entrance, suddenly feeling that he didn't want to stand at the bar and talk, not yet. Besides, he was a little hungry. There were maybe ten, twelve people in the place and he took a booth against the wall. Felipe gave him a great big hello and started to ask questions, but he cut him off by ordering spaghetti with meat sauce. One of the other waiters, Gino, came over to bull with him. Aaron gave him short answers, trying to be polite, wanting to be cordial, because after all these were great fellows, stalwart companions. Then, as Felipe brought the spaghetti, he looked up and saw Amy coming toward him. He stood up, while Felipe said, Hello.

"Sit down, baby," Aaron said.

She fell onto the bench at the other side of his table, and righted herself immediately and sat stiffly.

"What do you want?" Aaron asked her.

"What can you afford?"

"Anything."

"Ah, how circumstances have changed." To Felipe she said, "Bring me a double rye." And to Aaron, "Is that too much? Am I being greedy?"

Aaron didn't say anything. Her skin was a dead white, with the consistency of dough going bad. Her eyelids were heavy and her mouth was slack, and she looked like a wreck. She was going fast and he felt sorry for her. And she'd had so much, once. The poor bitch.

"Have something to eat," Aaron said.

She shook her head. "I'm not hungry." She reached across the table and pressed his hand. "Baby, how have you been? Was it awful in that carcel? Did they corrupt you?"

"Yeah," Aaron said. "They corrupted me."

"You're really purer than you think, schnook," she said. "You think you're evil, but you're not. I ought to know, because I'm evil." Reaching for the drink that Felipe had just set down, she said, "Thanks," both to him and to Felipe, and then threw down a slug.

"When are you going to cut that out?"

"You see," Amy said, swallowing some more, "you're actually a moralist. Your morals may be self-centered, but you have them, and, schnook, they're rigid. And I'll tell you what they are, but you must never quote me, because I don't want people to know I can see through them. Promise?"

Aaron promised.

"You think anything that builds is good and anything that deteriorates is bad. Am I right?"

"I don't know," Aaron said. "I don't even know what you mean."

"Ah well, I am a prophet without honor." She pressed his hand again. "It is good to see you," she said, emphasizing the is. "Did we get you out?"

"No."

"You heard about the money being raised?"

"Yeah, someone told me about it. That's pretty nice."

"Now, schnook, don't let me disillusion you, but you mustn't feel that money was raised for you. Even people who didn't like you paid from their hard-earned wages. Even I sacrificed a few drinks, not that I want to head the list. But it wasn't for friendship, schnookie."

"What then?" Aaron said, beginning to feel bleak.

"You're a mercenary, you're a standing army. People were paying dues to your strong right arm. It didn't wither in prison?"

"No," Aaron said. "I was on the rockpile."

"I've hurt your feelings. And that isn't fair, because it's so easy. Get me another drink."

"No. Look at you, you're a mess. Well Jesus, just look at you."

"Now don't preach at me, schnookie," she said, her voice beginning to wheedle.

"Look at you," Aaron said, growing angry. "You look like a goddamn tramp. When are you going to straighten out?"

She took a deep patient breath. "I'm going on the wagon tomorrow."

"How many times have I heard that? All the time we were together you kept telling me that. Christ baby, get hold of yourself, will you?" He raised his voice. "Hey, Felipe, let's have the check."

Amy started to say something, but stopped when Felipe came over.

"What's this?" Felipe said. "A fifty."

"Yeah. That's all I got."

"I'll see if we've got change," Felipe said, going away.

"You've got change," Aaron said after him.

Amy had a broad sly look on her face. "She's keeping you well."

"Who?"

"Your friend from Park Avenue."

"Who told you about that?"

"Oh, things get around in this picayune community of ours. I've seen her. She's tres chic. How about your other girl friend?"

"Who?"

"Your Hindu playmate. Does she know?"

"Lois. How do I know?"

"Because if she does," Amy said, wagging a finger sloppily, "I foresee trouble. Black reprisal. Not that I meant it that way."

"What way?" Aaron said, as Felipe came back with the change.

"Are you going to buy me another drink?"

"No."

"For auld lang syne? For old enzyme?"

Aaron took ten dollars from the change. "Here," he said, dropping it on the table, "buy your own drinks. I don't want to be around to see you lapping up the stuff." He stood up, but Amy remained on the bench. "Aren't you going to the bar?" he asked her.

"No," she said, and a look of pain was on her face for a moment. "This is more genteel, n'est-ce pas."

He wanted to touch her, how he didn't know, to run his hand over her smooth hair or to hit her right between the eyes. "Okay," he said, "but for Christ sake, take it easy." Then he turned away.

"I knew her once," he heard Amy say behind him, "but that was in another country, and besides the wench is dead." She laughed, and he walked out through the door.

On the sidewalk a squat man was standing, as if waiting

for him. His fat belly pushed out his closed grey jacket.
Aaron recognized him. He was a bookie whom he knew
from around. What did the guy want? Spongie, that was
his name.

"Hiya, kid." He had a thick voice, as if he had laryngitis.
Aaron shook hands with him.

"What's new?"

"I want to talk to you."

"Okay. What about?"

"You know, I kind of like you, I think you're a good
Joe, so I want to give you some advice. You better beat it."

"You threatening me?" Aaron said, feeling his fist ball
up. One in that fat belly.

A soft hand lay on his arm. "I just told you, I was with
you. Now don't start blowing off at me."

"Well, you know what you said."

"You didn't let me finish."

"Okay, sorry."

"Now listen, there's a lot of guys around here who are
going to be laying for you. They figure they got to even up
on you and they'll do it, I don't mind telling you. And this
time it'll be for keeps, you know what I mean. They ain't
smart, those guys, and they won't let bygones be bygones,
like you and me might."

"What am I supposed to do?" Aaron said.

"I'm telling you, go somewhere, don't hang around here.
You might be a brave guy and all that, but you don't stand
a chance."

"Where am I supposed to go?"

"That's up to you."

"Well, I can't go anywhere. I'm out on bail."

"Jump the bail."

"What, and change my name and everything?"

"You might as well. This thing's never going to come to
trial. Those guys wouldn't go into court. What do you think
they are? Do like I say, jump the bail."

"I can't."

"I'm telling you."

"I can't do it."

"Okay, kid." They shook hands again. "I tried to set you
straight."

"One thing. Who are these guys?"

"Aw, now listen, you know I can't tell you that."

"How about if I talk to them?"

"That won't do no good."

"Okay then."

"Okay," Spongie said, and went into the Marino.

Aaron went up Macdougal, telling himself they couldn't scare him, that he wasn't scared, and yet knowing that it was there, the thing called fear. They were going to get him, do something to him. For keeps. Kill him? Well, die, what was that? Stop kidding. It was kind of final. And what could he do? He couldn't run away. (A) he couldn't jump bail, and (B) he just couldn't run away. Okay, the only thing to do was to stand his ground and when they got to him, well, he could take care of himself. If only the bastards would fight clean, one against one, he'd take any of them on.

He walked on over to Lois' place, trying hard not to look into doorways, into recesses, into parked cars. He rang her bell, but she didn't answer. Just as good, he didn't want to see her now. He didn't want to see anyone now. He went back to his own place, keeping to the main streets until he came to Jones, and there it lay before him, a treacherous darkness. The street lamp in the middle of the block had been broken, and he knew who'd done it, and why. This was it. He walked down the street, trying to keep an un-hastening pace, succeeding. No light from the street filtered into the vestibule of his house. They might try it there. But the vestibule was empty. That didn't mean much. They might be waiting in the hallway or up on the stairs. Okay—talk about free will—he had to go up. At each of the four flights he expected them to jump out at him, but they didn't show. Where in hell were they? There was his door, open, the way he always left it. He walked in and turned on the light, feeling every nerve tight, every muscle tense, half-expecting them to be sitting there, waiting for him. But no one was there. He closed the door, started to lock it. No, the hell with them, he'd never locked his door and he wasn't going to start now. He undressed down to his underwear, which was filthy, washed in the kitchen, and then went down the outside hall to the toilet that served the floor. He had a sudden fear that they'd jump him while he was in his underwear; somehow he felt more vulnerable

that way. But nothing happened. And yet he felt that someone was listening to him, someone was watching him. Going
back inside his place, he turned out the light and tried to
fall asleep. He couldn't make it. He got up and walked
around, started cursing at himself, had a brief talk with
Marty Greenwald who could give him the benefit of wisdom
deposited at the bottom of the Atlantic. Then he turned
out the light again, got back into bed, and tried without
success to fall asleep. They were out there, somewhere.
They were going to get him. For keeps. The hell with them;
he wasn't going to make it easy for them. Telling himself
that he wasn't really afraid, he went to the door and locked
it. And then . . . then he still couldn't fall asleep.

16. Aaron Proposes,
But Lois Disposes

AARON CAME AROUND TO see her three
days after he'd gotten out of jail, came around late one night
when she was sitting around and just beginning to get cozy
with a sax player named Jackson Tyler. It had taken him
long enough to get around to see her. Just long enough.
Because now her plans were made.

She introduced him to Tyler and offered him a drink, but
he refused, saying, "I wanted to talk to you."

Tyler stood up. "I've got to get along," he said.

"You don't have to," Lois told him.

"Well, it's getting kind of late and I've got to be pushing
on." He took his hat off an end table and put it on. "See
you soon, baby."

Lois opened the door for him. "Call me tomorrow," she
said.

"Okay."

"Maybe we can do something." ·

"Suits me fine."

Then she closed the door.

"Who's that guy?" Aaron asked her.

"A friend of mine."

"Kind of new?"

"More or less."

"You haven't been wasting any time, have you?" he said, throwing his week of martyrdom at her.

That was close, but it didn't quite win the bet she'd made with herself.

"Well, what about it?" She poured herself a drink. "What did you expect me to be doing? Knitting you an afghan?"

"Why didn't you come around to see me when you knew I'd gotten out?"

Bravo, that won the bet. That corny attempt to put her on the defensive.

"Honey," she said quietly, to show him she didn't give a damn, "you live on a two-way street."

"I came around. I came around the first night I was out but you weren't here."

"And then you got occupied?"

"No, I just didn't feel like seeing anyone. You know I get that way sometimes."

"How about your rich bitch?"

"What about her?"

"I suppose you didn't see her. Or your friend Amy."

"Aw Christ, Amy. I ran into her at the Marino the first night."

"Don't get me wrong," Lois said—her drink needed ice. "I don't care what you do or who you do it with." She went into the kitchen to get some ice from the tray. "To me you're a big mistake." The damned tray was stuck. "You're my winter's folly." Not a bad line, and here came the tray. "You understand?"

No answer. A direct hit. Score one.

The stud was standing when she came back into the room.

"Leaving?" she asked, archly of course.

"Yeah. I'm going."

"Don't want a drink?" Uh—oh, mustn't weaken.

"No, I don't want anything." He came toward her. "How about the dough?"

Another question anticipated. Lois, you're a smart chick.

"What money?"

"You know. The dough they collected for me."

"That's in the bank."

"Yeah? Well, I'll take care of it from now on."

"That's all right with me. I'll go to the bank with you tomorrow and you can have it."

He looked a little surprised at her easy agreement. But if he knew, if he knew . . .

"Come around about two," she said. "I've got to go uptown in the morning."

"How much does it come to?"

"Almost three hundred."

"Is that all?"

"What did you expect, a fortune?"

She walked him to the door. "Goodnight, sweetie," she said as he went out, but when he tried to kiss her she stepped back and away. "Goodnight," she said again, closing the door in his face.

She heard him go down the stairs heavily, and then began to get her things together. Her winter things she could leave behind, she wouldn't need them. Some light summer dresses and rags like that. Sandals, bathing suits, robe, etc. Because she was going, yes she was going, far far away, repeat, far far away. Rolling down not to Rio, but to Haiti, down to that fabulous black republic smack in the middle of the Caribbean. Three hundred dollars from the local squares and eleven hundred, mind you, from Breedon Rawley had bought her freedom. Haiti, the land of Black Majesty, the land of voodoo, of Creole songs and tall black men, a Negro country. Yes, fabulous, that's what everyone who had gone there said about it, that's what Pearl P. and Katherine D. had called it. She'd wanted to go for a long time, but when she was working she'd been too busy and when she wasn't she'd been broke. But now, emancipation. Proclamation.

So friend Ross would be around at two in the afternoon. Let him. By that time, according to the ticket in her bag, she should be somewhere over North or South Carolina—thank God, over them.

17. *Amy Macduff Sets Salvation in One Eye And Damnation in the Other*

BEWARE OF TRICKERY, MY friends, and
set your soul against disaster.

"Amy, when I heard you were here," Marion Salter was
saying, "I rushed right over. I felt I had to talk to you now.
Because I hate to see this happening to you of all people."

"Why me of all people?"

"Well, you know Jack and I are very fond of you, Amy.
We both think you're a fine person."

Marion Salter was smiling the warm and winning smile
of a salesman, her buck teeth breaking out between her
stretched thin lips, a smile imposed on her bleak bony face.
Poor Marion. She hadn't seen Marion and Jack for over a
year, not since that winter night when she and Marion had
had some drinks at the Rochambeau and Marion had told
her tearfully (the tears increasing as she drank) that Jack
was going to leave her unless she went on the wagon.
Marion occasionally did magazine illustrations and Jack
taught art at a local college, so that they had the possibility
of being respectable and stable. Amy had posed for them
both.

"You know," Marion said, her quick brown eyes taking
in the ward, "I was in here once. And once in Towns. Of
course you know about that."

"Darling," Amy said, "your exploits are legendary."

With just a hint of regret, Marion said, "That was before
I joined the AA."

AA equals Automobile Association, Anti-aircraft, Actors'
Ancestry, AAron Ross. Also, and more to the point, Alcoholics Anonymous.

"And now you feel better?" Amy asked.

"Oh my God, yes."

"Really better?"

"Amy. I can't begin to tell you."

"But you still want to drink?"

"I'm not going to."

"But you still want to."

"That's one of the principles of the AA. We recognize that we're alcoholics. We know we can't drink like other people. Whether we want to or not doesn't matter. We can't."

"I can't stop," Amy said. "I can't stop. I know it. I've tried, but I can't stop."

"I thought I couldn't either, but I have."

Through the wire mesh covering the window behind Marion, Amy could see the span of the Queensboro Bridge, slightly faded in the haze of the warm day. The cars going over the bridge blurred the line of the span. Closer, on the river almost below, a tug was manfully pushing a barge upstream.

"How long can they keep me in this place?" Amy asked.

"I don't know. Until you're better."

"Until they think I'm better."

"I'm sure it would help if I could tell the doctor you were going to join the AA."

Beware of trickery, my friends. The bribe, the immemorial basis of human relationships. If you do so and so for me, I will do such and such for you. This was the eternal barb in the olive branch.

"They can't keep me here forever."

"I was in here almost two weeks," Marion told her.

"But you were in the alcoholics ward. This is the violent ward."

"That can make it even worse."

Almost two weeks, just this side of a lifetime. Two weeks of sleeping between yellow sheets, of walking around in this old seersucker robe, of smoking during smoking periods, of eating this ridiculous slop, of helping with the cosmetic tray and being useful around the ward just to show the attendants how well she was (since it was well known and probably true that they reported each day to the doctor), two weeks or more of this tyranny, of the fear that they would never understand that she was all right. And it was all the fault of the damned smug doctor. When she had come there, voluntarily mind you, this female disciple of Freud, Adler and Jung had asked her where she thought she should be placed, and Amy had answered with a faintly malign humor, The violent ward. And now here she was. Here she was, trying not to take sedatives and drugs and warm baths or use any of the other soothing devices and resources of the institution, because that would count against her.

"They can't keep me in here," Amy said, keeping her voice level. "I came here of my own free will. They didn't pick me up and drag me here. I came here." Her voice was rising, against her will, as she began to speak of the indignity that had been worked against her. "Listen, you've got to get me a lawyer. You've got to find someone who can get me out of here. Because if you don't I'm going to claw my way right through these walls. I'll kill the doctor, I swear I will."

"Amy." A sympathetic hand joined hers. "You've got to keep control."

"How can I keep control?" Amy heard herself saying in a voice that was too high to be her own. (Could this be some trick of ventriloquism? Was someone speaking through her?) "How can I keep control? Listen, I'm lost here, I'm lost. You know what they can do. They can keep me here the rest of my life."

"You know they can't. And they won't." Marion's hand pressed hers reassuringly. "Jack and I are going to get you out."

"You promise? You promise?"

"Yes, I do. But Amy, what will be the use if you do the same thing all over again when you get out?"

"I can stop drinking if I want to," Amy said, without conviction.

"Then you will?" A bright note of hope.

"I don't know. Why should I? I'd have killed myself long ago if I hadn't been drinking."

"No you wouldn't, Amy. That's what I thought, I thought the same thing about myself, but now I'm happy. I'm really happy, Amy."

Amy looked at her suspiciously. Her happiness was so patent, shining in her eyes like light through a window, that it must be spurious. Trickery, beware of trickery. Yes, she knew from her bitter experience that human beings are

always anxious to share their unhappiness with large hands
while craftily hoarding their happiness. Society existed for
manipulations designed to bring about the lowest common
denominator of good will and mutual joy. Not that Marion
Salter was a bad sort—she was not—but she was of this
time and of this place, as they say, and a victim of the ills
thereof.

Trickery. For how had she come to this ward, how fallen
to this low estate? Through trickery, my friends, through
fraud and deceit, through force made plausible. They had
subverted—ah, the old mind was unimpaired if it could
come through with such a word—they had subverted a
voluntary action into a victimized restraint. And through
trickery.

Consider, ladies and gentlemen of the universal jury,
consider this poor little frightened overgrown beast of a
woman and how she has come here. She has been brought
here through her own desire to get well, incredible and
heretic as that might seem. Yes, it was precisely because she
wanted to be better that she has become so much worse.
Ladies and gentlemen, have pity, s'il vous plait.

It was true. She had wanted to get well. There, that could
be flung in the teeth of all those windy amateur psychi-
atrists (almost as harmful as the professionals) who had
prattled that she was out to destroy herself. Amy against·
herself. She had, according to them, guilt feelings, electra
complexes, also inferiority complexes, inhibitions, repres-
sions, frustrations, sadism-masochism, patterns, and so on
through all that convenient lexicon. She'd heard all that
from young whelps and aged rakes, all of them motivated
by the laudable desire to give her succor and assistance,
receiving for their sainted selves (and in one of two cases
it might have been true) naught but the priceless pleasure,
nay the boon, of helping someone in need. But they were
all wrong, because despite their penetratingly mistaken
analyses of her mind, character and background she had
wanted, all her life, to be happy, and she was here because
she had wanted, immediately and specifically, to get well.

"What are you thinking about, Amy?"

"Oh, just something," she told Marion. "Just something."

"Tell me."

"I will. But not now."

Start with the august doctor to whom she had gone because he had a reputation of working wonders with alcoholics. He had given her a physical and metaphysical and
finally pronounced the fateful words, "I can't do anything
for you. You're not like any other alcoholic. As a matter of
fact, I'm not sure you are an alcoholic." Encouraged by that
diagnosis and spurred on by necessity, she had kept on
drinking, but no matter how much she had drunk her
nerves had gotten worse and worse, until she was forced to
sleep with the light on, and even that didn't keep away the
terrors. She had tried sedatives: barbiturates, Seconal,
then paraldehyde. They had worked for a short time, a few
days at most, and then she had gotten that feeling again
and again, and nothing would stop it, that feeling of being
a snowflake fluttering down through the sky, melting.
Finally, one afternoon, at the end of her rope, she had managed to walk over to St. Vincent's Hospital, where a young
interne had treated her benignly, in the tradition of Mon-
sieur Vincent . . . First he had made her extend her hand,
to judge the degree of shaking, admittedly considerable.
This she had explained was due mainly to lack of sleep and
inability to hold her food, and that was true, since she had
cut down on the drinking when she had started with the
sedatives. Then he gave her a slug of paraldehyde, which
was by now old stuff to her, and suggested that she go over
to Bellevue, where he said she would be well taken care of.
He had a friend there, another interne, who would take a
particular interest in her. She had asked him, quite reason-
ably, whether she could take a look at the ward before
deciding whether she wanted to stay there, and he had
assured her that she could. The first warning came when a
policeman took her by one arm and an attendant by the
other and gently hustled her off to an ambulance. They
were kind, but firm, talking to her pleasantly while re-
maining ready to twist her arm up behind her if she started
trouble. (Men never treated her with the delicate deference
they reserved for smaller women.) Going to the psychi-
atric wing at Bellevue, seeing the open mouth of the building, she had tried to hold back, but after being dragged a
few humiliating steps through the bare lobby, she had fallen
into step with the times and gone along without making
any more resistance. (And never a harsh word.) But when

she came face to face with the psychiatrist, a middle-aged austerely objective-looking woman whose face seemed created only to surround and frame her acid steel-rimmed glasses, her heart had sunk. When she had told the doctor that she had come there of her own free will, told her this as woman to woman and one citizen to another, the doctor had smiled, showing her bitter yellow teeth. "Of course, I understand," she had said, and immediately begun to question her. But Amy was no longer in the mood to answer questions; she just wanted to get out of there, as was her right. She had started for the door, but the policeman grabbed her, and rather than become involved in any unseemly scene she had stopped. The doctor had asked her a few more questions, while Amy had patiently said again and again that she wanted to get out of there. Finally the doctor had told her, "Get your clothes off. You're going to stay here for a while, make up your mind to that." Amy had made one more attempt for the door. "What ward do you want me to put you in?" Said just like a schoolteacher speaking to an unruly child. "The violent ward, naturally. Can't you see I'm violent?"

So here she was.

Recite all that to Marion Salter? Not now. Some other time perhaps, when they'd be sitting around and having a couple of convivial drinks—but Marion didn't drink anymore—some other time when they could laugh at it a little and agree on the basic treachery of man.

The girl who was afraid that she had turned into a gila monster was standing in the alcove, looking at them. Amy reached out to her, because she was a beautiful small girl, but she scuttled away.

"Amy." Said tentatively. Marion's hand was still on hers. Had it been there all the time?

"Yes, darling."

"I haven't convinced you, have I?"

"About what?"

"About joining the AA."

"Darling, it's not a question of convincing me. I can't join the AA or even the GOP until I get out of here. I've got to get out of here." No, no, she must keep her voice low and steady. Now, again. "I don't want to stay here anymore. Well my God, I can go nuts in here from just being here."

"You mustn't worry about that. They're not going to keep you here much longer."

"How do you know?"

"I spoke to the doctor."

"The doctor said she was going to let me out?"

"Yes. Now you mustn't worry."

"I don't trust that doctor. I don't trust her. She hates me. If it hadn't been for her . . ." No, careful, she mustn't say things like that. Signs of paranoia, or would it be dementia praecox? Another tack. Laughing. "Why couldn't this have happened to me years ago? And why couldn't I have been a writer? I would have made my fortune. I'm too late. Too late and too little." Wrong. "Did I say too little?"

Marion stood up. "I'll come back tomorrow." When Amy stood up also, Marion embraced her, and Amy, springing back instinctively, could see tears beginning to form in Marion's eyes. The poor sad babe. But for whom was she weeping? For her, or for herself, because she had failed.

For herself. She was saying, "Amy, I'd feel so much better . . ." She broke down for a few seconds. "I'd feel, oh you don't know how much better I'd feel, if only you'd say that you'd join."

"Maybe I will," Amy said reluctantly.

"Just try it. Make an effort."

"All right."

"Promise."

Grapple me with hooks of steel.

"Yes, all right, I promise."

Marion held her convulsively, like an early Christian welcoming a convert to mutual martyrdom in the dungeons below the Colosseum.

"I'll come back tomorrow afternoon."

The advantages of a fixed address.

With Marion gone, Amy went down the hall to her cot and sat on it. She must try to see things clearly, she must try to think things through. Could she stop drinking? And should she stop drinking? And what if she did? Wouldn't she still get those horrible depressions, those crippling depressions? And the constant fatigue, the shortness of breath? And would her acute fear of people, her fear of saying and doing the wrong thing, which always gripped

her until she had had a few drinks, would that disappear?
Was it worth a try?

A tall skinny girl sat down beside her on the cot.

"Hello, Mary," Amy said.

The girl looked up and down the hall with so much
caution that she seemed to be overacting.

"I've got something to tell you," the girl said.

The poor kid was nuts. "What is it?"

"I've found a way to get out of here." Her hand flew up
and pressed against her lips; she had told a secret, she was
found out.

"How?"

Again that long cautious look. Gestapo lurking in the
shadows. NKVD under the bed. "I can't tell you now. I'll
tell you later."

"All right. Tell me later."

"You mustn't say a word."

"I won't."

"Promise."

Again that word. This time a grasping for faith.

"Of course, Mary."

"Say it. Say I promise."

"I promise."

"Are you a Catholic?"

"No, I was a Protestant."

"Oh. I should have asked you first."

Amy watched her go down the hall, stop and talk to another girl. She saw the cautious look up and down, the hand
flying to the mouth, saw her whisper and look back.
Poor kid.

Amy lay back on her cot. God, her mouth was dry.

18. Oliver Kittridge Sees Good and Evil And Hears a Voice Call His Name

HEARING THE KNOCK ON his door,
knowing that it was his brother Wilbur coming to take him
to lunch, Oliver closed the notebook in which he had been

setting down his principles, called, "One moment," and placed the notebook in a suitcase, which he carefully locked. Although it was undoubtedly near, the moment for revelation was not yet at hand. He then crossed the room and opened the door. But it was not Wilbur who had knocked; it was Joseph Saint-Simon. Saint-Simon was, in spite of his name, an American. He occupied the room to Oliver's left—or to his right, if he faced away from the Seine—and they had met on Oliver's second morning in Paris when they had simultaneously stepped out onto their balcony, which connected the rooms, to see the placid beauty of the Seine in the morning mist. Saint-Simon had a round pale face and eyes that glittered through the thick lenses of his glasses and a smooth head whose sheen was scarcely dulled by a sprinkling of hair. Oliver liked him. The night before they had sat in a cafe near the hotel and talked, and he had ascertained that they were in agreement about the need for a rediscovery of Christ (but Oliver had not told him how dramatically and how soon the world was going to rediscover Christ). Saint-Simon had been a conscientious objector during the war, and had spent three years of suffering in various federal prisons, years of suffering for a faith, for a love of his fellow so great that he could not kill. The love that Christ had borne. Added to that was his name, Joseph Saint-Simon, trailing clouds of glory, a name which Oliver was convinced after their talk was no mere accidental inheritance. It had meaning. Could it be that Joseph Saint-Simon would be at his right hand?

"You're not busy?" Saint-Simon said, standing in the doorway.

"No, no, come in. I'm waiting for my brother."

They went out on the balcony and leaned on the grill-work railing, absorbing the city before them.

"Isn't it strange," Saint-Simon said, continuing in their vein of the night before, "that there should be so much beauty in Paris and so much sin?"

"This world's beauty," Oliver said, conscious that he was speaking important words, "is only the vessel. Now it is as if a crystal goblet of the most wonderful workmanship were filled with beer, stale beer. But I think" (he refrained from saying I know) "that the time is coming when we will throw the slop out."

"I will tell you a secret," Saint-Simon said, bringing his face closer. "For some time I've had a feeling that a great change is coming. It's almost a mystical feeling that something is going to happen, a great event." Oliver began to tremble with excitement. "I don't know what it is," Saint-Simon went on, "but I feel that you and I are on the threshold of the greatest event in the history of the world. I can't communicate to you what I feel because it's only an awareness that something is going to happen. Something."

"You're right," Oliver said. "Something is going to happen."

"You feel it too?"

"Yes."

Had the time come to take his first disciple, to welcome the first believer, to offer the first salvation? Or would it be better if . . .

Just then Wilbur came into the room and took them to a lunch of mediocre food and conversational banalities.

And after lunch the moment of fusion was gone. Oliver felt that he and Saint-Simon were now two distinct people, not the believing one they had been in that glorious moment on the balcony, two people akin but still distinct for the present and waiting, as lovers do, for a second moment of wonder. Oliver made an appointment with Saint-Simon for three o'clock and spent the intervening time in his room, writing at length about the brief talk on the balcony.

At three Saint-Simon knocked on his door again and they agreed to go to the Louvre. But there, in that long gallery which seemed monstrously designed to reduce each painting to insignificance, Oliver felt the artificiality of all these attempts to set glory down, to place it in a frame, and he suggested they go out and stroll along the Seine. Saint-Simon was willing.

They walked past the bookstalls on the left bank and went down the stone stairs that led to the bank of the river and sat on the low concrete barrier at the edge of the river, watching the barges go by peacefully. It was a quiet and removed place. Once two young men walked by, arm in arm.

"Isn't it wonderful to see that?" Saint-Simon said.

Oliver watched the two young men going under the arches of a bridge.

"Of course you know what they'd say in America," Saint-Simon went on bitterly.

"Yes," Oliver said, "yes, I know."

"All that the Greeks taught us about love, all that's been forgotten."

Oliver said nothing. A chill breeze had swept along the river and he got to his feet. "Let's walk a little," he said. Saint-Simon agreed.

The towers of Notre Dame were before them as they walked.

"Have you ever been inside?" Saint-Simon asked.

"Not yet," Oliver said. "Not this time. I went years ago, when I was here with my father, but we rushed right through. I think we were on a guided tour."

"Being led around by the nose."

"Yes. Doing our duty."

Saint-Simon laughed appreciatively and gravely.

"Come on," he said, taking Oliver's hand, "let's go in."

They came to the open place before the cathedral and stood looking up at the massive towers. Two centuries of the work of men, of the loving work of men, had pushed those towers toward the sky. A monument to the grandeur of God, still standing above the city, and with God forgotten. They started to walk across the open space toward the great door of the cathedral when a small man in a tight jacket came up to them.

"Americain?" he asked hopefully.

"Oui," Saint-Simon said.

"I have something," the man said, fumbling at the breast pocket of his jacket and pulling out an envelope. "Tourist views of Notre Dame. Souvenirs. Very nice."

Saint-Simon waved him away. "No," he said, "no, merci."

"Very nice pictures."

"Non, merci."

"Cheap. Cheap. I sell them to you cheap."

"Je regrette, m'sieu," Saint-Simon said.

"Ah wait," the man said, catching up to them. His hand went into a side pocket. "Wait, I have something else. Very different." He stood in front of them so that they would have to step around him to continue going toward the cathedral. He pulled out another envelope. "Look." Oliver looked over his head at the grey marvel of the cathedral, at the sublimity of its lines, the aspiration of its magnitude. He heard Saint-Simon say in an angry voice, "Get away. Allez, allez," and then he looked down, directly at the pictures in the hand of the man, recoiled at the crude indecencies, and struck out with his hand to blot them out, saw the pictures scatter to the ground and heard the man cry out, a diminishing voice, because he was running, running away, over ground that gave under his feet, having no substance at all, and then he fell. Saint-Simon helped him to his feet, calling the man a fool, a dirty scummy fool, and with his arm around Oliver, who was quivering, walked him back to the hotel.

At dinner, Oliver had no appetite, which worried Wilbur, and after dinner he went up to his room, where he lay on his bed, feeling weak and nauseous. Somehow, mixed with the brutal image of the pictures, which he couldn't get out of his mind, was a continuing sensation of the pressure of Saint-Simon's supporting arm around him, and now and again he saw that arm outstretched naked and hairless. Finally, in desperation, he got his notebook out of the suitcase and began to write abstractions about love and suffering and corruption and misery and rebirth. He wrote feverishly, setting down the thoughts as they came to him, letting his mind flow out through the ink of his pen, a scribbled incoherency. Then, growing tired at last, ignoring what he knew must be Wilbur's knock on the door, he undressed and lay on the bed and went to sleep.

As he slept he became aware that he was not alone, that there was a presence in the room, that somewhere beyond the wall of his shut eyes there was something else, something he had been waiting for. He heard something like the movement of a curtain, a soft soft sound, and very close, and then he felt a breath upon his cheek, and he heard a voice say with infinite quietness, "Oliver, Oliver, Oliver," calling his name, and he knew that at last, after these years of waiting, it had come, that he was being called. He opened his eyes at the touch of a hand on his bare shoulder, opened his eyes with fear and gratitude, wondering how it would look, and saw in the moonlight, so close to his own face that it lacked definite form, the face of Joseph Saint-Simon, and beyond moonlight coming through the window that had been opened inward from the balcony. Saint-

Simon's weight pressed down on him, and he heard again
this mocking use of his name, and as he convulsively threw
Saint-Simon off him, he heard the voice saying, "I love you,
I can't help myself, I love you." Then he heard another
voice—a stranger's voice, but his own—distorted in a
scream.

19. Lois Wilson Finds Herself
Safe and Sound in a Sane World

                    TALK ABOUT LIVING, MAN, this was it.
Even though she had been here in Haiti for only five days,
Lois already knew that this was the place and this was the
life for her. Here she was somebody. No more struggle, no
more fight, no more crying through the night. Why hadn't
she latched onto this before? Now that she was sitting on
this verandah of the Hotel des Belges, facing the warm sun
that would soon go down in the Caribbean west of Port-au-
Prince, she could laugh at that other Lois Wilson, the fran-
tic chick of a week ago, remember, who had been all hung
up like Mister In-Between. Here she was, and here she
belonged.

For one thing, here for the first time in her life, her
color made sense. In the Confederate States of America,
they unimaginatively divided everything into white and
black. But no more of that here. Here shades and variations
counted. Here was a sensible spectrum going all the way
from black to ivory, and she was close to the very top of
the spectrum. The whites here—*blancs*—were outsiders,
foreigners. They didn't matter very much; at least they
didn't make the rules. People of her color for the most part
owned and ran this country. They drove around in the big
cars and lived in the big houses and had a good time. Yes,
here she belonged, and she was sure that if Lucien had
anything to do with it, here she would stay.

She had met Lucien Mauriac here at the Hotel des

Belges. He was related to the Perriers, who owned the hotel, or to be exact the pension, and Madame Perrier had introduced them that first night Lois was in Haiti, started a conversation going and then withdrawn. Very well done. Lucien was an aristocrat, and that word had meaning here. He was tall and pale and graceful with clean features and long hands. His age—well, it was hard to make it out at first, but he had turned out to be a surprising forty-seven. Debit side. As they had talked she had discovered in a very natural manner that Lucien was one of the wealthiest and most powerful men on the island, his wealth consisting of an import and export firm, an automobile agency, a transportation franchise, a banana plantation, other houses and land and enterprises, and his power resting on direct access at all times to Son Excellence Le Président. And it checked. She noticed quite quickly that everyone treated him with deference and that his opinions (which she couldn't understand since they were expressed in Creole or French to his countrymen) were always listened to and apparently agreed with. He drove a new Cadillac and owned a plane, one of the two private planes in Haiti. He was but definitely of the upper-upper. He had never made what might be called an advance or taken anything approaching a liberty. And yet, Lois knew every man is after something. She had a clue when he had taken her to his house in a new residential section in the hills overlooking the town and introduced her to his daughter Celeste, a plump blonde girl of eighteen, daughter by his second marriage, who like him spoke excellent English. She and Celeste had seemed to hit it off and Papa had been very pleased.

Now she was sitting on the verandah in a cool neat black dress, waiting for Lucien's Cadillac to turn into the drive.

"Good evening."

It was Frances Leeb, who had come up behind her quietly.

"I didn't mean to startle you."

"Oh, you didn't startle me."

"May I sit down?"

"Certainly, of course."

Frances Leeb took a wicker rocking chair. She was a squat hairy girl, dumpy and sexless at twenty-five, who

was giving Rorschach tests to the Haitians, those she could
entice into taking them, in preparation for a Ph.D thesis.

"Well, how do you like Haiti?"

"I like it very much," Lois said, feeling a little con-
strained.

"I liked it at first," Frances Leeb said, giving a little
sigh, "but now I can't wait to get home. I'm sick of it."

"Why?"

"The monotony. The same thing all the time. Wait till
you've been here a while. How long do you intend to stay?"

"I don't know yet."

"Don't stay too long or you'll find that things get spoiled
for you. You don't want to get too close to these people.
They're like children, but not nice children."

"They seem very pleasant to me," Lois said, feeling that
she was rising to the defense of more than the Haitian
people.

"Oh yes, they seem pleasant, they have good manners,
but inside they're rotten and decadent. I'm not talking of
the peasants, the people in the hills. They're all right,
they're wonderful. But these people in Port-au-Prince,
they're terrible."

"Really?"

"I know."

"I suppose you do," Lois said, only a little maliciously.
"After all, you've been analyzing them."

"I've been giving them psychological tests, yes, and the
results would amaze you. I thought at first these people
were happy and well-adjusted, but they're horribly neu-
rotic. I've never seen such Rorschachs. Incidentally, would
you like to take a Rorschach some day?"

"Why? Do you think I'm going native?" The prejudiced
white bitch. What was she doing here?

"No, but I'd like to do it."

"Well, all right. Someday." Someday being never.

Frances Leeb rocked her chair a little. Lois watched the
small figures crossing the dusty Champs de Mars. The red
light at the tip of the radio tower came on and she saw
some glimmers from the white block—now grey—of the
President's Palace.

She heard Frances Leeb say, "Would you like to come

to a voodoo tonight? A friend of mine is taking me to an authentic voodoo . . ."

"I'd like to," Lois said.

"He's a poet, a little decadent like all of them, but not too bad. Of course he writes terrible poetry, romantic, like fourth-rate Victor Hugo."

"I'd like to come," Lois said, politely, "but I can't tonight. Someone's calling for me."

"Lucien Mauriac?"

Lois said nothing. Why should she go on talking to this sad character?

"He's one of the worst."

"Have you given him a Rorschach too?"

"I'm telling you this because you're an American and you're new here." Bridges were being thrown up furiously: American to American, woman to woman, veteran to greenhorn. "You know, he tricked his first wife out of all her money and then he got an annullment. They still say funny things about the way his second wife died, she was a Danish woman." She paused to allow Lois to be overwhelmed by the insinuation, then added a little anti-climactically, "He's a terrible snob."

"Oh really?"

"He's not actually from one of the best families, and that's terribly important here. His mother was a Frenchwoman and they say she was nothing but a prostitute. And I believe it."

"Why?" Lois asked, and then saw Lucien's car turn into the drive.

"There's generally something to the rumors you hear. These people are only too anxious to talk about each other. Why, anyone would tell you about the woman. . . ."

Lucien was getting out of the car and Lois stood up.

"I'm sorry," she said, "but I have to be going," and went down the steps. It was rude, but she had been waiting to be rude.

Lucien took her to dinner at Tulio's, a restaurant on the shore road to the country club. They sat at a table on a little concrete platform that jutted out into the water, eating while the sun sank colorfully into the water and the sky began to turn a greenish night hue. Lucien talked about some of his experiences, particularly those in which he had

cooperated in some way with the United States. He was
very proud about that, and it was a small thing which Lois
didn't like, almost resented. He had been a sergeant in the
marine constabulary during the occupation, a Quisling of a
sort, and during the past war he had helped round up
Nazi sympathizers in Haiti for shipment to camps in Texas.
In Texas: Lois was vexed about that until Lucien explained
that the Nazi sympathizers were whites of German origin,
some of whom had even been planted by Hitler in this
strategic area. Lucien was almost childishly pleased to be
able to tell about his friendships with Americans, something
Lois could understand only when she realized that he did
not fathom the depths of her estrangement from the great
white fatherland. When she asked him about his treatment
when he flew to the States—he went there about twice a
year—he shrugged it off. "This is my country," he told her.
"Here I am a man. I am proud to be a Haitian." Great,
that was great for him. And she—could she say of the so-
called United States: This is my country, here I am a
woman, I am proud to be an American. Oh sure.

After dinner, which was leisurely, with several courses
and much rum, they drove back along the shore road. It
was dark, a darkness more complete than Lois was used to.
Beyond the pale spray of the headlights there was only
the flicker of candles in huts that seemed remote and hidden. They drove fast, Lucien showing no regard whatso-
ever for the black men and women padding along the side
of the road.

"Aren't you afraid you'll hit them?" Lois asked.

"Oh no. They watch out. In Haiti the car has the right
of way."

They passed a couple of large stone houses set back from
the road, marked by electrically lit signs: PARADISE and
CLUB ORIENTAL.

"Are they night clubs?"

"Night clubs?" She could see Lucien's teeth, but he
wasn't permitting himself to laugh at her. "No, they are
places where they have women."

A question formed in Lois' mind. "What kind of women?"

"Well . . ."

"I meant Negro or white."

"Ah well, they are from the Dominican Republic. They

are pretty dark, most of them, not very attractive. Some
light ones. It doesn't matter as long as they are from the
Dominican Republic. It is a question of pride for these
people to have a Dominican." And Lois remembered the
massacres ten years before, when thousands of Haitian
farm laborers, brought into the Dominican Republic to help
cut the cane, had been murdered. Now these few women
were an instrument of national revenge.

On the outskirts of Port-au-Prince, in the jumble of huts
and shanties called La Frontiere, Lois heard the beating of
drums, the first time she had heard that expected sound
since coming to Haiti.

"What is it?" she asked, a little excited. "Is it a voodoo?"

"No, not a voodoo. It is a bombash."

"What's a bombash?"

"A dance. Just a dance of these people."

"I'd like to see it."

"It's only their Saturday night dance. It is nothing to
see. These people all get drunk and they dance in a way
you would not like."

"Please," Lois said, "I'd like to see it."

"All right," Lucien said grudgingly. He slowed the car,
drove carefully for a short time, listening. The sound of the
drums became more distinct and Lois could hear something
else, a dull thumping which strangely enough did not seem
to come from a percussion instrument. The rhythm was
crazy, basic, really out of this world. Finally Lucien pulled
to the side of the road and said something to a man who
had been squatting on his heels. The man came to the car
instantly, peered inside, only his eyes and his teeth showing
as he talked to Lucien. In a few moments Lucien said,
"I know where it is now. Come along."

They went down an embankment and along a narrow
path that followed the edge of a drainage ditch. Small
children leaped out at them, chattering, holding their hands
out, palms upward. The children were black, emaciated, in
rags. "Don't give them anything," Lucien said. "They are
disgraceful, they are beggars." An old woman's black stick
of an arm fell like a barrier in front of Lois. Hastily and in a
queer panic she dug into her purse, while Lucien looked
disapproving, and gave the old woman a dime. The woman
began to whine piteously and clutched at Lois' dress, but

Lucien shouted at her and she disappeared. "You see what happens if you give them something," Lucien said angrily. "She can live on that for a week." A man came up to Lucien and said something in such a low voice that he seemed to be whispering; then he walked in front of them as a guide. Once or twice he turned to shout at the children, who were still following them. "Competition," said Lucien, laughing. "He is afraid that if we give to them we do not give to him."

Then they were at the bombash, a mass of blacks swarming in a murky reddish light, chanting, screaming with glee, swigging from bottles, some of the men stripped to the waist, the sweat of their bodies glistening in the light of the candles, the women in shapeless white dresses that didn't reach their knees. A short black man with a nose that had been eaten away by yaws or syphilis pushed towards them with a bottle of clairin, the cheap raw native rum, but Lucien waved him away. Some women began to gather around Lois, pointing to her and jabbering.

"What are they saying," Lois asked Lucien, feeling suddenly afraid and a little revolted.

"They want to know who you are," he told her. Then he said something to them in Creole, something which seemed to make a great impression.

"What did you say?"

"I told them you are an American."

Some of the women began to smile at her and one said over and over, "Blanc, blanc," and touched her arm gently.

And there was the orchestra, the source of that mad rhythm, at one side of a large open shed whose thatched roof was held up by a couple of rude poles. A gaunt black man was beating a large drum with his fingers, while another was straddling a smaller drum, shaking his shoulders and rolling his head as he ran his fingers over it. Two men were on their feet, heads down as they blew into bamboo poles; that accounted for the dull thumping she had heard from the road. All around the orchestra were stray men, beating together pieces of wood or bottles on tin cans. They were all inside the rhythm, seeing nothing, beating, beating, blowing.

"Damn," Lois said, "what a jam session."

"What?" It was Lucien.

"Nothing." This was the kind of thing you either felt instinctively or you didn't. Her feet were beginning to trace a pattern.

"Can we dance?" Lois asked.

"Here?" Astonished.

Couples were locked in the concentrated area of the shed, their bodies pressed against each other, their hips grinding out the rhythm against each other, as if they were trying to squeeze their juice out. Some were leaning back from each other so that only their groins touched, moving. Lois felt excited and yet repelled. It was like the time about three years before when she had come back from a tour and found the girl she was rooming with staging a little orgy with some friends, three and three. But here it was purer, no kissing, no by-play, no sense of shame. There was a question she wanted to ask Lucien, but she knew it was not the kind of question to ask him; still she could see that the couples remained on the floor, never changing the tempo of their movements against each other.

Lois was about to say it was wonderful when she heard Lucien say, "It is disgusting. They are uncivilized. Animals. No intelligence." She kept quiet. "If we permitted them," Lucien went on. "they would do this every night."

"Is there a law against it?" Lois asked, allowing herself just a trace of sarcasm.

"Oh yes. They are permitted to play the drums only on Saturday night, otherwise they would never work, they would dance every night and starve to death. We have to take care of them."

"But they're happy this way," Lois said.

"Yes, they are happy but they do not know. Someone must direct them. Come on, let us go."

The guide placed himself before them—he had evidently been standing somewhere outside, waiting for them—and led them back to the car. Lucien gave him a coin and cut him short when he started to protest. The guide opened the door of the car for Lois.

"These people are children," Lucien said as they drove through the town. "By themselves they would do nothing. They have no ambition, they do not care for anything. Let them dance, let them have their cockfights, their voodoo, that is all they want." He lit their cigarettes with the dashboard lighter. "This is not like in the United States where every man wants to get ahead. If we let these people do as they like, do nothing, then where would we be? We cannot make money if no one will work. Without our class this country would have become like Africa," he added with disdain. They went past the long low building that housed Lucien's automobile agency. "I taught the people who work for me everything," he said. "Everything. I learned all about the automobile first and then I taught them. And even now there are always mistakes, things I must do myself. No, this is not like the United States. Here there is only us and them. Do you understand?"

Yes, she understood. There were people who understood machinery, who could read and write, who could add and subtract, who could handle money, who were in short civilized, of the twentieth century. And so they were the people who could ride in a Cadillac like this, live in a house with running water, give orders, demand obedience, could be lords and masters of creation. Damn it, the thing went against her sense of justice and yet she liked it, because for the first time in her life she belonged without reservation to an upper class.

She understood even more when they reached the party to which they were going. It was a quiet, almost sedate affair, held in a modern spacious house in the hills just off the road to Petionville. The men were in stiff white linen suits, the ladies in expensive Paris dresses. Lois was reminded of the Negro upper group at home, the doctors and lawyers and the successful business men, who dimmed their natural good spirits in the machine-made conventions of the white upper class. But here there was a difference, more ease of manner, more confidence. She noticed that they spoke French, disdaining the native Creole, and almost all of them spoke passable English, some with a relish and enthusiasm which garbled their sentences. Everything was subdued. A white-haired man was sitting at the piano, quietly playing Chopin, furnishing the necessary cultural background to the talk. And there was the Eighteenth century here too, the servants being dressed in livery, frogged and brocaded, slipping in and out of the room with drinks and canapes on mahogany trays. Suddenly she noticed that all the servants were barefooted; the whole illusion ended abruptly at their black wide feet. It came almost as a shock.

"Why are they barefoot?" she asked the man she was sitting with, a short fat tan man who was a Senator.

"The floor, it is concrete, you see," he said. "If they' wear shoes, clop, clop, clop, they make too much noise, we cannot talk." He leaned over to the man sitting to his right and said something, pointing at one of the servant's feet. The other man laughed and began a relay. Lois was embarrassed. This was something, evidently, she should have been able to figure out for herself, something that should have been in her experience. The poor bastards, having to go around barefoot just so they wouldn't make noise, just so they wouldn't disturb conversations. And yet whose conversation would they be disturbing? Hers. People treating her like—Well, they probably didn't want to wear shoes anyway.

Later Lucien showed her through the house, showed her the gleaming modern kitchen (the servants stood off to one side), the terraces, the wading pool outside the main bedroom ("for the hot nights"), the library. Then he showed her around the grounds in the darkness, leading her to a pale patch that was the tennis court and then to the dark oblong of the swimming pool. Finally he sat with her on a bench in the garden.

"How do you like this house?" he asked her.

She said she was crazy about it.

"You know, I could buy this house," he said. "I am sure Roland would sell it to me.",

"But what about the house you already have?"

"Well, I am a little tired of it. This is better. Would you like to live here?"

So, here it came. Duck, everybody. The guy wanted a mistress.

"How could I live here?" Lois asked, playing it dumb.

"I can buy the house for you. Roland is under obligations to me."

Tempting, but not enough.

"I don't understand," Lois said, leaning just a little closer to him. "I can't stay here. I'm only here on vacation. I have to go back home soon."

"Why not stay in Haiti?"

"Well, I'm an American," she said, knowing he wouldn't sense the falseness of that statement.

His hand began to play with her hair. Damn it, no, not the hair, she had had to oil it too much tonight.

"I would like you to stay here," he said, his voice sounding urgent and dreamy all at once. "Tomorrow the President is giving a reception. I would like for us to go there and I could let the President make the announcement."

"The announcement?"

"Yes, that we are getting married."

Married! Well, well, well.

"You will like it here," he said.

And give up the United States? Give up what? Living in a borrowed apartment, crawling after jobs, feeling those eyes on her, being a second-class citizen, being a Negro. To come here, to live here. To be part of this, the new cars and the big houses, the ruling class in a colonial society, to be—what had that woman at the bombash called her?—blanc, blanc. Yes, to go from under-dog to top-dog in one easy leap, by signing a contract and climbing into a bed. And not too bad a bed at that.

Why not?

"Well?"

"All right," she said after a moment.

"Ah, good."

His hand dropped from her hair to her shoulder and she rested her head against him. She sat that way for a little while, imagining that she could hear the rapid beating of his heart. Then she felt him stir restlessly.

"We had better go back inside," he said.

They got off the bench and walked back into the house. In a few moments Lucien broke away and started talking to the Senator. She went to the piano, where the white-haired man was still playing, Bach now.

He smiled up at her. "Would you like to play?" he asked.

"No," she said, "not now."

"Do you like Bach?"

"Oh yes, very much."

"I have heard that in the United States you are a famous singer."

"Well, I wouldn't call myself famous," Lois said with mock shyness.

"You sing like Marian Anderson?"

"No, not that kind of singing."

"I heard Marian Anderson in Carnegie Hall two years ago. I did not like the spirituals, but the lieder. What, then, do you sing?"

"I sing jazz."

A tremor of disappointment nudged the lower part of his face.

"Jazz," he said. "It is necessary." And he played a little louder.

Lois thought about Lucien, still in conversation with the Senator. Sitting there in the garden, he hadn't even kissed her. A hand to her hair, hand to her shoulder, and that was all. Now why was that?

20. Breedon Rawley Gets In With the Outs

"SO FIELDING WANTS TO see you. So what," Carney said with utter unconcern. "What's there to get jittery about?"

"I—I—I . . . n-nothing. I ju-just have a feeling . . ."

The summons to Fielding's office had arrived a few minutes before, written in the great man's own hand on a small white rectangle of inter-office stationery. Ever since Carney had handed in the finished version of THE LONE PRAIRIE (formerly called WHERE THE BUFFALO ROAMED) Breedon had been dreading the reception it would receive from Max Fielding, especially since he had done most of the work on the script.

"Maybe he'll ob-object to the psy-psy . . ."

"Object to the psychoanalytical treatment of the outlaws? Not a chance. He'll be crazy about it. It gives the script that added something, the modern outlook. Freud comes to the frontier."

"Yes, but he might not . . ."

"Kid, you're getting the Hollywood jitters," Carney said protectively. "You're getting that old fear of losing a thousand bucks a week. That's bad, that's very bad. Sometimes I look back with nostalgia, yes with actual nostalgia, at the days when I could lose only forty bucks a week. Or less. Now buck up, brace your shoulders, throw out your chest. Fielding probably wants to congratulate you on the script."

"Y-you really think so?"

"Sure I do. He probably wants to give you the Superior Pictures Superior Medal with a cluster of options."

"But why-why doesn't he w-want to see you too?"

"He has been seeing me. And besides, you're the new boy, the bright hope of the squirrel cage. I'm old hat. Yes, he's probably going around town knocking you."

"Kno-knocking me?"

"So he can hold on to you. Do you think he wants the other studios to know what a good thing he's got? Now stop worrying and go on in there and if he says anything nasty threaten to quit. You'll see how quickly he shuts up. Tell him you want to quit to work on another book, tell him you're losing money working here. You'll see how that scares him. Now go on in there," said Carney, giving him a little push, like a coach sending out his star quarterback for the second half.

Impelled by that push, spurred on by a spurious optimism, Breedon went through the slippery corridors to Fielding's office. He was admitted into the sanctum immediately. A good sign. Fielding looked up and nodded briefly as Breedon crossed the lawn of green broadloom.

"Sit down, Rawley," Fielding said coldly.

Breedon sat down, apprehensive, but remembering Carney's advice, starting to repeat it to himself.

"Well, I'm surprised at you, Rawley," Fielding said, his eyes narrow and hostile behind the thick glasses. (CU ROD WEAVER NARROWING HIS EYES. TWO-SHOT AS NIXON FINGERS HIS GUN)

"S-s-surprised?"

"Surprised and hurt." The eyes widened a little with pain.

"You-you mean the s-script . . ."

"I'm not talking about the script, Rawley. We don't have to discuss that. It's a good standard George Carney job, the kind of thing I'm accustomed to getting from George."

"From Cah-Carney? But I . . ."

"No use discussing the script. That's not important now. It's this other business . . ." Fielding shook his head sadly. "I am surprised," he said.

Breedon felt as if he had been caught walking naked down Hollywood Boulevard. "At what? W-what did I do?"

"You've done your best to destroy the reputation of this industry. You've done your best to harm this studio. You've done your best to undermine the institutions of this country."

Breedon saw all his past sins roll before him, but not one of them seemed pertinent.

"I-I-I . . ."

"Rawley, when you leave here today I want you to think about this attitude of yours. I want you to think about it carefully. You're a young man, perhaps you've been duped by older people, perhaps they've played on your youth, your idealism." He paused for a moment, then lowered his voice to impart a confidence. "When I was your age I was tempted to join."

"J-join what?" Breedon asked, trying to determine whether he was angry or frightened.

Fielding's voice sank to a whisper. "The Party."

"The P-party?" What party? Wait, perhaps he was being accused of participation in some ribald affair, women and dope and alcohol. But he hadn't . . .

Fielding said, "Don't be cagy with me, Rawley. Are you a member?"

"M-member?"

"You know what I mean," Fielding said, standing up behind the rampart of his desk, taking off his glasses as if preparing for combat. "Are you a member of the Communist Party?'"

Breedon wanted to laugh with relief.

"Well?"

Breedon discovered that he was really laughing.

"I don't think this is any laughing matter," Fielding said in a clipped haughty voice, the voice of a British colonel.

"I—I . . ." Breedon couldn't stop laughing.

"Mister Rawley."

Training came to the rescue. "Sir?"

"You haven't answered my question, and for God's sake don't say it would incriminate you."

Shoulders braced, back stiff, chest out. "I am not."

"Then you're a fellow-traveler."

The Confederate soldier. "No, sir."

"If not, why were you collecting money for them?"

"For whom?"

"Don't try to use those well-known evasive tactics. You know very well who I mean."

"No, I—I du-don't."

"I don't know why you should be in with them. How would you like working in Russia? Did you ever hear of the purges? Do you know what happens to writers who don't follow the party line? You ought to be thankful you're a free writer in a free America. I can't understand it. You, with your background. Maybe it takes someone like me, whose parents came from the old country, who knows from their lips what European tyranny can be like, it takes someone like me to appreciate this great land of ours. Rawley, you forfeited my respect when you went around this studio, this studio that's paying you every day a hundred times what a Russian worker makes in a week, collecting money for them."

"For the R-russian w-workers"

"I'm referring to the Ten."

Ah, so that was it. Oh, oh—on a rising note of relief—oh. Now he could explain how in all innocence he had contributed a hundred dollars to The Ten, not knowing as he did now that they were the ten directors and writers who had been called before the Committee on Un-American Affairs to testify whether or not they were members of the Communist Party. Now he could tell Max Fielding that he would not now . . .

"I g-gave some money," Breedon said, confident that everything would now be cleared up, that he and Mister Fielding would end up in a warm embrace, "but I—I didn't know what it was f-for."

"That's a lie," Fielding said curtly. "I've terminated your contract, Rawley. I want you off the lot within an hour. I'm giving the studio guards orders to put you off the lot, by force if necessary, if they find that you're still on the property."

"B-but . . ."

"You not only gave a hundred dollars, but you ₍spent three days of studio time collecting money. Now get out of here."

The office door opened, Fielding's secretary came in, pad in hand, and Breedon, as if he were clinging to the rope of a pulley, went out.

He stood in the outer office for a few minutes, trying to think of how he had gotten into this unaccountable mess (knowing it would all be cleared up someday, but probably not within the next crucial hour), and suddenly it came to him. He knocked on the closed door of the inner office. The secretary opened.

"I—I have to s-see Mister Fielding."

"Mister Fielding is busy now."

"B-but I have to see him."

"Close that door, Margaret," he heard Fielding say.

And the door was closed.

All right, he'd send Fielding a letter, explaining that he hadn't been collecting money for The Ten, not at all, that he'd been collecting for the defense fund of Aaron Ross. He'd send him an affirmation that not only had he never been sympathetic to Communism, but he and his family were from time immemorial staunch Democrats (never even deviating into Republicanism). Or better yet, he'd get Carney to talk to Fielding, to explain away this misunderstanding. All would be well, all would yet be well.

He went to Carney's office and was about to go in when Carney's secretary stopped him.

"Did you want to see Mister Carney"

"Y-yes."

"Well, he's gone home."

"H-home? I-I'll reach him at home."

"I'm not sure he'll be home after all. He said something about playing golf."

"I've go-got to speak to him. Wu-where does he play"

"I don't know, Mister Rawley. Can't you wait till to-morrow?"

"No, I can't, I—I . . ."

"Well, if Mister Carney calls I'll tell him you're looking for him and I'll have him try to get in touch with you." She turned away from him, abruptly ending her little talk.

Breedon went to the door, opened it, looked back. Carney's secretary was about to go into Carney's office, and through the open door he could see Carney sitting at his desk, pouring some whiskey into a dixie cup. Never one to force an issue, knowing when he had been done in, Breedon went out silently.

He would write that letter to Fielding, telling him all about Aaron Ross and Lois Wilson and the defense fund, and so on and so forth. A tenuous story, admittedly, but a believable one. The kind of contretemps which could occur to anyone. A Kafka-esque misunderstanding. Yes, Fielding would understand, he would believe. Time enough later to settle with Carney. When Fielding saw how an Iago played upon his weak spot, like a noble Othello he would turn on the treacherous dog and thrust him out. Only, as was very well known, the Noble Moor had strangled Desdemona first.

21. *Amy Macduff Looks Forwards And Backwards and Around*

HERE LIES—AMY THINKING of her possible epitaph—*one Amy Macduff, never got to drink enough* . . . aha, not bad, that rhymed . . . *Saved by friends she* . . . *she* . . . she what? . . . *Saved by friends for this quiet grave where she finally learned to behave.* A little awkward, but.

She laughed. Marion Salter, one arm of the vise that gripped her, looked at her with partially-concealed apprehension, by now congealed apprehension, while Jack Salter, the other arm, seemed to share her amusement. Ah, but they didn't know, of course they couldn't know what she was laughing at. *Here Lies One Amy Macduff Who Never Got To Drink Enough* . . . And then the years come on, wind and rain and weather, as they say, and little by little the inscription fades into the face of the stone, and Amy

Macduff is gone, erased, the granite memory of her gone,
just like the people who have been better before her.

She laughed again, not loud.

"What is it?" Marion asked, worried.

"Nothing, darling. A random thought."

"You were laughing." Said accusingly.

"Not at him. I'm sorry."

No, not at him, not at the tall middle-aged man in the
grey suit who stood on the platform and was telling them
of the sorrows of his life, all brought on by John Barley-
corn. He had been (he said) an account executive with a
Four-A advertising agency, no less, with a good income,
more than enough for his needs and his pleasures, a wife
who loved him and a son whom he adored. Into this happy
American household, enter John B. It had started with the
social and necessary side of business, drinking with his
clients. Soon he had found himself drinking more and more,
but he hadn't worried about it, he could take it, or leave
it alone. He still thought he could take it or leave it alone
even after he found that he was lapsing into black moods
and nervous jitters when he didn't have a drink at noontime, or a couple of drinks, or later a few. Still nothing to
worry about, since it was only a few drinks and he was
never under the weather. A couple at night too, a few at
night, to settle his stomach and calm his nerves, to soothe
him for sleep. Then in the morning, a quick pick-up and he
found that he could function until that noontime break.
Still nothing to worry about since he never got drunk,
really drunk that is. Until the night he was out with some
of the boys and they'd paddled from bar to bar and he'd
really gotten drunk and stayed drunk and ended up three
days later in Chicago, of all places. He'd missed a couple
of important appointments, but hadn't been fired, not until
he had repeated this performance half a dozen times. But
he'd caught on with another agency, stayed for a while, got
fired, caught on, got fired, couldn't catch on again. Began
to devote himself to drinking, wife divorced him after
showing a certain amount of patience, until the morning he
woke up in the house of a man he used to binge around
with. But now a clear-eyed alert man, looking years
younger, who told him about the wonders done for him by
AA. He'd gone to a couple of meetings and now, now he

was sober, now he was getting back to the point from which he had fallen into the gulf, and he owed it all to AA.

Amen, thought Amy, sitting between Marion and Jack. Amen. This reminded her of a revival meeting, but much more polite and therefore less interesting, with no one doing spectacular worthwhile things like falling to the floor and writhing and screaming hallelujah. She looked again at the motto primly framed on the side wall. GOD GRANT ME THE SERENITY TO ACCEPT THINGS I CANNOT CHANGE, COURAGE TO CHANGE THINGS I CAN, AND WISDOM TO KNOW THE DIFFERENCE. Marion had told her the motto had come from St. Thomas Aquinas. Possibly, and why not?

Now a woman was on the platform, fairly young, well-dressed, trim, sober, and she was telling how the hand of God had brought her to AA. She had tried to commit suicide twice, the first time by gas, the second time by swallowing a tumbler of CN, and each time God had saved her and finally brought her out of the dark world of alcoholism and into the light. Then she went into a recital of the harrowing details of her life with liquor. Amy, listening, knew that she could never get up on a platform and tell of all the outrageous episodes in her life, nor could she even get up before three people and say that God had brought her anywhere or anything, because she didn't believe in God. She was sober now, dry as a wrung rag, had been sober, including the time in Bellevue for thirty-one days, and she felt lousy. To what avail all this righteousness if she didn't have any fun. Of course she didn't have any fun drinking, people who thought that all vice is fun were dead wrong, but it did ease the pain. Yet Marion told her, kept telling her, that in a short time, when she had finally gotten over the temptation to drink, and more than that the fear of drinking, then she would join this happy happy gathering, then she would want to stand up and tell about herself in the hope of helping others, then she would be in truth an AA, ready to take her sober place in a sober world. Could such things be? Ah, who could make a balance sheet of promise and fears, of hopes and dupes? Not she.

The woman on the platform had finished her story and the chairman closed the meeting by leading them all in the Lord's Prayer. Amy mumbled what she thought might pass

for the words. Well, if she became an AA at least she'd
relearn the Lord's Prayer.

"Well?" Marion asked her.

"Isn't there any other way to stop drinking?" Amy said.

"No, there isn't. That's what makes AA so wonderful."

"I don't see how that makes it wonderful," Amy said,
feeling that she had made a reasonable statement.

"It does," Marion told her, eyes shining, "because at last
there is a way. Think of it, Amy, there are eighty thousand
of us who would still be drinking if it weren't for AA.
Eighty thousand lost souls," she added fervidly.

"It's helped Marion a lot," Jack said, more calmly.

"Oh, when I look back!"

"You ought to really try it," Jack said.

"Darlings, why the hell are you so good to me? You make
me feel like a heel. What if I don't stay on the wagon?"

"Not on the wagon," Marion said. "We don't go on the
wagon. That's negative. We do something positive. We not
only give up drinking but we find something to take its
place. We help others, we fight this thing . . ."

"I'll make a lousy soldier," Amy said laughing. "At the
first pop of a cork I'll turn and run." Jack laughed with
her and put his arm around her shoulder, but Marion had
that worried look. "Now what's that?" Amy said, indicating
the back of the room where people were pushing toward
a counter. "You wouldn't be broadminded enough to have
a bar?"

Marion tried to smile. By God, the girl had lost her sense
of fun since she'd dedicated herself to sobriety. "We have
coffee and cake," Marion said.

Jack asked, "Want some?"

"Just cake," Amy said to him. "After all coffee contains
caffeine and I have to watch my bad habits."

"Amy, Amy," Marion said with that harassed smile.
"You're going to be all right, I just know it."

Funny how Marion was beginning to sound like one of
those fussy women at a do-good church social.

As Jack went after the cake and possibly coffee the tall
middle-aged man who had been, and was again, an account
executive came up to them.

"Hello, Frank," Marion said warmly, "do you know Amy
Macduff?"

"No, but I want to," he said directly and shook her hand with just the right amount of professional skill and just the right amount of special interest. Amy saw, on this closer view, that his face was seamed yet tan and healthy and his eyes were clear, like the eyes of the people in his advertisements, "Are you an alcoholic too?"

"Yes, she is," Marion said quickly.

Irritated, feeling that a doctor had just asked a nurse about the contents of her bed pan, Amy said, "What next? Why don't we discuss my sex life?"

Frank was distressed. "I'm sorry," he said. "I only wanted to know whether . . ."

Marion put in, "Frank wants to know whether you're joining us."

"That's all. I didn't mean to offend."

Well, she was a louse, putting a guy down like that.

"It's my fault," Amy said, giving him a big smile. "I'm not used to the customs and mores of the native population yet. I'll catch on tres-vite."

Frank grinned and encased her right hand in both of his. "Good, good. Say, how about some coffee and?"

"Jack's bringing some," Marion said.

"Well, I'll go help him."

As soon as he was out of range, Marion said confidentially, "He's a very nice guy. I think you'd really like him."

"What about his wife?" Amy said feeling her natural resistance to this matchmaking.

"They're divorced. You remember."

· "Oh yes," Amy said, thinking back to his recital.

"You need a good stable man."

"Ah, you make me sound like a horse," Amy said, and then Jack was back, and so was Frank Hilton.

They chatted for a while, munching their cake out of hand and sipping their coffee, and Amy could see that Frank Hilton, tall and marriageable and stable, was interested in her, and she could see further that he was knowing enough and aggressive enough to stake out his claim on her in this chapter of AA. And perhaps it wouldn't be too bad; he was good-looking in a middle-aged way, preserved well in alcohol (intramural joke), he had a job and therefore money and a sense of humor only partially marred by that all-pervading earnestness of the reformed drunkard, and (trust intuition and experience) he would not be merely on the make but would be after that which is bigger and better, being slightly permanent, since he was a man with a mission and of a consequence reformed in all things. It might be dull, but it could be worse, and probably she should make ready to bid an unfond adieu to her salad days. Hell and farewell.

As she went up Sullivan Street with Marion and Jack, going back to their snug harbor with them, Amy began to realize the extent of the sacrifice she would be making in joining the AA and living up to its principles of sobriety and in marrying (if it should come to that) Frank Hilton and living with him the good earnest life. She would be making the supreme sacrifice, the greatest known to man or woman; she would be giving up herself. For what was Amy (Amy thought) if she wasn't Amy anymore? Who would recognize her in a sober quiet woman shuttling between meetings of the AA and the quiet of a decent home? And how would she recognize herself? What would happen to the Amy who had beaten up the conductor on the train? What would happen to the Amy who had, horribly enough, made love on a Greyhound bus, late at night of course? What would even happen to that deep submerged Amy who lived in that constant climate of depression? How would she fare in the sun? It would be a great sacrifice. For herein—ah, herein was the basic truth, the frightening truth of reform: that reform is not so much a rebirth as an assassination. And had not all the religious drones of this world fixed their canons against self-slaughter? Once out of the soul or the psyche of the Amy Macduff she knew, the only Amy Macduff she knew, she would be naked in this world, and lost.

Besides which, she wanted more than anything else in the world, more than mother, father, country, love or the promise of a golden hour, she wanted a drink.

"Amy."

Yes, a drink.

"Why are you stopping?"

"Look, Marion, you and Jack go on. I'll be home later." A lie. A transparent lie.

"Amy, no, you must come with us."

"Come on, Amy," Jack said, persuasively taking her arm.

"I'll be home later."

My God, it was starting to come on, the shortness of breath, the fading out.

"Amy, I know it's hard," Marion said, "but if you get through it this once, this one time, it's going to be all right. I know. Just fight it now. Here, Jack and I will help. Amy, please, please don't fail me."

Fail her! The motives of man. Or woman.

"I'm not going to do anything," Amy said desperately. "I'm not going to drink. I feel crowded. Oh God, I don't mean anything by that, but be a sweet young girl and leave me to my own devices."

"All right, Amy," Jack said. He let go of her arm. "Come on, Marion."

Marion said, "Amy, don't take a drink. I know you think you can take just . . ."

No sermon, not now.

"I know I can't," Amy said, fighting off her impulse to begin shouting. "I know what I'm doing. My God, Marion, don't treat me like a wayward child. I won't betray you and the AA. I'm on the side of the Lord."

"Amy . . ."

"Marion, come on."

Thank you, Jack.

"Good night, Marion. Good night, Jack."

"You'll come home, won't you?"

"Yes, yes."

"Even if . . ."

"Yes, yes, yes."

She waited while Jack and Marion went up the block, knowing Marion would turn around again and again to see where she was going. She didn't even put it past Marion to hide at the corner, as her mother might have done, and follow her and then play a great and dramatic confrontation scene. No, no, Jack wouldn't allow that. Good Jack, praise Allah and so forth that he had never been an alcoholic, that he had no need to reform and no urge to reform others, that he could still be a normal human being who would not consider it a catastrophe if someone else went to hell.

They were gone now, out of sight, slickly vanished, so Amy walked to the corner, paused, made a precautionary reconnaissance, and then went at a near run down Bleecker Street toward, of all places, the Marino. There if her money ran out, always a dreaded possibility and tonight a certainty, she could depend on the bounty of the house. And there were the people she knew, the filthy little bastards. A warm protective atmosphere of good cheer and bad fellows, the very stuff which bars are made of.

"There's Amy."

She heard, but she looked neither to right nor left, going straight to the bar. She wasn't ready yet to admit in detail the facts of her absence. She wasn't ready yet, not until she'd put down a few, to relate the contretemps of the wrong ward at Bellevue or to regale the general ear with her close call with the AA. That would come. All in due time, necessarily so, life being a matter of putting mistakes in their proper order.

"Hello, Johnnie," she said to John, who was behind the bar.

."Hello, Amy. I heard you was sick."

"Sickness of the soul."

"Yeah?"

"A dismal decline."

"Yeah? I missed you. I almost came up to the hospital to see you. What'll you have?"

There were the old familiar rows of bottles, always at service, the names America loves, the regiments and battalions of the enemies of the AA.

"The usual deadly rye," Amy said.

She watched intently, feeling no pain, as John filled a jigger, watched with fascination as she noticed how the whiskey, filling the jigger to the very top, seemed to swell above the edges of the glass. She feared it would spill, some of it anyhow, as he set it in front of her, but no, it held that convex form. A good omen.

"Well, well, well."

It was Jason Spivak, looking and acting as always like a bit of a drip.

"Go away, boy," Amy said. "Run along and peddle your papers."

Spivak had already pushed up to the bar.

"Well, well, for Christ sake," he said, his voice a little

thick," I heard you were a guest of our fair city. Hah! **How** does it feel to be a guest of the city?"

"You'll find out, you mother's love," Amy said. "Now **go** and play somewhere else, will you?"

"All right, but I won't pick you up on the news about our mutual friend."

"Which mutual friend?" Amy asked, knowing full well she had been baited.

"Aaron the Ross."

"What about him?"

"There's a rumor, which I know happens to be true, that the local lads are out to get him." He began to laugh stupidly. "I hope they cut his balls off."

"Oh, get the hell out of here," Amy said, pushing him.

"You don't still go for that guy?"

"No I don't. But I go for you even less."

"Well, Jesus, what have I ever done to you? Come on, let me buy you a drink."

"I've got a drink."

"Then you buy me one."

"Manana. Demain. In the distant future."

"Okay, then I won't tell you about Lois."

"Who?" Say, she was forgetting her drink. That must never be.

"Lois Wilson, your successor."

"Oh. What about her?"

"She absconded to the Virgin Islands."

"Good for her. Cheers."

"Hey, wait, wait, you said you'd buy me a drink."

"Goodbye, sonny."

"No, listen, you tricked me out of information." He reached quickly for her drink and Amy, in a sudden panic, seeing his fingers already curled around the jigger, struck out at him, the lousy thief. She saw his hand jerk back instinctively, defensively, while the neat convex form at the top of the jigger was destroyed and the whiskey splashed out.

"Hey, hey." From John.

Spivak said, screwing up his face, "What the hell, what the hell."

John was coming around the bar and people were fading back from either side of them.

The hand of God. Strange, curious, but in all those AA stories it was the hand of God, in one form or another, which finally reached out and rescued the alcoholic. The hand of God. What would it be doing at the end of Jason Spivak's wrist? One said that God moves in mysterious ways his wonders to perform. Nonsense, bushwah, tripe, but it was to think.

"Don't get yourself in an uproar," Spivak was saying to John. "This is a demonstrative babe. I'll buy her another drink."

"No, I don't want any," Amy said, surprising herself.

"What?"

"I said I don't want any."

John said, "Have it on the house."

"Thanks," Amy said, "but not today. You are witnessing a great event. This is history. I'm through, I'm through drinking, now and forever."

She heard Spivak laugh, laugh with intention to scar, as she went away. Some character in a booth near the door smiled at her and Amy grimaced. Through, through, through. And through the door of that place for the last time. The end of an era.

Well, by God—she thought, standing on the sidewalk outside her favorite ex-bar—I've actually gone and done it. But it wasn't the hand of God, or even the hand of Jason Spivak, or even the fickle finger of fate. No, much better than that, far superior, she had realized while she watched John pour that wonderful convex drink that she had been going on a false assumption, the assumption that she would be sacrificing herself, the Amy Macduff she knew and loved and hated, in going on the famous straight and narrow and sober path. She had been wrong, since that Amy Macduff of San Francisco and New Orleans and New York infamy no longer existed, having died with the passing days, and was now the Amy Macduff of memory. That had been a fond and vigorous and energetically insane girl, and now she was an aging (to be truthful with herself) and somewhat debilitated—that ole debil—woman in her early thirties, the age of truth and sad consequence, and her insanity would be too sporadic, too forced, too hopeless now. And, as poets have written, the paths of folly lead but to the grave.

So that was all over, finish, le fin, fini la boire, and now

she stood on the threshold of that normal life. Envision it.
She would become a Mrs. Him or He or Someone, with
children at the breast, water on the knee, a mop in one hand
and a cookbook in the other, virtue as her girdle, a movie as
her entertainment. She would get up early in the morning,
prepare coffee for her hard-working spouse, fix the children's lunch boxes, making up the shopping list for the day,
listen to the soap operas while she did the housework, be
well, feel well, look well. And who could tell, but being all
full of that sweetness and light, she might want to carry her
message to the fallen, and eventually she might find herself
standing up in front of a group of confessed alcoholics
pouring forth her past woes in that same smug tone she
had heard that night at the meeting and . . .

And what?

No, by Christ, that wasn't for her.

Amy turned, hesitated, and then reinforcing her decision
by taking a first step, went back into the Marino. Ah, well,
she thought, why go from misery to monotony?

22. Oliver Kittridge Comes to The Summit of Calvary

IT WAS M. CLEMENT, one of Wilbur's
business contacts, who with Gallic hospitality and a notice-
able eye to business, was driving them in his big new Delahaye on a swing through the flat green country south of
Paris. Mr. Clement was a bulky bulging man with a pine-
apple of a head who had survived, according to his story, a
year of Buchenwald. He had walked before them with
banners flying through all the long galleries of that monument of French pride, the Palace of Versailles, reading in
a loud swollen voice the lists of battles won, the names of
the generals and the marshals. They spent an hour at Versailles, with M. Clement nodding approvingly every time
Wilbur snapped his Rolliflex. Oliver was more than bored

by the tremendous yet petty pile of stone, he was almost revolted by it. So much of what was wrong with mankind was here displayed—the mean show of triumph, the ornaments of vanity. He felt better when they got into the car again. He sat in the back, watching M. Clement's white-gloved hands guide the car along the road that passed between lush green fields dusted red with poppies. They were going at his request to the cathedral town of Chartres. When he had been a boy he had seen a picture (he remembered it as an etching) of the cathedral at Chartres, had remembered it. Ever since his scream in the night, which he had explained as the awakening from a nightmare, Wilbur had made every effort to humor him. He had never, of course, told Wilbur about Joseph Saint-Simon's attempt, although Wilbur had thought it very curious that Saint-Simon should disappear so suddenly from the hotel. ("He must have owed them money.") It was all past, and mostly forgotten.

M. Clement and Wilbur chatted a bit in front, mostly about business, although every now and then M. Clement would point out—to Oliver as well—something of notable interest, a French military airfield, a house partially destroyed by bombing. From time to time Oliver closed his eyes and listened to the country flow past. The weather changed just after noon. Grey clouds closed together solidly, it grew colder, and then it began to rain.

"Shall we turn back?" Wilbur asked cautiously.

"Ah no no, it will go away, you will see," M. Clement said optimistically. "And here we are in the car." He tapped the steering wheel with a gloved hand in obvious gratitude for his material wealth. They passed a man on a light motorcycle, head down into the rain. M. Clement laughed at him. "Poor fellow," he said.

They went through the rain for about half an hour, and Oliver was beginning to doze—the car windows were closed and it had become stuffy—when he heard M. Clement exclaim, "Ah there, look, now you can see it. See!"

And Wilbur saying, in a hesitant doubtful voice, "Oh yes yes."

Oliver looked over their backs, seeing nothing of importance at first, and then he made it out through the rain, the cathedral, peaks and spires showing dimly above clus-

ters of houses. Soon, since they were driving fast, he could
see that the cathedral sat splendidly on the crest of a hill
in the center of the town. In the rain and at that distance it
looked black, but shining, radiant. They twisted around and
around and up through narrow streets, the Delahaye seeming to worm through the alleys, until they suddenly drove
out into a wide square, and there at the further side of the
square, towering, magnificent, was the cathedral. Oliver
wanted to get down on his knees and pray, but he was still
in the car, and M. Clement was racing toward the cathedral.
He parked almost directly in front of the main entrance.

"Quite a building," Wilbur said, reaching for his Rolliflex.

"I fear you are too close," M. Clement said.

"I can get a shot of those people at the entrance."

A man in a wheelchair was being lifted up the steps to
the entrance by two young men in shorts who wore crosses
on white brassards. The man in the wheelchair was slumped
down, his head to one side, his mouth open weakly. Another young man with a white brassard was standing near
the entrance.

"We are in luck, we are in great luck," M. Clement said
enthusiastically. "I had forgotten all about this, but now you
will see something really interesting. Oh, this is luck."

The men with the crosses, the old man in the wheelchair
—why?

"What's going on?" Wilbur asked.

"This is the Journée des Malades, the day of the sick.
They come here on this day and the priest prays for them,
it is the bishop, the bishop, and they work great cures. I
know a man from my own native city, Orleans, who was a
cripple, like that man in the chair, and now, well now he is
dead, but I have seen him walk."

"You don't say," Wilbur said. "I've always wanted to see
something like this. Of course I've always wondered
whether . . ." He looked back at Oliver. "You want to go
in, don't you, Oliver?"

"Yes, I'd like to," Oliver said, managing to suppress his
excitement.

Because now that they were here, at this cathedral he
had wanted expressly to visit, he could see the sure hand
that had brought him here. No accident, no casual coinci-
dence had led him at this specific time to this specific place.

His life was no longer subject to hazard. He knew he was working out ordained patterns and if he was now too close to see the entire design of his life, soon he would be able to stand back and view it, and so too would others.

Inside the cathedral the light was leaden, but far off, at the altar, there were banks of richly glowing candles and swirls of red and purple and white. Oliver saw in that distance a priest holding what seemed to be a silver microphone; his amplified voice filled the vaults of the cathedral, even those vast dim upper spaces, lost toward heaven. The priest slid toward them—they were walking up the aisle— and Oliver could see the details of his rich vestments, the folds, the patient lace, the brocade. He was chanting in Latin, his eyes half-closed, and yet Oliver sensed that he was watching them come up the aisle.

"Here," M. Clement whispered.

They squeezed past an old man gripping a stick and sat on a bench just behind the invalids, the incurable who were this day to be cured. In the space before the altar there were—Oliver started to count them—almost twenty, lying on cots and stretchers, propped up with pillows so that they could watch the supposed miracles being wrought. Only, as Oliver well knew, and perhaps as only he of all the people in this grey cathedral knew, there would be no miracle wrought for them, not by this priest with the microphone and the rich vestments, not in this way, because their faith had been subverted and their hopes were at heart despised. He looked at the backs of the invalids in the row in front of him, backs bent and shaking, just a small crescent of head showing as they bowed in prayer, and he knew, elated, and he wanted to tell them—but not just yet—that they were to be the witnesses, they were to be the beneficiaries. For the time was coming, it was coming.

A nun came down the aisle and passed mimeographed sheets to them. Oliver heard the sheets rustle as M. Clement and, Wilbur opened theirs, heard them whisper, and then Wilbur nudged him, saying in his ear, "The prayers." Oliver glanced at his sheet, saw JOURNÉE DES MALADES. He looked away from the sheet, heard the priest chant, "Notre Dame des Champs, Notre Dame de Lourdes, donnez-nous la grace, donnez-nous la guerison . . ." The ill did not stir. They lay there, watching. Oliver could see the broken

corded hands of the old man next to him, holding fast to
his stick, and then the eroded face, the eyes fixed, intent.
"Donnez-nous la grace . . . la guerison . . ." Oliver
searched the cathedral, looking for a sign, but there was
nothing, nothing yet. The organ swelled, its tones seeming
to come from all the recesses of the cathedral. The priest
who had been chanting faded bit by bit from the front of
the altar, while the bishop, assisted by a group of busy
worldly satellites, came on with infirm steps. The satellites
buzzed around him, helping him on with his high peaked
hat, helping him take it off and holding it for him reverently,
arranging his robes, busy-handed, treating him more like a
girl being prepared for her first dance than a sometime
graduate of a seminary. There was a great aimless to-do in
front of the altar, with priests and acolytes taking tentative
steps here and there, in this direction and that, pausing to
question each other in whispers, while the sick watched, and
Oliver felt a constantly mounting sense of irritation, played
against the knowledge that soon he had only to raise his
hand to sweep all this away and signal a rebirth of faith.
The prayers went on. The word "Gloria" repeated over and
over began to remind Oliver of the shrill raving of a lunatic
in a French picture he had once seen. It went on—Gloria,
Gloria. The bishop paced to the altar, flanked by two of his
satellites, each a measurable intelligent two inches shorter
than he. One of them held a book, pointing out the place to
the bishop, while the other held high a long wax taper. A
priest flew up with a microphone. The bishop read in a halting senile voice, losing his place from time to time, waiting
interminably while pages were turned. This too, Oliver
thought, this too shall pass away. The bishop went from cot
to cot and stretcher to stretcher, the way being shown to
him. At each cot or stretcher he made the sacred sign of the
cross while scattering a mist of holy water, and a priest at
a microphone began to talk, seeming to Oliver to describe
unnecessarily what the bishop was doing. Was this the dignity, Oliver asked himself—although he knew his answer—
was this dignity that speaks to God? A small acolyte was
summoned; he held the large book against his forehead
while the bishop read. Is this the True Faith? The Faith of
the Crucifix, of the Catacombs? Ushers passed back along
the aisles, collecting money; it sounded like a neat metal

rain. Suddenly Oliver saw a panoply appear as if from nowhere, mysteriously materialized. It was raised over the
bishop's head by four men and a procession began to march
slowly around the cathedral, the priests chanting. As the
procession moved down the center aisle, Oliver was certain
that he saw a priest motion to him to join. He stood up,
heard Wilbur say something rather sharply—but he didn't
listen—and awkwardly he passed the old man, who drew
back his stick a little. He saw the eyes of the people on the
benches follow him and a small girl in white seemed to
reach out her hand. They passed under the arches of the
cathedral, their feet shuffling over the ancient stones, while
Oliver looked around, now with a feeling of almost desperate hope. But no one stepped out of the shadows, no one
came from behind one of the columns, and now they were
in the space before the altar, walking in front of the men
and the women trying to lift their pained heads from their
stretchers and their cots. And Oliver looked back at them,
feeling pity, feeling passion. Then, as they all stopped to
kneel, Oliver felt a mild hand on his shoulder and turning
to his right he saw the figure of Christ. Christ looked into
his eyes long and earnestly, while Oliver felt a terrifying
constriction of his chest, and then Christ said, "Now," and
moved toward him, and into him. Then the constriction
broke, swelling as if all the air of the world had been
pumped into his chest, and he felt himself rising above all
those kneeling around him, felt himself soar toward those
vast spaces far far away under the lost roof of the cathedral,
and he heard his voice coming from inside him, rolling with
the sound of planets rolling together, telling all those below
him who were seeing this miracle who he was and why he
had come and what he would do. Then, close, seen through
a telescope, one by one, he saw the agonized faces of the ill
lighten and shine as he took from them the burden of their
pain and gave them the blessing of his suffering. Suddenly
he felt himself borne along, as if gripped by a great current
of air, borne down the center aisle of the cathedral, and it
was not until he had passed and recognized for the instant
Wilbur's whitened astonished face and saw the people
standing and pointing and waving that he realized that a
man had him by either arm, holding him so that his arms
were out at stiff right angles from his body, with their

weight pressing him before them down the aisle, and he
knew he was being carried in that way out of the cathedral,
rejected and scorned and jeered as Christ must always be,
carried through the gaping doors toward his own calvary,
forming with his rigid body and his extended arms his own
cross.

23. *Lois Wilson Schemes to Attend*
Barmecide's Funeral

THE GREAT CLIMACTIC DISCOVERY
had come early that week when she had been shopping in
Port-au-Prince with Celeste, now of all things her step-
daughter. Whether Celeste had told her with malice afore-
thought or had acted out of womanly sympathy, Lois didn't
know, because the girl was deep. But Celeste at least had
shown her where she stood.

Being a woman she had known something was wrong.
She had come to a certain conclusion, one based mainly on
Lucien's age, but she'd been wrong. He could function. It
was good to know that anyway.

The wedding had been a classic, but the honeymoon had
been a fiasco. They had been married in the solemn presence of everyone, but everyone, of importance on the island.
The President himself had stood as Lucien's best man, and
Celeste had given her away. Thrown her away would be
more like. She had been kissed at the reception afterwards,
given at Roland's big house, by the President, several Min-
isters, a few Senators, and even by a clerk from the American Embassy. Then a big motorcade down to the airport,
where they got into Lucien's plane and took off for Cape
Hatien, where Lucien had a house. The big event of their
honeymoon—and so it proved to be—was to be their visit
to Christophe's citadel, in the mountains near the Cape.
For the rest they could swim in the rough pool built in
the sea by the marines during the occupation, they could

fish and loaf around the house and visit Lucien's nearby sisal plantation, and they could do other customary things of which they had actually done very little. In fact, Lois had been amazed by Lucien's lack of vitality in bed. He evidently possessed the qualifications and the skill, but he only went through the motions. That had been exactly what Lois had been prepared to do, and she was surprised and furious and frustrated when she found the shoe was on the other foot, so to speak. At first she had put it down to age and the weakening effect of life in the tropics. But then she had known a couple of West Indians, one from Trinidad and the other from Jamaica, and they hadn't had any such trouble. She had had to face it—Lucien just wasn't interested.

That had made things look bad enough, but there were compensations. There was life in the upper class, there was the car Lucien had promised her (but not yet delivered), there were servants, there were no color lines to cross. She had started to learn French and had picked up a few words of Creole, and she knew she was quick at learning things, so that the language barrier hadn't bothered her too much. What had begun to get her was boredom, and lack of love. They had spent only three days on their supposed honeymoon and then flown back to Port-au-Prince. Things were cooking in the business world and Lucien couldn't afford to stay away from the pot too long. Back in Port-au-Prince they'd gotten into the domestic routine that Lois supposed was expected to continue for the rest of her natural life. Lucien would wake up about seven, and she would too, and Jude would bring breakfast to Lucien, Celeste and her on the terrace. No morning papers, some chatter in Creole, and for the rest only food. Then Lucien would get into the Cadillac and drive off to his offices, while Celeste would go upstairs to sew and read. During the first week Lois had played the piano, but the piano was out of tune and she was soon out of sorts. After the first week she had just gone back to bed, not wanting to sleep, but lying in a bored stupor until about noon. At noon Lucien generally came home, ate heavily, and then tramped upstairs for his siesta. No love. Jude would drive Celeste and her out to the country club on the Bizeton Road, where they could swim and play tennis. He would call for them about five, by which time Lois would have played three awkard sets of tennis and

read in an uncomfortable deck chair and gone through a
halting conversation in English with one of the other
Haitian aristocrats. Lucien usually had dinner with them,
and once he took her to a movie (it had been an old American picture with French dubbed in, a real drag). Saturday
nights they had gone to parties, and those were the only
nights she could count on seeing him. Except—no love. And
if the tropics were supposed to be weakening in that respect,
well, they weren't weakening her. She was about to go out
of her mind. She had never bothered Lucien about what he
did in the evenings. She knew better than to give a man a
chance to lie, figuring that if she played it cool she'd soon
know the score. He had volunteered the information that
he generally had work to do at night, and Celeste had told
her that the married men usually got together and drank
and talked till late. But she wasn't interested only in what
he was doing. It was what he was not doing that was annoying her.

So that was the life of the Haitian aristocrat, the life she
had let herself in for. No great deal. No great deal, did she
say? It was deadly.

Still Lois had kept the hope that things would change for
the better, a vague kind of hope that gave no real buoyancy.
Then one morning that week, instead of creeping upstairs
back to her damp bed, she had gone shopping with Celeste.
They had messed around, looking for yard goods (because
Celeste liked to make her own dresses—what else was there
to do?), going into one store after another and being treated
like royalty by greasy Levantines. Only that bow-and-
scrape treatment was getting to be a drag too. Finally, in a
crowded shop on the Grande Rue, Celeste had been greeted
by a fat black middleaged woman, all breast and belly and
ass, with a broad sweaty African face. The woman and
Celeste had shaken hands, and Lois had noticed an expression approximating alarm on the thin sharp face of the
Syrian behind the counter. She had seen Celeste smile at
her and say, "Ma mere," which she knew now meant
mother. Then Celeste had said, "May I present Madame
Lorraine." The woman had said, barely moving her thick
lips, "Enchantée." And Lois had said, as she had learned to
do, "Enchantée." They had shaken hands, since that was de
rigeur in Haitian society. The fat black woman had said

something—Lois couldn't get the drift of it—to Celeste in French or Creole, and then murmuring, "Au revoir," had gone. As she left Lois could see the big stain of sweat, like a black flower, on the back of her white dress.

She had asked Celeste who that was.

The Syrian, who spoke English, had hastened to the back of the store.

"It is a friend of my father's," Celeste had told her.

"A friend?"

Celeste had nodded. "The friend."

"The . . . friend! But you don't . . ." And seeing the smile on her face, which might have been sympathetic, which might have been plain malicious, Lois had known that Celeste meant just that.

Celeste had said blandly, "You do not think she is very attractive?"

Lois had laughed at the idea.

"Neither do I." Celeste had shrugged her shoulders, saying, "But men are very strange. I could never understand, myself, but most people do not think it so unusual that my father should prefer this woman. There are many men who like black women."

Feeling almost detached, as if they were talking about an acquaintance instead of a husband and father, Lois asked, "Has he known her long?"

"Oh yes, a long time, before I was born. They are old friends, very congenial."

"Then why . . . why hasn't he married her?"

"Oh no, he cannot," Celeste had told her, as if explaining something very elementary, "she is too black and she is not of good family."

"Well then, why did he marry me?" The detachment was being pushed away by anger.

"It is better that a man should have a wife."

She had known in that instant what everyone who mattered in Haiti must also have known, that Lucien had married her as a special convenience, as a wife for show. And she had also known what they couldn't know yet, that whenever she thought of Lucien from now on she would think of that meaty wet African face and the spreading stain of stinking sweat on the back of that white dress. Not that she was prejudiced. Crummy as it might sound, at

home some of her best friends were black. But to think of
a man, a supposedly normal man, preferring—that had
been the word Celeste had used—that fat black bag to . . .
Well, it could also be meat. Some men liked plenty of vulgar
loose meat.

That had been the great climactic discovery, and she had
begun immediately to make her plans. Obviously she was
going to get out of this whole thing, this boredom, this so-
called marriage, out of Haiti. Christ, at least at home—it
shocked her a little to find that she was thinking of the
USA as home—she had some excitement, some life. She had
to pick up and move.

But there was the catch. She knew that Lucien, who had
married her before God and the President, wouldn't simply
let her go. She'd have to escape, and that wasn't being melo-
dramatic. There was no way she could leave Haiti without
his knowledge and consent. No shipping line, no banana
boat would take her unless he gave his okay. She wouldn't
be able to go by air. It wouldn't even do any good to throw
herself at the mercy of the American Embassy; they
wouldn't want to spoil good relations with the local government just for one chick. She couldn't swim the two hundred miles to Cuba or the three hundred to Jamaica. She
was trapped, trapped in this damned island.

A way out had occurred to her when she had met Frances Leeb one evening, and Frances Leeb had mentioned
that she was leaving Haiti later that week, her Rorschachs all given and the Haitian neuroses tabulated. Now
she didn't like Frances Leeb and she sensed that Frances
Leeb, being ugly and hairy, didn't have any great liking
for her. But they were both tried and true Americans,
citizens under the skin, and moreover Frances Leeb was
evidently the kind who in the States leaned over backwards and sometimes fell right on their asses trying to
prove to themselves how much they loved the good ole
Negro people. So she had told Frances Leeb about her
troubles, leaving out the part about her discovery of the
black mistress for tactical reasons. Then she had asked
Frances—getting real chummy now—to send her a cablegram just as soon as she got back to the States. The cablegram would say: FATHER DYING DOCTOR SAYS FOR
YOU TO COME ON HOME signed MOTHER. (That had

seemed less like murder than having her mother on her
death bed.) Lucien certainly wouldn't refuse to let her
go home to see them put her father in his grave. He
would undoubtedly get her on the next plane flying to
Miami from Port-au-Prince. And once home she could
forget all about this mock marriage. No need to bother
anyone about it.

So now she was sweating it out, waiting for the inevitable cablegram which would arrive just after Frances
Leeb, who was going home by French Line, docked in
New York. That would be in five more days, so she ought
to be getting the cablegram the coming Wednesday.

Ought to be getting it, unless Frances Leeb forgot.

Or unless she was too cheap to lay out the couple of
bucks for the cablegram.

Or unless Frances Leeb followed through on her general bitchiness.

24. Aaron Ross Suffers a Temporary Loss But Makes a Permanent Gain

SEEING THE BOOKIE NAMED Spongie
across the street, openly taking a bet from a guy in a route
driver's uniform, Aaron decided to ask him and get this
waiting business over once and for all. It had been Spongie
who'd stopped him outside the Marino that night and
warned him those goons were out to get him before the
trial. Well, he'd been waiting for them to make their move,
but they hadn't showed. Maybe Spongie would know what
they were up to, if anything.

Aaron watched Spongie note down the bet and say goodbye to the driver. Then he crossed the street. The bookie
looked up, wiped his over-red lips with the back of one
small pudgy hand.

"Hiya, kid. What's new?"

"Nothing."

"I see you're still around."

"Yeah," Aaron said, waiting. "I'm still around."

"Well, that's your lookout."

Spongie slipped two fingers inside his shirt and began to scratch his chest. After a while he asked, "What's on your mind?"

"I want to know what's the matter with those buddies of yours."

"What buddies of mine?"

"You know. What are they waiting for?"

He was putting up a front. He knew that, but he wasn't going to let this hunk of lard know it. He'd found himself hoping the goons would lay off, that they'd let the whole thing ride, and he'd known he was going chicken. But that wasn't entirely his fault. The damn business was like sitting up all night in a haunted house, not knowing what was going to jump you or when. He had the same feeling he'd gotten on a munition ship the winter of forty-three, when their convoy had been jumped by a wolf-pack in the middle of the North Atlantic. He hadn't been scared at first, the danger had been a little abstract, until he'd seen the ship on the starboard quarter go up, practically dissolve in front of his eyes. Then he'd started to think, We're going to get it, we're going to get it next. But it had been a little easier on the ship. He could look around at the other guys, who'd crowded to the deck just in case, and see their scared faces, and some of them were guys who didn't scare easy. And he'd known that even if they got hit he'd show them all that he had guts, one way or another. Pretty grim gag. But now there was no one to show anything to, except himself, and he knew inside that he was going chicken.

"The trial's coming up in a couple of weeks," Aaron went on. "If anyone's going to try something they'd better try it fast." He made himself laugh. "I'm getting tired of this waiting around."

"Well, what do you want me to do?" Spongie said, not quite hostile.

Aaron found himself saying, "Tell them I'm waiting for them."

"I'm not telling no one nothing."

"Tell them I shit on them."

Spongie had laid his head a little to the side, looking up and sideways at him.

"Look, kiddo," he said finally, plastering a small smile on his face, "get me straight on this. This ain't my deal at all. Get me? I don't want to have nothing to do with it. I don't want to get in the middle." He looked closely at Aaron, as if trying to see whether his words were sinking in. "I tried to do you a favor because I thought you were an okay guy. That's all. I wash my hands of this whole thing."

"Pontius Pilate," Aaron said, and wondered where he'd gotten that from.

"What?"

"Your grandfather."

Spongie smiled wearily.

"Whose side are you on?" Aaron asked.

Spongie made a horizontal swipe with his hand. "I ain't on no side."

"You got to have a side."

Spongie didn't say anything.

"You play this like a regular bookie, don't you?"

"That's it, kid," Spongie said, nodding his head a little. "I'm a bookie. I could lay you odds on this hassle, but I don't take sides. See? I never care which side wins. My alma mater's back here." He patted his hip pocket.

"Listen, why don't you do me a favor?" Aaron felt ashamed as he heard his voice rise in pleading. "Why don't you tell me how I can get to those guys? Anything, just so long as I don't have to wait for them to come to me."

"I can't do that."

"Why not?"

"What the hell."

"You won't?"

"I told you I can't."

The dirty little fat wop, the greasy ginzo.

"Lousy bastard," Aaron said in a low voice.

"Sure, sure," Spongie said placatingly.

"Lousy bastard."

"Have it your way," Spongie said and walked away from him.

Okay then, he'd have it his way. At least he'd shown the fat prick he wasn't yellow. And that would probably get back to the goons. They weren't going to have the satisfaction of thinking he was scared of them. They were going to know that whatever they started he'd finish. That's the way it always had been, and that was the way it was always going to be. It had to be. He felt all his determination to be brave hardening inside himself. No one was ever going to make him crawl. Ever.

The only thing he was afraid of now—and this was legitimate, he told himself—was that they'd actually bring him to trial. Time in jail was what he wanted least of. He'd been starting to make plans for the summer, ever since Phyllis had gone to Europe to visit her brother, who had blown his top and was now tied up in some sanitarium near Paris. He was going out to Provincetown, at the end of Cape Cod, and take a shack out on the dunes, and sit there and paint right through the summer. It would be cheap; he could get a shack for nothing, and the hundred bucks Phyllis had thrown his way just before she left ought to buy his groceries for the couple of months. He needed that, a couple of months of self-communion. He was tired of people, they were beginning to get in his hair. Christ almighty, there wasn't a single person on earth he gave a damn about. Okay, his folks, his brother, but they were remote. Amy? She'd been in Bellevue and now she was out again, sopping it up, and he couldn't feel she was a human being anymore. She was just a big pathetic memory and he didn't like to see her even. As to Phyllis, she was nothing, just old moneybags. There was no one close to him, hadn't been since the enforced companionship of the war, hadn't been since Marty Greenwald had died. He was alone, but the thought gave him no pain. Feeling no anguish. He was alone, so he might as well go off to the dunes and be without people. Dammit, he might turn out to be a hermit. When he'd been a kid he'd often wondered what made people go off and live completely by themselves. Now he was finding out.

Going into the park he stopped to make a quick sketch of a bum sprawled out on one of the benches. The bum woke up in the middle of the sketch and tried to make a touch. Aaron gave him the sketch, just for the hell of it. Now the bum had a fortune in his pocket, only he didn't know it. He could go into any restaurant and trade that original Ross for a glass of water. At the circle on Fifth Avenue he saw no one he knew, so he sat there on the hard stones, listening to the brats and their loving mamas, lifting his face and closing his eyes against the sun. A few minutes of that and he began to get restless. The last thing he'd seen before he'd closed his eyes had been the Renaissance tower of the church at the south side of the square. It made him think of a Chirico, lonely and sad and clean. He wanted to get something like that down today. A tower. A Tower of Strength.

He walked home, walking faster as he came to Jones Street, because he could see the painting now, a terra-cotta tower against a faded green sky, with black and green squares of a piazza in the foreground, and he wanted to paint it before he lost it. The tower just a little off-center, leaning very slightly, almost imperceptibly, the kind of thing that wouldn't hit you at first but that you'd discover after you'd seen the picture a few times. The squares in the foreground tending toward the diagonal, as if the painting was about to melt sideways out of its frame. And the green sky very clear, glazed, without a spot. An infinity of sky. Like Chirico. No, like Ross.

He took the stairs two at a time, came to his landing, and stopped dead. His door was open, just a couple of inches, but open. He hadn't locked it, but he remembered closing it tight. Someone was in there. Who? He felt the scalp crawl, the coldness going down his spine, the catch in his breath. Scared? No, he was all right. He went to the door, soft foot over foot, screwing up his face and clenching his hands to shut out the sound of his own moving. Who could it be? Whoever it was, he was going to get the jump on them. It was going to be his play.

He threw open the door. It slammed back against the wall as he leaped through the doorway. His hands were up, tense, ready to strike, ready to grab. But there was no one. The place was empty.

Yeah, but they'd been there all right. The paintings he'd stacked against the wall were lying on the floor, slashed to ribbons. The strips of canvas looked like broken fingers. His easel was smashed, the legs torn apart, like an animal dismembered. His palette was off in a corner, thrown there. Down on the floor he could see his tubes of paint, stepped on, squeezed out. Brushes were scattered around, most of them broken in half. They'd even gone after the studio couch Phyllis had bought for him; the guts of the pillows were all pouring out.

Then he saw the wall. A wall to paint on. And they had, they had. On the bare wall, in straggling letters, someone had printed: KIKE BASTARD. Spelled it right too. The words stood out harshly against the dead white wall. Up to the T it had been painted in vermillion; then the vermillion must have given out because it had been finished in black. Not such a great color scheme.

Aaron sat down on the ripped couch, looking over the damage, strangely enough not really feeling angry at all. That he couldn't understand at first. This whole thing, this eruption, left him without feeling, as though it hadn't happened to him, as though some remote volcano had just lifted its lid. He just didn't give a damn. Matter of fact, he almost felt good about it. The hell with the old paintings—they'd stunk anyhow. The easel, the couch, the brushes, the paints—he'd be able to replace them somehow. Maybe shoot a cable to Phyllis on the other side of the pound. Or maybe work for it. As to the KIKE BASTARD on the wall . . .

Yeah, he'd leave it there. He'd leave it right there on the wall, as a trophy. Because it showed he'd beaten them. He'd make them sneak in here and take their evil out on things that couldn't hit back. It was like they'd hung him in effigy when they could have had the real thing. They'd shown the yellow streak. Five against one, and the most they could do was print KIKE BASTARD on the wall. The hell with them.

Another thing. They'd never come into court against him. It was dollars to doughnuts that when he came to trial the case would be dismissed because the witnesses wouldn't cooperate. Those hoods wouldn't show in court. Probably every one of them had a record, and besides they'd make jerks of themselves around the neighborhood if they ever played ball with John Law. No, he wasn't going to jail, that was sure.

And then Aaron understood something else, although not quite as clearly. He understood that he had a little less to prove to himself, a little less to prove to others now. Because he'd stood up when he could have laid down; he hadn't given in. Remember the Alamo and all that crap.

He'd been scared, admitted, but he hadn't let it make any difference. He'd shown everyone once and for all that he wasn't a yellow little Jew; he was as much a man as anyone else, maybe more, and he didn't have to keep on proving it. Let the fact be accepted. He might never have to prove it again. But if he did—well then, he would.

He looked up at the wall. KIKE BASTARD. Yeah, he'd leave it there.

25. Breedon Rawley Finishes a Chapter, Closes a Book

SO THIS WAS TO be the end of Breedon Rawley, early novelist, late screenwriter, heir to gentlemen, and no fortune. He felt quite calm about it, composed and resigned. Keats had died young, and Shelley. No one would ever know whether their early promise had been but a false dawn. And so let it be with Breedon Rawley, killed by incomplete modern technology as he neared the city of New York and his twenty-fourth birthday.

Breedon looked through the fog-stained window, peering down through the open triangle bounded by the wing of the plane and the edge of his window. Down there, ten thousand feet below, the city looked like the glowing embers of a fire that had been kicked and scattered. For an hour they had been circling in the mist, waiting to land on the shrouded field.

"There's nothing to worry about," Breedon heard the stewardess say reassuringly to the plump woman in front of him. "We're waiting to make an instrument landing."

"But that's dangerous."

"No, no. Why, we've done it a hundred times. Would you like some coffee?"

The bald man sitting next to Breedon, whose cheeks sagged like dewlaps, caught the stewardess.

"Say, you're doing a fine job. When we get down I'd like to show you my appreciation."

"Thank you, sir."

"What I mean is, I'd like to send you something."

"That's not at all necessary. I'm only doing my job."

He stopped her as she began to move on down the aisle. "If you give me your address . . ."

"Care of the airline," she told him smoothly.

"Oh." He grunted and watched her legs as she went away.

In the last moments of their lives the man with the dewlap had tried to make connections with the stewardess, the plump woman had whined with fear, and Breedon Rawley had thought on Keats and Shelley. And so, in a way, Breedon Rawley had been closer to the immortal.

Yes, Keats: Now more than ever seems it rich to die, to cease upon the midnight with no pain.

Oh, what a way to write, Breedon thought despairingly. I could never . . . Seems it rich to die. Rich. How the word suddenly took on a new and fuller meaning. Seems it rich to die.

To cease upon the midnight with no pain. To erase the turmoil that was Breedon Rawley. To wipe out, obliterate, all in one merciful second.

For he was now, having achieved a victory, a man who was suffering through defeat. Having climbed the Matterhorn he had been told to prepare to scale Everest. Having received a mark of 100 in his first examination, he had been told to get a mark of 110 in his second. He was in a new world, a stratosphere world.

Despite his lengthy letter to Max Fielding, explaining how he had become the innocent victim of a tragicomedy of errors, he had been exiled from Hollywood. Fielding had never deigned to reply to his letter, nor had he answered any of Breedon's seven phone calls. Breedon's Hollywood agent had told him things were hopeless, for the time being, what with studios closing because they were making only normal profits. He had waited in Hollywood, miserable, hanging on, knowing that in life as in all good movies innocence cannot be too long punished. But he had received only one minor satisfaction, which had turned out to be no satisfaction at all. One evening, as he was wandering along Sunset Boulevard for want of anything better to do, he had seen Carney get out of his car. Hardly aware of what he was doing he had confronted Carney and resolutely hit

him in the mouth. Carney had blinked, then smiled cynical-
ly, pushed him aside, and walked past him. It was like a
dream he sometimes had in which he struck and struck and
struck a man without making the least impression. He
would wake up from it, frightened and depressed, with his
pajama trousers wet. This had been the first time he had
ever actually struck anyone; he knew he could never do it
again. He was half a writer and half a man.

"We'll be landing soon," he heard the stewardess say.

But Breedon, a trained observer, more acute than any
of the other passengers, had detected the slight tremor of
fear in her voice. They were going to land but, as he knew
exultantly, they were not going to land safely. Thus an end
to all his problems.

He gasped as they struck an air pocket and the plane
dropped.

The bald man said patronizingly, "Nothing to be scared
of. An air pocket."

Breedon tried to say he knew. He hadn't gasped through
fear; it had been purely a physical reaction.

The bald man looked at his wristwatch. "I hate getting
in late like this. My wife will be worried."

A sterling and typical citizen, desirous of the stewardess
and considerate of his wife.

The bald man said, "Now we're starting to go down."

Down there, in the glow they were hurtling toward, were
his ex-creations—and some pun intended. Down there were
Amy Macduff, and Lois, and Oliver Kittridge, and Aaron
Ross. He never wanted to see any of them again, but he
wondered what they would think when they knew he had
been killed. Probably Amy would say, pityingly, "Poor
Breedie." And Lois would think, "Now I can keep the
apartment." The news of his death would probably pass
around the Marino and excite interest and/or satisfaction
for a while, a day or two. And that would probably be all.
No memorial plaque, no memorial, no memory. The newspapers might feature his name in writing up the crash, and
then again they might not. For all he knew he might already
have vanished into the void of American culture six months
old.

The embers were taking form as blocks of light as they
swept down over the city. Now Breedon could see the close-

hatched pattern of the street lights, and there were the thin strings of light flung across the rivers. He braced himself, instinctively, waiting for the crash which he knew would soon come. Would there be pain?

At least he had done something, made some little mark, and perhaps they would say he might have gone on to greatness had he lived. Perhaps in future books of criticism they would write: "Breedon Rawley showed the utmost promise, but unfortunately he was killed . . ." Of course they would never know that he had ceased upon the midnight with no pain. To them the act of his being killed would always seem something sharp and cruel.

The stewardess was approaching, reminding the passengers to fasten their safety-belts. This was the fatal time.

"Are we all right, Miss?"

"Oh yes. We're about to land now." Said confidently, and falsely.

To land is to crash. To crash is to splinter and burn, a horrifying sight for the relatives and friends watching from the administration building, but no one would be there waiting for Breedon Rawley, little Breedon Rawley.

"Better fasten your belt tighter," the bald man told him. Breedon went through motions of cinching his belt. "Your ears hurt?"

Breedon shook his head negatively.

"Mine always do." Chewing gum.

If he lived, what would he write about? When he had been younger the world had teemed with subjects for him, been full of compelling conflicts and intense dramas of tremendous scope. But now it was empty, like a sea gone placid. If he lived, what would he write about? Could he write about Max Fielding and Carney and Blaker? Could he do for them and for Hollywood what he had done for the Village and Amy and Lois and Ross? And just what had he done, for them or for himself? He had made a good deal of money, and spent most of it, without enjoyment. He had accomplished something, it was true—he had written a book—and yet he had accomplished nothing at all.

BREEDON RAWLEY KILLED IN AIR CRASH.

Better this way . . .

Whoops. They had hit, jarred, bounced, were whirling through the air, hit again, shuddered, raced forward, the lights of the airfield flashing past, blurring. They were heading at unimaginable speed toward some invisible object. They were about to crash into something, a hangar, another plane, a high tension pole, but something, anything. They were . . .

They were slowing down, smoothly.

The plane came to a halt for a moment, then turned slowly to taxi across the field. The bald man took a deep breath and smiled. Breedon could see the head of the plump woman disappear as she reached down for something.

Breedon Rawley unfastened his safety-belt, relaxed his rigid legs, prepared to reach up for his typewriter on the rack above his head.

Cheated. He'd been cheated.

26. Footnote at Dusk

TOWARD THE END OF that summer, I came back to the Village from Provincetown, where Portuguese and intellectuals both fish, in their separate troubled waters. I was feeling vaguely dispirited, having finished my account of the adventures of Breedon Rawley and his satellites, and yet having the feeling that I had left them all in mid-air, with their futures unresolved. I didn't know whether Lois Wilson was still in Haiti, or whether Oliver Kittridge was still in that sanitarium near Paris. That was entirely my fault. I'd been so busy setting down this narrative that I had almost completely lost sight of the people I was writing about. But not completely, because Amy Macduff had been in Provincetown and Aaron Ross near it.

About my third night in Provincetown I'd gone into one of the restaurants for dinner. And there was Amy Macduff, bounding out of the kitchen with an arm full of dishes. She scattered the dishes on a table occupied by three middle-aged women and then caught sight of me.

"My God," she said, coming over, "another familiar face. So, you see me slinging the hash. Those people, they don't realize that their lives hang in my precarious balance."

I asked her what she was doing later.

"Is this an invitation?"

"Yes."

"Well then, this establishment closes at nine o'clock. It takes me eleven seconds to rinse the old catsup off my hands. Meet me here." She stood off a bit and said in a quasi-professional voice, "Have the New England clam chowder. It's no worse than the other slop."

Later, over a few drinks, Amy told me she had come to the Cape with Aaron Ross. Aaron was going to live in an isolated shack on the dunes and the idea of being away from people and away from liquor had appealed to Amy at the moment. So they had hitch-hiked up to Provincetown, carrying a suitcase each, and gone off on the dunes to live the clean and constructive life. Three days later, Amy told me, she'd practically crawled across the dunes to get a drink. Aaron was still out in the shack, painting and reading and reflecting, and only occasionally making a trip to town to get more supplies.

"What about you?" I asked Amy.

"What about me?"

"What are you going to do?"

"Ah, isn't it evident?" she said, pinching her glass in her powerful fingers.

A few minutes later Amy got up with her usual abruptness. "I'm going out on the wharf," she said. I walked her to the door of the cafe. "Don't come with me," Amy said, her voice tense. "I want to go out there alone." I started to say something, but Amy interrupted: "I know. You're thinking wharf and deep water and the lady is depressed. Well, stop thinking. Nothing's going to happen. I just want to be alone. Besides, one form of suicide is as effective as another." I watched her walk down the street with big hastening steps and then she went out onto the lonely wharf.

I saw Amy several times more that summer, but just in passing.

To Aaron Ross I spoke only once. One morning I saw him coming out of the First National store, a swollen burlap bag on his back. He was stripped to the waist, burned copper, and with his straight black hair and hard deep eyes looked like an Indian in a Frederic Remington illustration.

"Hiya," Aaron said, almost genially. "Got to take my eats back home."

"How do you like it out there?"

"Okay. It ain't bad."

"Are you going to stick it out?" I asked.

"What do you mean, stick it out? I just told you I liked it out there."

"How's the painting going?"

He looked away for a moment. "I don't know," he said. "I can't tell."

I asked him about Lois Wilson.

"The hell with her," he said with only a little bitterness. "Why bring that up?"

"What about the defense fund? Aren't you sore about that?"

"Sure. But what can I do? Let her keep the dough. It don't do me no good. Besides, most of it was Rawley's dough, so she had it coming to her."

I didn't ask him about Phyllis Kittridge. I don't know why.

So here I was back in New York, knowing that Amy was slinging hash in Provincetown and that Aaron was painting pictures in a shack on the dunes. And not much else.

That first night back in the Village I was walking through Washington Square Park when someone called to me from one of the dark benches. It was Jason Spivak.

"Sit down," he said, moving over a bit. "Got a cigarette?"

I gave him a cigarette.

"Got a light?"

I lit him up and he blew some smoke in my face, accidentally, I suppose.

"This goddamned park," Spivak said. "This goddamned excuse for a park. A few lousy patches of grass sected and bisected with paths and lined with benches. All for the rabble. Look at them." People were walking in and out of the circles of light, mostly young couples with the aimless stroll of lovers. On a nearby bench a couple of kids were necking furiously, with much motion of hands on each other's backs. Somewhere behind us a portable radio screamed. "Marconi," Spivak said. "What a great benefactor he was."

I lit a cigarette and we smoked in silence for a while.

Finally Spivak asked, "What are you doing?"

I told him of my story about Breedon Rawley and all. And I told him that I was afraid that I'd left all my people dangling.

"Well, what's wrong with that?" Spivak asked.

I wasn't sure. But I felt uneasy about it.

"What's troubling you?"

"For instance," I said, "what's going to happen to Breedon Rawley now?"

"I hope he drops dead."

"But if he doesn't?"

"He won't. Anyway, there was a squib in the book review section of the *Times* the other Sunday. It seems that the young genius is writing, and I quote, a satirical novel about Hollywood. As if we need another one of those."

"It might be another success."

"That depends on what you mean by the word. I wouldn't want such a success."

"We've got to live," I said weakly.

"Sure we've got to live." An angry tone. "Do you know what I'm doing now, just so I can live? I'm writing comic books. What do you think of that? Jason Spivak writing comic books!"

I tried to laugh.

"It's not so funny," Spivak said, and we settled into an uneasy silence.

Finishing my cigarette, I asked him, "Is Lois Wilson back in town?"

"Who?"

"Lois Wilson."

"Oh." Recollecting. "That fake Hindu. No, I hear she's still in Haiti."

"I was wondering."

"Why?"

"That's where I'd left her. But she was trying to get back here, only I didn't know whether she'd make it." I didn't tell him about the cablegram she'd been expecting from Frances Leeb.

"What's wrong with leaving her there?"

"Well, I don't know whether she'll ever get off the island or not."

"Neither does she. And even if she comes back to the States, what then? How do you know what's going to happen to her? Suppose she comes back and gets the best break she can dream of. How do you know it's going to last? That's the trouble with books. They wrap everything up into a neat little package. After I come to that business, the end, I begin to wonder what's going to happen to the characters. Okay, so John and Mary have gotten married, they're all set for life. They love him at the bank and she cooks the most wonderful pies. So the day after they get married John steps in front of a truck and the oven explodes in Mary's face. Only we don't know about it, because the author has ended the book. Or let's say our hero dies, maybe nobly. That's the end of the book. But what happens to the guy who's killed him? Or to the spectators? Or whatever and whoever it is? There's no end to any book, so stop worrying about it. Maybe Lois Wilson will stay in Haiti and maybe she won't. What's the difference? You've got to leave her sometime."

"Yes, but . . ."

"No buts. Who else are you worried about?"

"Oliver Kittridge."

"What's with him?"

"He's in a sanitarium near Paris."

"What kind of sanitarium?"

"For the insane."

"So?"

"Is he going to stay there?"

"How should I know? What's wrong with him?"

"He's crazy."

"How do you know he is?"

"Well, he thinks he's Jesus Christ."

"So what's crazy about that? Jesus Christ thought he was Jesus Christ, and does that make him crazy. A lot of people thought so, think so. Maybe he is Jesus Christ. He's got as good a chance as any of us."

"But is he going to stay in the sanitarium the rest of his life?"

"I'd rather have him stay there thinking he's Jesus Christ than have him get what we call cured and come out feeling he's no one. And anyway, what do you mean by the rest of his life?"

"Well, just that."

"You don't have any conception of what that means. You think of it as three score and ten, don't you? There isn't any such thing anymore. Right this minute there may be a plane up there with a load of bacilli or maybe an armful of atom bombs, and all our troubles will soon be over. I'm a great believer in pessimism as the only workable philosophy. You might as well expect the worst, because that's what you're going to get."

"If you think that," I said, "why do you keep on living? Why don't you just go out and kill yourself?"

"Because," Spivak said, "in addition to being a pessimist I'm also a masochist."

I started to say something, but Spivak cut in with: "Listen, how much dough have you got on you?"

I knew enough to be wary. "Not much," I said.

"Lend me ten, will you?"

"I haven't got ten on me." It was a lie, a natural and necessary lie.

"Make it five then."

To give him five dollars would be an act of cowardice.

"Well listen, you've got some dough, haven't you?"

"I can let you have a couple," I said, surrendering.

He took the money, crumpled it into his pocket, and stood up.

"I've got to be going," Spivak said. "I'll be seeing you."

"Be seeing you."

A few seconds later he was back.

"Give me another cigarette," he said.

I gave him one.

"You need the pack?"

"Yes," I told him, stiffening.

"You know what," Spivak said, bending down for a light, "we're the generation that doesn't have the courage to get lost."

"Maybe you're right," I said.

"Of course I'm right," he said.

Then he was gone and I was alone on the bench, wondering.

THE END